IN THE SEVEN MOUNTAINS

IN THE SEVEN MOUNTAINS

(Photo by S. W. Smith)

IN THE SEVEN MOUNTAINS

MOUNTAINS

Legends collected in Central Pennsylvania

HENRY W. SHOEMAKER

CATAMOUNT
PRESS

an imprint of Sunbury Press, Inc.
Mechanicsburg, PA USA

CATAMOUNT
PRESS

an imprint of Sunbury Press, Inc.
Mechanicsburg, PA USA

For information about special discounts for bulk purchases, please contact Sunbury Press Orders Dept. at (855) 338-8359 or orders@sunburypress.com.

To request one of our authors for speaking engagements or book signings, please contact Sunbury Press Publicity Dept. at publicity@sunburypress.com.

FIRST CATAMOUNT PRESS EDITION: October 2022

Set in Adobe Garamond | Interior design by Crystal Devine | Cover by Lawrence Knorr | Edited by Lawrence Knorr. Interior artwork by Katharine H. McCormick, Philadelphia, Pa.

Publisher's Cataloging-in-Publication Data
Names: Shoemaker, Henry W., author.
Title: In the seven mountains: legends collected in Central Pennsylvania / Henry W. Shoemaker.
Description: First trade paperback edition. | Mechanicsburg, PA : Catamount Press, 2022.
Summary: Henry Shoemaker compiled these legendary tales set in the Seven Mountains of central Pennsylvania. Shoemaker's tales recall the transition of the landscape from forest to industrial logging and the decline of the native peoples as the European settlers advanced westward. This collection of tales has been modernized for 21st-century audiences but maintains the charm, wit, and suspense of the originals.
Identifiers: ISBN : 978-1-62006-969-1 (softcover).
Subjects: FICTION / Fairy Tales, Folk Tales, Legends & Mythology | FICTION / Cultural Heritage | FICTION / Small Town & Rural | FICTION / Short Stories.

Product of the United States of America
0 1 1 2 3 5 8 13 21 34 55

Continue the Enlightenment!

Here began . . . the happiness of my life. . . . Here passed the peaceful but rapid moments which gave me the right to say . . . I have lived. —J. J. Rousseau

BY THE SAME AUTHOR:

Wild Life in Central Pennsylvania (1903)
Pennsylvania Mountain Stories (1907)
More Pennsylvania Mountain Stories (1912)
The Indian Steps (1912)
Tales of the Bald Eagle Mountains (1912)
Susquehanna Legends (1913)

* * *

Immaterial Verses (1898)
Random Thoughts (1899)
Pennsylvania Mountain Verses (1907)
Elizabethan Days (1912)

* * *

Legend of Penn's Cave (pamphlet) (1907)
Story of the Sulphur Spring (pamphlet) (1912)
Stories of Pennsylvania Animals (pamphlet) (1913)
Stories of Great Pennsylvania Hunters (pamphlet) (1913)

CONTENTS

ILLUSTRATIONS

INVOCATION

Oh, tell me are you, Hills divine.
Named for the Seven Mountains of the Rhine,
Thy gorge with Penn's Creek bursting through
Suggests the Drachenfels anew—
And your vast tracts of spruce and pine
Reach to the cliffs like Ehrenbreitstein.
And each pale crag of cold, conglomerate stone
Stands 'gainst the skyline like a castle lone.
From which the robber baron's trail
Led to where travelers toured the vale:
Here the black wolf on midnights cold
Crept down to prey on peaceful fold.
Where Rhineland slopes are shawelled in vine
Here are stumps garlanded with red woodbine.
And the frail ghosts of pool and rill,
That flit to tell their stories ill.
Are paler reflections of a shadowy line,
Which gave the dark mysteries to the Rhine.
Here did the German pilgrim find
In thy deep heart, a peace of mind.
Surveying your cloud-bathed summits grand
The soothing dream of fatherland;
The High Top, Broad Face, Knob, and Dome
Waked in his breast the sense of home,
And gave him courage and fresh life
To wage again his tireless strife.
Forget life's thanklessness and woes.
And "make the desert like the rose,"
Thy torrents, caves, and mystic heights
The epic of a nation writes.
Oh, tell me are you, Hills Divine,
Named for the Seven Mountains of the Rhine?

FOREWORD

Around the time Henry Shoemaker published *In the Seven Mountains*, the foremost psychologist of the day, Carl Jung, was busy discovering striking similarities among myths from around the world. Jung argued that the repeated experiences of our ancestors had formed "primordial" or original images they handed down. And so, Jung argued, we humans share a "collective unconscious"—in other words, a set of hard-wired expectations and preferences about the stories we share to make sense of our origins, desires, fears, mortality, and the forces of the world we face each day. Jung was so bold as to suggest this is not learned but hereditary; we're born with ancestral memory.

Twenty years later, the theory of this "archetype" broke into literature. Henry Shoemaker, a writer ahead of his time, could have taught a course. Consciously or not, he had been delivering his legends in any of the classic character types and plot patterns the experts were identifying in literature, dating to the earliest recorded myths, the grandfather of Shoemaker's genre, the legend.

On the one hand, you can argue that Shoemaker did nothing remarkable in constructing his work according to age-old models. After all, Jung and the critics merely identified an instinctive tendency. But most prose writers will tell you that finding material is exceedingly difficult. To uncover it over and over in archetypal patterns seems superhuman. Shoemaker must have either tediously trained his subconscious such that he navigated the world through a prism of archetypes, or he was already onto Jung.

An archetype is not a window dressing in a scene; it is elemental; the story's construct is one with it. No matter how much he embellished his legends before he sat down to translate them such that they would appeal to the sensibilities of contemporary readers and convey universal themes, Shoemaker had selected tales that, pared to their cores, were naturally archetypal.

The archetypal examples in this collection read like a handbook on the theory itself. As you read these legends, or "traditions" as Shoemaker occasionally referred to them, you will experience not just the principal archetypal character—the hero—but many colorful archetypes working with or in opposition to the hero: bullies; creatures of nightmares; moral innocents; damsels in distress; outcasts; star struck lovers; devils; dreamers; evil geniuses; fatal attractors; friendly beasts; explorers; sages; martyrs; temptresses; tyrants; and wizards.

It's fun to experience a book in the context of a literary framework like an archetype, and Shoemaker certainly facilitates that enjoyment with his epic style. As you read, consider identifying his plotlines by their archetypes. Here are the most recognized: The battle of good and evil; death and rebirth; innate wisdom versus educated naivety; the initiation; a hero's journey; rags to riches; riches to rags; nature versus mechanized society; the task; and of course, the quest.

Further, you will find no shortage of archetypal settings, which reinforce tone, foreshadowing, and theme when we are aware of them. Again, the classics: The garden; forest; river; sea; island (yes, there are islands here); mountain; wasteland; tower; and the small community (which carries the weight, good and bad, of provincialism).

Unless you are hesitant to be in the company of William Shakespeare, there is no shame in writing archetypally. The best writers know they are working in the arena of shared patterns of the universal human experience. It makes readers realize how much they have in common with other cultures worldwide.

Before you jump into the delight of these legends, I want to ask that you think about something in Shoemaker's explanatory preface: "It is difficult to make people interested in places and legends they see daily or know by heart; the writer's fondest wish is that fifty years hence an active concern may be aroused for the localities mentioned."

Shoemaker, understanding that our collective unconscious is not delimited by generations, must have sensed an archetypal role he was to play as a harbinger. Sunbury Press, thankfully, heard the call and recognized the importance of what he asked us to cherish. It just took a little longer than 50 years.

And so Henry Wharton Shoemaker is the conscience of Pennsylvania, warning its people against taking their commonwealth for granted, asking them to embrace and preserve a distinct culture. He had faith that in time we would appreciate and learn from the "traditions" he captured so that we, like he, "can truthfully say that through these mountains, forests, and rivers," we have "tasted deeply of life."

PJ Piccirillo
Brockport, PA
September 2022

EXPLANATORY PREFACE

MOST of the materials for the legends contained in this volume were collected last April, when, in company with his friend, Mr. John H. Chatham, of McElhattan, Pa., the author enjoyed a driving trip through portions of the Seven Mountains and adjacent territory. The drive was made in a livery carriage hired at Milroy, and the driver was Mr. J. S. Hoar of that place. For once, the writer found the right man in the right place. The driver quickly understood the purpose of the trip and mapped out the route so that it would touch scores of localities of historic or legendary interest. In this way, the writer was able to traverse many picturesque regions, including some of the remoter little valleys, and learn from the old people the traditions connected with them. He was so pleased that upon his return, he wrote an editorial for the *Altoona Tribune* called "Eldorado Found," which described the beauty and charm of the scenes visited. Though he had previously toured the Seven Mountains on several occasions, they appealed to him most deeply and lastingly on this latest journey.

Then, he conceived the idea of compiling a volume of legends dealing solely with the region. In his previous books were many legends from the Seven Mountains, most of them being the best-known traditions, but on the trip last April, he was fortunate enough to secure enough additional ones to compose this book. As in his previous volumes, the compiler has endeavored to transcribe the legends exactly as he heard them from the old folks. For this reason, they are less of a picture of life in the mountains than they are of supernatural and legendary elements. It is difficult to infuse one's point of view without lessening the effect of ghostly and tragic occurrences. The stories may be lacking in descriptions of scenery and the manner of living, but an effort is made to atone for this by the unusual character of the legends. In this respect, much is left to be desired, as the ancient mountaineers have a directness and charm of speech that no writer can attempt to reproduce unless he has a stenographic memory. As many of the stories have happened "within the memory of man," it has been necessary in many cases to change the names of persons and places, to transpose localities and dates. The writer has done this reluctantly, indeed less than he should have in a few instances, but if some of the sources of his information notice confusion in their stories, they must understand the reason. In other cases where the true names are used, it is hoped that no offense will be taken, for certainly far from such is meant.

The book has been prepared with the idea of preserving ancient traditions, especially those dealing with ghosts and Indians, for the benefit of future generations. The number of Indian stories in the Seven Mountains is amazingly large; the writer feels that he has barely pricked the surface with the half dozen herein, physical wealth having been so well exploited for so long. He hopes that this book will receive something of the same treatment accorded to its predecessors. It is difficult to make people interested in places and legends they see daily or know by heart; the writer's fondest wish is that fifty years hence an active concern may be aroused for the localities mentioned. Meanwhile, the friendships made, the kind words heard, the happy memories, and the aspirations kindled are ample enough recompense for his efforts. He can truthfully say that through these mountains, forests, and rivers, which he has loved with a full understanding, he has tasted deeply of life.

HENRY W. SHOEMAKER
At Sea, August 30, 1913

IN THE SEVEN MOUNTAINS

(A Story of the Vale of Petersburg)

LEWIS DORMAN, the panther killer of the Seven Mountains, is
not the only celebrity buried under the carpet of myrtle, beneath
the shaggy-boughed white pines, in the ancient cemetery at Dormantown. In an obscure corner, at the foot of the hill, where the ground
is inclined to be marshy, where the peepers linger until far into June,
rests all that is mortal of Indian Joe. An unchiseled block of mountain
brownstone was placed at the head of the grave, a smaller block at the
foot, but even this was not done until fully two years after the uneventful
funeral. Perhaps no name was cut on the headstone because folks had
forgotten—if they ever knew—what Indian Joe's real name was—so they
left him to rest anonymously.

When the Indians and half-breeds retired from the Seven Mountains, their sole residuum was this one sturdy specimen—he was about
nine years old when persons first recollected him as attached to the

Delette family. Whether he had been left there by his parents when they responded to the allurements of the reservation on the Allegheny River or had wandered out of the forest into their midst was a profound mystery. The nearest neighbors to these dwellers in the secluded little valley at the foot of the Petersburg were too busy clearing new ground and killing wolves to care to inquire; besides, they lived five miles away, and distance lessens curiosity. From this inconspicuous beginning, the Indian youth became an integral part of the Delette household. The old couple were childless, and were it not that two nephews from Lewistown visited them at regular intervals, Indian Joe might have become their heir. When he was fifteen, old Jacob Delette died; his wife followed him to the grave three years later. The two burly nephews swooped down and took possession; Indian Joe was sent adrift.

When the old man died, the young redskin's sagacity asserted itself. He saw what awaited him and made preparations for the future. Unknown to his benefactress, he built himself a one-roomed cabin near a spring on the mountainside, probably half a mile above the Delette farmstead. It was constructed piece by piece from logs, slabs, mud, and mortar. "It's my hunting cabin," proudly said the boy when a curious old trapper from the other side of the mountain—his name was Cephas Zettle—surprised him sitting in front of it on a stump in stolid meditation one Sunday afternoon in June. Cephas rather liked the boy and contrived to visit him from time to time. The Indian explained that he only visited the shanty during leisure hours, that it would make Mother Delette unhappy if she knew of its existence, and Cephas understood right away. The old trapper taught the Indian how to shoot, the secrets of woodcraft and trapping, of which he had been singularly ignorant—but he proved an apt pupil.

After the passing of Mother Delette, the Indian took up his permanent abode in the cabin and decided to live by hunting and fishing. The nephews gave him nothing, but in the scrap heap made by the men's wives in the "housecleaning" after the funeral feast, he found some broken knives, forks, cups, and plates, also an ancient clock with a picture of a stagecoach painted upon the glass which covered the pendulum. Indian Joe was honest; he never took a thing from the old couple—he began housekeeping with conscience clear. The neighbors nearest to the Delette farm were named Osmer; they were the earliest settlers in the Vale of the Petersburg. Theirs was a great, long, unevenly roofed manse, built of logs, plastered and whitewashed, and enlarged every decade or so as the family grew. There seemed to be a warp where each new part of the roofs joined; the ridge line presented a bold appearance, zig-zagged and high chimneyed, outlined against the pink evening sky—for the house stood on a slight rise. It was a doleful place at night, as the ice pond was filled with frogs, which vied with the crickets and katydids in drowning the uncertain tinkling of the sheep bells. Isaac Osmer and his father, known as "old Isaac," had cleared a farm of a hundred acres, a big plantation in those days in the Seven Mountains. Cephas Zettle had helped them cut the giant pines, pile them in heaps, and burn them until he was tired of the sheer monotony of the task and became a mountain idler or trapper. Though big game was plentiful, he had never killed anything fiercer than a wildcat; deer and birds were his specialties.

The summer that Mother Delette died, the Osmer harvest was unusually heavy. Hands were few and far between; Isaac Osmer urged Cephas to help "just for old times' sake." He refused but said he would bring over the Indian boy—Indian Joe—who used to live with the Delettes; that he was a likely lad, very anxious for work. He said all this without first consulting the boy, but he fancied he knew his mettle. In this he was correct, as Indian Joe rejoiced at the chance to get to farm work again, especially as he was promised that part pay would be in real money. All he had gotten from the Delettes was board and clothes, with a few coppers on nights of church entertainments. But as once a year was the oftenest he had ever gotten to a meeting, he had almost forgotten what money looked like. Indian Joe reported at the harvest field and handled the cradle like a veteran. Like most of his tribe, he developed early. At eighteen, he was splendidly built and muscled. Dinner for all hands was served in the out-kitchen, and a dozen hungry workers began a bounteous repast at noon.

Here, the Indian met Gabriella Osmer, or "Gabs" as she was generally called. He had no recollection of ever seeing her before, but she said she had seen him on two occasions at Bethel Church on the north or "other" side of Mt. Petersburg. As it was there he had attended on the few occasions he had been to church; it must be so. Gabs was very gracious to the young stranger, but the same might be said of all the mountain boys who sat at the table. Farmer Osmer's wife was also very attentive, asking him frequently how he liked the dinner and the work. The Indian was sensitive and appreciative and smiled broadly throughout the meal. This was unusual as his face was naturally serious, and his eyes almost scowled. Gabs, at this period, was just past her sixteenth birthday but, like most persons of mixed stock, was well developed for her age. She was an ash blonde with full blue eyes, black brows, and lashes. She was rather above the medium height, in fact, the tallest girl in the township, where most of the people were short, like the German peasants.

That evening on his way back to the mountain, Indian Joe stopped at the Osmer well—it was a primitive affair operated with a pole—and was having difficulty mastering it. Gaba heard him and came out of the summer kitchen. She asked him how far he had to walk to his cabin. He replied that it was about five miles, adding facetiously that "the walking was good."

"Why don't you stop with us during harvest?" inquired the girl.

The Indian stammered something, but Gab's mother, who had been watching the proceedings, came out and renewed the invitation in stronger tones. She was shrewd enough to foresee that if the stalwart Indian were made comfortable, he would become a "standby," a person much needed on the big, uneven farm. The Indian quickly decided to remain and followed the two women to the kitchen porch, where he carefully laid down his cradle and whetstone. Isaac Osmer and his three sons, boys a few years older than the Indian, made the supper very enjoyable for the stranger, and before dark, he felt himself a member of the household.

The farmer, his wife, and the boys retired early, leaving Gabs and the Indian to sit on the little front porch for an hour before going to bed. The young Indian had never been noticed by girls before. Those who had seen him at Bethel kept away from him as the story was told that he was a poor beggar kept by the bounty of old Father and Mother Delette. Since occupying his shanty on the slope of Petersburg, he had never attended a meeting and consequently had not spoken to or seen any women. But the manly instinct was there; he was ready for love; he possessed all the romance of his culture. Gabs asked him where he was born; he could not remember. He had been told that his parents were basketmakers and lived on Poe Creek; they had traded at Millheim and moved away, leaving him temporarily with the Delettes. They had never returned, no doubt, had died in the North. Mother Delette once told him that Southern Indians could never thrive north of where the coffee tree grew. Gabs seemed much interested in him, drawing out all that was best in the untouched mine of his nature. He had courage enough to squeeze her pretty hand when they said goodnight. The old stairs creaked unsympathetically as each, with a flickering tallow dip in hand, climbed to their dreary bedrooms.

In this way, Indian Joe became a fixture in the Osmer household. He did not abandon his cabin, he had too much concern for the future for that, but whenever he worked for the family, he spent his nights there. In the autumn, he was absent most of the time hunting; for some reason, his ardor for the chase had quickened. It is said that Indians always desired to excel as huntsmen when they were in love. Every few days, however, he would appear at the farmhouse to give Gabs some specimens of his skill. One day it was a string of rabbits, another a string of ruffed grouse, another a string of grey squirrels; once, he brought in a heath-hen, one of the last ever killed in the Seven Mountains where they had once been so abundant. His big, deep-set eyes would flash when he told of the pack of wolves he had been chasing for several weeks. They circled round and round the slopes of the conelike Petersburg; gradually, he was rounding them up on the summit; he would annihilate them yet.

"I'd love a wolfskin as a mat in my room to put beside the bed," said Gabs enthusiastically. "I know several girls who have them; they are so nice to step on when one gets out of bed on cold mornings."

This aroused the Indian's anxiety to procure a wolf. He absented himself for three days, taking his own hound, Salem, and farmer Osmer's hound, Rube. When he returned, he was minus the two dogs, but he carried three large wolf hides, one of a male and two of female. He told how he had chased a pack of six to the cone of Petersburg, where in the narrow space, he had attacked them with his hounds and rifle. The wolves fought valiantly; all six were hit, but three got away, though they tore the big dogs to pieces in the melee. This rather dulled the young nimrod's sense of triumph, but he soon cheered up when he found that Isaac Osmer took the loss of his hound lightly. Gabs was delighted and danced and clapped her hands for joy. She was naturally of serious mien herself; he had never seen her so exuberant. The hides were treated with eggs, cornmeal, and water, the Indian method, and hung on the wall of the summer kitchen, now deserted, fur inward, to cure. It was a great achievement, especially as on his first trip to Lewistown, long-planned, he would go to the courthouse and collect twelve dollars in bounties.

On cold winter nights, when there was snow, the Indian remained overnight with his benefactors. Then, he noticed Gabs' fondness for books, which emphasized his own inability to read. No one had ever suggested his going to school, and if there had been any truant officers in the Vale of Petersburg, they would not have molested him, as an Indian was considered best uneducated. Gabs liked to show him the pictures in the old leather-bound books to read aloud. There was one book he liked best of all. It was called *Orations of Celebrated American Indian Chieftains*. It was embellished with crude woodcuts of Logan, Cornplant, Farmer's Brother, Red Jacket, Scarouady, and other loquacious warriors and published in Philadelphia in 1801. Logan's high-flown perorations pleased the young native most; the victim of Captain Michael Cresap's regulars was fond of talking of the so-called "white man's honor" and the apparently established "red man's honor." The word *honor* had hitherto been unknown in Indian Joe's vocabulary; now, he liked to use it on all occasions. He liked the sound of it; it was the theme that ran through all his conversation. He recalled having heard the old Delettes talking about John Logan, the oratorical chief's younger and more sensible brother, of his spring not far from Reedsville. His ancestors had probably hunted and fought with Shikellamy, the father of the two Logans; it gave a glamor, a prestige to his personality. Since hearing this book read, he was no longer a lone Indian; he was the embodiment of a noble and high-principled people who had ruled the Seven Mountains for centuries. Gradually old memories took concrete form, and he began to imagine he could remember his parents. Scores of legends rehabilitated themselves so that he could entertain the Osmer family for whole evenings with Indian ghost and hunting stories.

He began to feel worthy of Gabs; someday, he would tell her that he had always loved her, surely she seemed to care for him. She apparently liked to be with him, especially alone, and when he had made bold to kiss her, she had offered no resistance. He felt he could restrain his passion until he became more prosperous; he would soon have twenty dollars "laid aside." Just a week before Christmas, on a clear, cold day, when the snow was pretty well blown away, farmer Osmer harnessed the team to the big wagon; they would all drive twenty-four miles to Lewistown, see the sights, and do some shopping. Indian Joe was, of course, invited; he had never seen the seat of justice and could collect his bounties for the wolf scalps. Osmer, his wife, and their youngest child Katie, a little girl of eight, rode on the box seat; boards were laid across the body of the wagon, on which sat Gabs and the Indian, also the three other boys, and the sweetheart of the oldest. Straw was piled copiously on the wagon floor—to keep their feet warm. Two of the wolf-hides were used as cushions on the driver's seat—Gabs had the other safe and sound in her room—and a big buffalo robe also covered the legs of those on the box seat. The start was made at five o'clock in the morning, and they were at the county seat a few minutes past noon; the team was tied and fed in the alley back of the courthouse, which seemed a giant structure, a palace, to the open-mouthed Indian. Lunch had been brought along, so there was no delay after reaching town. Farmer Osmer had some business to attend to, he said, so he left his oldest son to escort the Indian to the courthouse to collect the scalp money. The woman and the other boys visited various shops. One of the commissioners was at his desk and agreed to pay twelve dollars without much hesitation. "Eighty dollars in one year for wolf scalps is using up the county's money pretty fast, but I guess we must rid the mountains of the blamed critters," he remarked as he signed the necessary inquisitions. The treasurer paid the money in twelve bright Mexican dollars, which Indian Joe slipped into his outside coat pocket, and clinked with his hand as he strode through the rotunda.

He paused a minute on the top step, surveying the square, which seemed of immense proportions, and the many elegant mansions; he was as good as any man in Lewistown today. The lad who accompanied him was glad to excuse himself to return to his sweetheart, so the Indian was left to his own devices for a few minutes. He had previously noticed a book store—it handled high-class goods—as the members of the old Scotch-Irish aristocracy had an insatiable thirst for reading—and soon found himself within it. The old bookseller, Jabez Boal, with his shock of white hair, black suit, and white tie, came forward to serve him. He told him that he wanted a good book for a Christmas present. The bookseller held up a handsome volume bound in half morocco; it was almost as big as a family Bible, the cover was stamped with gold lettering, and the edges were gilded. "This is the handsomest book we have this Christmas," he said. "It is the poems of Reginald Heber; it contains many beautiful pieces." He opened the pages randomly as he spoke, displaying some magnificent steel engravings. Indian Joe had never seen such a book in his life. It far excelled the old English Bible in the Osmer home that had been printed in London in 1789; the engravings were far clearer, the paper and type better. He asked the price; it was seven dollars. He did not hesitate a minute but drew out seven of the twelve silver dollars and handed them over to the bookseller. The old man wrapped the book carefully in brown paper and handed it to him, together with a Christmas card, on which was a biblical quotation, telling him that the card was a souvenir of his visit, to come again.

Armed with his gift, Indian Joe strode out into the sunlight, the happiest young man in the world. He had given Gabs her wolf hide; now, with the bounty money, he had purchased her the handsomest book of the year. When the family party reassembled that afternoon at three o'clock, according to previous arrangement, Gabs noticed the heavy package that the young Indian carried but did not comment. All the party members, except Isaac Osmer, carried bundles of some kind. Instead of the hilarity of the others, he wore a doleful, worried look. Indian Joe noticed this and wondered what could be wrong. On the homeward drive, the party talked and jested about their day in town, what they had seen, some telling of their purchases or acquaintances they had met, all but farmer Osmer, who was moody and taciturn. However, by the next morning, he was all over his melancholy and had many pleasant things to say concerning the trip. Mother Osmer and Gabs were proud of the fact that they got to the county seat twice a year; they visited Milroy a like number of times annually. In this, they were more fortunate than some of the other mountaineers, who, if they traveled to Lewistown once and Milroy once in twelve months, considered themselves fortunate.

Christmas eve was ushered in by a party at the Osmer home—the rooms were prettily decorated with evergreens and holly-berries—and about a dozen neighbors were present. On that occasion, the distribution of gifts took place. Gabs, who was overjoyed at receiving her handsome book of poems, presented Indian Joe with a hunting knife. It was of the best steel obtainable and was something the young hunter had long wanted, "It's bad luck to give a knife unless you give a copper in return," said old Cephas Zettle, who was one of the guests. The Indian did not have any coppers about him, so the old man handed one to the fair donor.

Some of the persons present noticed the intimacy between the young girl and the native and thought it strange that the Osmer family tolerated it. Class distinctions were unknown in the Seven Mountains, at least among the farmers, but Indians were regarded as outcasts, unworthy of being regarded as human beings. "There are so many grand-looking boys on the mountain it's a wonder she fancies that rascal," said one woman as she was driven home; such is the way those who accept hospitality invariably talk, no matter what their station.

All through the winter, the intimacy continued, even to the point of sitting up together, which in the backwoods is a sure sign of impending matrimony. Ostensibly they sat by the big kitchen fire to read the poems of Bishop Heber, but the pages never looked much thumbed the next mornings. In the springtime, the Indian went away for a few days at a time trout-fishing but always returned with a basket full for Gabs. Once during the latter part of June, he accompanied two young men from Lewistown, relatives of the family who now occupied the old Delette farm, on a fishing excursion to the headwaters of Panther Creek. The trip lasted nearly a week, and the three lads, all about the same age, had a merry time camping in the virgin forest. The Indian found a mammoth elk horn among the ferns near the camp. It seemed in good condition, though it must have lain there some years, as the last known elk had disappeared from the region almost beyond the memory of the generation.

It would be a fine relic for Gabs, thought the young Indian, so he stowed it away carefully.

When the party broke up, the Indian lover could not cover ground fast enough to meet his sweetheart. When he reached his cabin, he unstrung his trout, some twenty inches long, for they were caught in a "virgin" branch of the creek that had never been fished before and packed them with wild grape leaves in a neat basket of his own making. He artistically fitted the elkhorn as a handle, although the ends extended much more than the basket's length, and with heart thumping hard, hurried along his well-worn wood path towards the Osmer manse. It was late in the afternoon—in the Golden Hour—when he reached there, the mother was sitting on a bench beneath the big Coffee tree near the summer kitchen, with her ironing table before her. She did not smile as the enthusiastic young Indian drew near, but her manner was gentle.

"Where's Gabs?" he eagerly inquired, not waiting to receive her greeting. "I've forty giant trout in this basket for her, and I found this elkhorn in the woods."

The mother looked at him critically, replying, "Gabs went to the county seat with her father early this morning. I don't expect her back much before midnight; her father had a lot of business to transact."

There was something unnatural in the woman's manner, something disquieting to his sensitive nature. Unlettered savage he might be, but he was more intuitive, more psychic than most gentlemen of culture. He felt something was wrong; he could not bear to stay to find out what it was.

"Give these things to her when she returns," he faltered, and then with a forced smile and a "goodbye," he turned on his heel and disappeared out the brushy pathway.

He kept his distance for twenty-four hours and returned as he had promised to help get in the hay. When he appeared at the barn, he noticed how happy Isaac Osmer seemed and how full of fun were the three boys.

"Well, we've lost our girl," said the farmer jocularly, "Gabs went and married Jakey Rumberger, the big drover, the day before yesterday; she's going to live in a fine red brick house, with marble steps, opposite the courthouse, she certainly has done well,"

Indian Joe was, by nature, a stoic, but this was shocking news. He bore it unflinchingly, however, and started to help harness the team as if nothing had happened. There was only one Jakey Rumberger whom he could remember. This Jakey was a huge, deep-voiced, black-bearded fellow over forty years of age; he had seen him once or twice buying cattle in the mountains. He was reputed to be wealthy but was a hard bargainer, crafty and cruel.

At dinner time, Indian Joe found Mother Osmer in excellent humor; he pleasantly discussed the wedding with her. She said she had sent the trout and the elkhorn to the bride the next morning, along with all her clothes, as she had not returned that night. Afterward, when he noticed the horn lying under the floor of the kitchen porch, he scented some deception but remained tranquil. He worked all summer for the Osmers, was cheerful and communicative, never once betraying the burning sorrow at his heart. He never wept even when alone; he never complained; he was like a wounded wolf, resigned to all that had and would occur.

Gabs did not come back on a visit that summer or winter, but she was at the farm the following summer with her small baby for several weeks. She acted friendly towards the Indian, but both kept their distance. At the beginning of that winter, Indian Joe joined the crew of a big lumber camp and helped build rafts to send down Penn's Creek. He liked the work so well that he never resumed farm labor. He made baskets at his cabin when idle and occasionally spent a day or two visiting the Osmers. He saw Gabs from time to time; she seemed happy; four children were born to her.

Years rolled by, Isaac Osmer passed away, the sons farmed the property, and Mother Osmer moved to Lewistown with her daughter. Indian Joe's visits ceased; he maintained his solitary existence when home from the pine jobs. Once thirty years after the marriage to Gabs—he must have been a very old man—and had been buried at his birthplace in Dormantown. Life is strange—its action is circular.

Twelve months later, the first year that Decoration Day was observed, Indian Joe was working on the headwaters of the branch of Panther Creek—it was called Little Panther—where he had found the elkhorn so many years before. The past tortured him so acutely that he drew his time and quit as soon as good weather set in. The boss for whom he had worked for seven or eight years remarked, "Indian Joe must be getting old; this is the first job he failed to stick at to the end."

Unlike most loggers, the Indians in particular, he was not restless and changeable. Some peculiar impulse drew him across the White Mountains to Dormantown; he wanted to see if Jakey Rumberger was really dead and buried there. He visited the cemetery and had no trouble finding the stone; it was the most conspicuous one there. To make it more so, several of the shaggy, venerable pines had been cut down, showing it off to full advantage. On the slab, he read, "Jacob, Beloved Husband of Gabriella Rumberger, Departed this Life June 1, 1865, aged 75 years." He wept no tears over Jakey's decease but hated to read that the widow had inscribed him for posterity as her "beloved." He felt sorry he had visited the graveyard. He planned to recross the mountains that night, but on the high road, he chanced to meet Benny McElhoe, who had once worked with him in the woods.

Benny had a contract for cutting ties for the new railroad projected through the valley and wanted the Indian to help him. He could board with Benny, whose home was next door to the Dormantown post office. Indian Joe accepted and soon became the most active man on the tie job. Benny's wife, a sober-minded Pennsylvania German woman, was much interested in church work. She was a leader of the "Helpers," a society of women who kept the church and its grounds in good condition. Decoration Day, the new festival, was to be properly observed in the little mountain hamlet. Already six Civil War soldiers were buried in the pine-shaded cemetery. The good woman invited the Indian to accompany her to the graveyard to help her clean the graves and scrape the moss off the old tombstones. He hated to go there, but as Benny had always been kind to him, he hated equally to refuse. As they neared the enclosure, they noticed a team of horses and a surrey standing by the whitewashed paling fence. A driver, who held the reins, was asleep on the front seat.

"Pretty toney folks for such a place," said Rachel McElhoe. The Indian's sharp eyes detected a familiar face when they entered the gate. It was none other than widow Gabs. She was seated by her husband's grave, scraping away the weeds, smoothing out the beds of myrtle. A trifle stouter, her hair a trifle darker; otherwise, she was the same Gabs. Elegantly dressed, two young girls were standing near, but they did not try to assist. When she saw the Indian, she called to him, and he hurried over to her, shaking her warmly by the hand. Rachel McElhoe stood at a distance, speechless at the wild Indian's intimacy with the "toney folks." He stood and talked to her for a while, and when the young ladies, having grown impatient, moved toward their carriage, she asked him to sit down and help her. Horror of horrors, did he ever think he would live to the day when he would be arranging his hated rival's grave for Decoration Day! But he took to the task with a will, and both worked until they perspired. Then they braced themselves with their hands and rested. They fell to talking about the past; every detail of the old days was discussed—up to the time of her sudden marriage.

"Do you know how I came to marry Jacob Rumberger?" she asked suddenly.

"No, I don't know," replied the Indian. "It's something I've puzzled my mind over for thirty years. It broke my heart, for I loved you."

Gabs, struck by his frankness, looked him full in the eyes and continued. "I think I loved you too, but I was very young and unsure what love meant. I had no intention of marrying him, but I did it to save our home. You see, Jacob was very rich; he owned many mortgages, including one which covered almost everything we possessed. Father was a poor manager and let everything slip out of his hands. Things got to a point where it meant we would have to give up the place and take to living in a cabin smaller than yours, and father asked him if there was any way we could remain. Jacob was blunt and told him that he could stay if he let him marry his girl. Interest-free for the rest of his days. I had read so much in that book about *duty* that I meekly consented. I never loved Jacob, but I made him a true wife. I am here today decorating his grave because he was the father of my four children."

Indian Joe looked at her, amazed yet full of love. "Is that what you call honor?" he faltered. The words were no sooner uttered than he wished them back, but it was too late.

"Is that what you call honor, to wait thirty years and then chide me for doing what I thought was my duty?" she answered.

"I didn't mean to hurt you," said the Indian.

Gabs did not make any sign as if she understood and went on, "I had hoped and prayed every day since Jacob died, and maybe away down in my heart once or twice while he was alive, that I would see you again. We have met; I am disappointed."

"Mother, mother, mother," called the girls in the surrey, "what on earth are you doing there? Come along."

"I must be going," said Gabs, with a flushed face, as she clambered to her feet. Once standing before her former lover, feeling that she might never see him again, all her old love came back like an avalanche; she forgot her recent words of reproach.

"I deserve all you said, Joe, and more. I have been the unhappiest woman in the world." She held out her hand; he clasped it; she half uttered some words, then repressed them. In her quandary, she left him standing on a grave without saying goodbye. In the carriage, the girls turned on their mother angrily.

"You didn't dare invite that awful-looking scarecrow to come to see us, did you? Your old-time friends are always turning up."

Gabs turned away and looked towards the White Mountains; across that wall-like range and several more was the bleak, uneven roofed farmhouse where she had spent her girlhood, from which she had gone to a life of affluent slavery. What had she gained by her sacrifice to duty, thirty years of uncongenial marriage, children who disapproved of her obscure origin, her one love who lived to chide her?

All the way back in the carriage, she remained speechless. "Mother's got her sulks," whispered one girl over the seat to her sister. That night the lonely woman sat up until midnight reading Heber's poems, drinking dregs of bitterness. What was Indian Joe doing now? Why hadn't she urged him to come to see her or insisted on remaining with him in Dormantown? Then she thought of her sons, rising young attorneys, of her daughters' social prominence; she had sealed her fate over thirty years before; it was a life sentence.

(Photo by S. W. Smith)

OLD FORT HOTEL

II

DAN TREASTER'S NIGHTS

(Story of the Wolf Knob)

"DAN TREASTER'S nights were awful," said the little spectacled livery driver as we bumped along in the rickety old surrey over the rocky road to Bannerville. We were on our way to meet a certain Joe Knepp, a famous hunter, and hear from him some of his thrilling adventures in the Seven Mountains long ago, but our driver bid fair to tell us more stirring tales than this ancient nimrod. "No matter how terrible the nights were," continued the driver, "Uncle Dan wouldn't move away. He was the first white man to settle in the little valley called after him; he was proud of the fact and swore he'd die there. When he first appeared there as a young man, the valley was choked full of pines and hemlocks. They grew so tall that they seemed to reach the surrounding mountains' summits. He viewed his future home from the top of the point they now call Treaster's Knob or Wolf Knob and then climbed down to the bottom, where he found a sweet spring and set to work. He had a lean-to of boughs and burlap built by the first night on the ground, and into it, he retired for a night of peaceful sleep.

"He had laid down and turned over once or twice when he heard some sniffling and snarling outside just like a pack of hounds. 'Somebody's hunting in the valley, and their dogs have scented me,' he thought. 'Get out of there,' he yelled, but instead of the desired result, there commenced a howling and barking the like of which was scarcely ever heard in the world before.

"Dan Treaster had come from Perry County, where the wild game had long since disappeared, but he had heard the old folks talk a lot, and he knew that his nocturnal visitors were wolves. There must have been five hundred of them, he figured. He stood the infernal racket as long as he could; there was no use trying to get to sleep, so he got up and walked to the flap of the tent. He saw eyes of wolves everywhere; they looked like lightning bugs, only every one was a dozen times bigger and brighter. He took a couple of random shots with his rifle; there were some awful yelps of pain, the pack turned on their heels, and Uncle Dan turned on his, lay down among his buffalo robes, and fell fast asleep.

"It was broad daylight when he awoke the next morning. There had been a hoar frost, though it was early in September, and the air was crisp and cold. Two dead wolves lay within a hundred feet of the lean-to. They hadn't been touched by the others, which proved that they were well fed, that game was abundant. 'I am going to live on what the wolves have been getting,' he said as he commenced preparing breakfast. After his meal, he skinned the two carcasses and hung the hides on trees to dry, and as a warning to other wolves not to disturb his slumbers in the future.

"Uncle Dan was a big powerful young man in those days; he wore a long black beard, and work was nothing to him. Within a month, he had a respectable-sized clearing and the logs and brush piled in the center of it ready for the blaze. He then, single-handed, of course, built a log cabin and barn and started for Pfouts' Valley to spend Christmas. When he came back, the sight reminded folks who saw it of pictures of Noah's Ark. First in importance, he brought a wife, a very pretty young girl. Next in value was the livestock, a mare and foal, two cows, three sheep, five hogs, a crate of Greeley chickens, and a trio of "toppy" ducks. Last, but not least, were three small dogs. Aunt Nancy, as we called Dan's wife, led the brigade driving the wagon, on which were piled household and farming implements; Dan himself brought up the rear driving the stock. He carried his trusty rifle, and the caravan feasted on game the entire distance. He had cut a trail through Beaver Hollow into the valley, it was pretty rough work negotiating it, but the entire outfit was landed safely at the new home. It was a great day for Uncle Dan; within four months, he had come, seen, conquered. The livestock was carefully shut in the stable while the pioneer and his wife proceeded to get supper. They lingered quite a while over the repast, discussing their trip and plans for the future when it occurred to them that they had better go out to see how the stock was faring. It had become quite dark, and Aunt Nancy experienced some difficulty in finding her box of tallow dips. Uncle Dan tried to help, and fifteen minutes were consumed in the search. Both got real upset at mislaying such an important item. While they fussed and fumed, an awful barking began outside the cabin; Aunt Nancy was frightened half to death.

"'What's all that, for lands sakes,' she shrieked.

"'Wolves, only wolves,' was Uncle Dan's reply. He shot several times into the darkness, but the dreadful racket would not grow less.

"'You can't go to the barn tonight,' said Aunt Nancy, 'the wolves would make their supper off you.'

"'I guess I don't care to either,' said the pioneer with a laugh.

"'Too bad we hadn't watered the stock before it got so dark,' said his wife.

"'Let's go to bed,' said Uncle Dan. 'Maybe when we wake up in the morning, the bar and all its contents will be gone,' said Aunt Nancy.

"At this, the hunter laughed, saying that if such was the case, it meant another trip to Pfouts' Valley for a fresh supply. In the morning, when they went out, they found that the compact log barn had proved an admirable fortress, that all the livestock were intact. The toppy ducks during the night had laid eggs, perhaps through fright! The little dogs lay helpless on the straw; their tongues hung out, their eyes bloodshot. They had tried their best all night to get out at their noisy foes, but after beating their little bodies frantically against the walls for hours, they finally laid down exhausted. That evening Uncle Dan and his wife went to the stable to feed the stock before preparing their own supper. It took quite a while to satisfy each hungry animal and fowl, and dusk closed in quickly. Just as they were bedding the mare and foal, an awful barking arose outside. It was the wolves back again. The little dogs dived for the open door, but the pioneer knocked them back with his fork. Aunt Nancy had the presence of mind to slam the door; they were safe in the barn but supperless. Uncle Dan, of course, had his rifle with him and shot it off a couple of times through a knothole in the door. It didn't do any good, and he didn't care to waste ammunition, so he decided to let the wolves hold the fort for the night. The couple fumbled about in the darkness and located the two duck eggs which had been placed in the corner of a feed-box for safe keeping, and these eaten raw, with cups of milk, constituted their supper. Then they drove the cows into the entry, lay down in their stall, and fell asleep. Outside, the wolves yelled themselves hoarse. In the morning, the courageous pair laughed heartily at having gotten the better of them. It must have been humiliating to the creatures to make such noise without frightening their intended victims. Thus began and went on a constant conflict with the wolves, which the animals felt more than the Treasters.

"Aunt Nancy admitted she was a little frightened when her first baby was born; it was too precious to be devoured by wild beasts. A lame girl from Cocolamus, I believe she was a distant relative named Sib Royer, came to stay with the Treasters at this time. The wolves made her so nervous that she could not sleep, so after a week, she decided to foot it back to civilization. She never reached Cocolamus. Her family vowed that wolves had eaten her on the way and blamed Uncle Dan for letting her start off alone.

"Old Daddy Reese, who used to peddle through the mountains pulling a little wagon, he was afterwards murdered near the Black Horse Tavern, and his body buried in the woods told a very different story. Two days after Sib had left Treaster Valley, he claimed he saw her in a Gypsy wagon, moving in the direction of Seven Stars. But at the same time, Sib Royer was never heard tell of again.

"Uncle Dan had some thrilling adventures with the wolves himself. Once, he was treed by the pack for a whole night. They got so close that he had to leave his gun and climb a honey locust for his life. On several other occasions, he had to run home in a hurry, literally slamming the door in the animals' faces. Most men would have moved away or else raised an awful howl for protection. It was all a joke with Uncle Dan. He always maintained that after the food supply of the wolves had gone, the sickly deer and grouse, and other game, they would die out of themselves. Every year more wolves died from starvation than from the hunters after a country was opened up. His father, who had lived in Buffalo Valley in his youth, used to tell him about finding the carcasses of fifty wolves buried in a snowdrift on Jack's Mountain in the early spring of 1835. The hunters had destroyed the wolves' supply; they had become too weak from hunger to draw themselves out of the drift and had to perish. Uncle Dan proved his statements by the fact that the wolves he killed the first night of his arrival in the valley were not eaten by their fellows; latterly, they turned on their fallen comrades so quickly that he could hardly secure the carcasses for the hides. For this reason, he killed or trapped few wolves. 'They will go soon enough,' he sighed. His industry was prodigious.

"He cut and burnt all the timber which stood on the face of the mountain back of his home, clear to the top of the Knob. There a ledge of sharp rocks overhung the steep slope. It was a risky place to work, so he left standing the thick tuft of scrub pines on the point, which at a distance resembled an Indian's war topknot. There was a time when anyone standing on the top of Paddy's Mountain and looking in every direction could see only one patch of light green; that was Dan Treaster's clearing; the rest was the blue-black mass of pine and hemlock wilderness. He pastured his cattle and sheep on the almost perpendicular slope; they seemed to thrive on fireweed and raspberry bushes. He had them all belled; it was sweet music to hear all the little bells ringing in harmony so far away on still summer afternoons. The descendants of the three small dogs he brought from Pfouts' Valley guarded them, and they were scarcely ever molested by wolves. The little dogs barked when they scented danger, and Uncle Dan or one of his boys would run up the hill with a gun and soon finish any would-be marauder. But this was seldom, considering the remoteness. Several people asked the old man why he preferred small dogs to big ones. 'Well,' he drawled, 'the big dogs are fools; they would fight a wolf and get licked. The little dogs bark for help, and my boys or I finish the job.'

"Naturally, he acquired several wolf hides annually, and his boys sometimes brought down a catamount or a wildcat. He never went to the county seat to collect bounties, as he feared it would attract outsiders into 'his' valley. He always traded the hides with Daddy Reese, who hauled them in his little hand-wagon to Derrstown or Youngmanstown, where they fetched good prices. The wolf-hides were coal black and very long-haired; they were of the species *Canis lycaon*. Old Daddy would never tell where he got these hides though some of the younger professional hunter scallywags threatened to beat him if he didn't. Some thought it was during a row caused by his silence on this subject that caused his murder;

at any rate, he was headed for the remoter little valleys when he met his cruel death. Perhaps his ghost will tell the story sometime; it draws the little wagon about the oakwood where he was slain every moonless night. Of course, a few hunters and timber prospectors did get in the valley, but Uncle Dan had a way of making the game seem scarce when they appeared. But he could not prevent the wolves from barking. Every night they would huddle themselves together on the ledge on the topmost point of the Knob and howl defiance at the occupants of the log cabin below.

"'Every year, their barking grows fainter,' Uncle Dan would say. 'Every time I kill a deer, it means one more wolf must starve this winter.'

"Uncle Dan was a great deerslayer; contrary to the custom of most men of his type, he loved to preserve the horns. His barns and outbuildings were decorated with scores of antlers, some of them very pretentious. I can recall a set that had sixteen points on each horn—it had a very broad spread; I think it was the record set for the Seven Mountains. Sammy Strohecker at Rebersburg had a grand pair with twelve points on each horn, but Uncle Dan's was much bigger. And the bear paws, there were enough of them to walk to California—he had them nailed up everywhere. He also tacked up catamounts' paws. They were fluffy and very big, twice the size of a wildcat's.

"The catamount or Canada Lynx is a northern animal, I know, but they were found in the Seven Mountains. Two were killed by the Foster boys on Broad Face in November 1912. While Uncle Dan bought and paid for five hundred acres, it was only a small fraction of the acreage of Treaster Valley. From head to mouth, it contained a good six thousand acres, all heavily timbered; it was seven miles long. About thirty years ago, the first white pine jobs started there. There was one camp in charge of Indian Joe, another bossed by a cranky York State Yankee, whose name I forget. The wolves would bark, and the Yank and his wife threw fits every night. He got so mad and excited that he actually drove to the county seat and asked state aid in ridding the valley of wolves; said he'd demand the calling out of the militia to help him; it was an outrage to have wolves in a civilized commonwealth. He drank a lot that day and told his stories to the newspapermen, so all the county papers came out with big headlines and scare stories about the wolves of Treaster Valley.

"This naturally brought a swarm of hunters into the region, but not a single wolf was killed. 'Why, it's only my little dogs that do the barking,' said Uncle Dan, by way of discouraging their permanent occupation of his hunting grounds. But the hunters killed a number of deer, wild turkeys, rabbits, wild pigeons, and grouse, which cut severely into the food supply of the remnant of the wolves which remained.

"The wolf scare was followed by a panther scare. The Yankee and his wife had gotten up sufficient courage to spend an evening with the Treaster family. It was clear full moonlight, almost as light as day. The wolves did some little barking that night, but whenever the Yankee woman clutched her husband's arm and shivered, Uncle Dan would say, 'dogs, dogs.' It was about ten o'clock when they left for their camp, which was situated about a mile west of Uncle Dan's home; the spring was where Beaver Run heads. They had a big spotted dog with them, which commenced acting queerly after they had gone a few hundred yards. It huddled close beside them, whining pitifully. The Yankees stopped and listened; all they could hear was the doleful cadences of the katydids and the gurgling of the brook. The dog laid down flat and had to be dragged along by his collar; this thoroughly frightened them. 'Wolves,' sobbed the Yankee woman; 'it's them, it's them, it's them,' bellowed the husband. Terror-stricken they eventually reached the camp, ran in, and slammed the door. They woke up all the crew, which started a regular swearing match as the red-shirted figures rose up from their bunks. Just then, they heard an awful scraping and scratching; it sounded like a planing mill in operation! They looked through the tiny window of the lobby and, in the bright moonlight, could see the head of a huge panther emerging over the back end of the horse stable. The animal walked along the tar-paper roof until he reached the ledge, where he stood motionless. They say moonlight magnifies; it must have, in this case, every woman's son in the camp swore the brute was eighteen feet long! Polish Mike, the biggest man in the bunch, picked up a shotgun and, despite the pleadings of the rest of the gang, opened the door and fired point blank at the monster, which was not more than fifty feet away. There was a hideous howl of pain, and the panther sprang off the roof, a distance of thirty feet; the ground shook when he struck it and disappeared in the underbrush.

"The next week, there was a new boss in the camp, and he was Polish Mike. Uncle Dan was glad when the pine jobs were all ended as they kept bringing strangers into the valley, and game decreased apace. The old man doubted if there were more than half a dozen wolves still in the valley. When he began to feel at peace again, it was only two years after the last pine job had been finished, no less than five hemlock camps were opened in different parts of the valley. A tram road was built into the valley. All told, the camps contained over a hundred bark-peelers, skidders, axers, and teamsters. To make matters worse, the very next year, a big prop-timber camp opened on the broad plateau back of the Knob, the wolves' last retreat. Hemmed in by civilization, the dwindled pack gave up the struggle and dropped out of sight.

"It was about this time that farmers in Penn's Valley saw little companies of wolves trotting across the fields towards the northern mountains. Presumably, they were heading for Canada, but they probably died of starvation before getting beyond the 'northern tier.' All was quiet in Treaster Valley; the wolves were gone, the stray panthers and catamounts, abashed, wailed no longer; the only racket came from a new stave mill. Uncle Dan Treaster began to grow feeble; his giant form sometimes shook with palsy, his beard became very white. When he was able, he began taking solitary walks; he seemed to be looking for something; it was the wolves. He often asked his boys who worked on the bark jobs if they heard tell of any being seen in his valley or in High Valley across the mountain. The only consolation he could find was when Indian Joe came and spent a Sunday at his home and told him that as soon as the bark jobs and the stave mill got away, the wolves would be back. But where were they, were they watching from some distant high top?

"Finally, the bark-peeling finished, and the stave mill blew off for the last time. Uncle Dan had survived these modern devices; perhaps the good old days and the wolves would return. But in the wake of the lumbermen came a killing forest fire, the first Treaster Valley had ever known. It burnt the valley to a blackened waste from end to end, from the summits to the deepest gullies. Every tree seemed lifeless except a few old tupelos. The abandoned stave mill and camps were wiped off the face of the earth. Uncle Dan and his boys had to work night and day for a week to save their buildings. The strain was too much for the old man; he went down rapidly after it. It is said that he wept when he looked up at the mountain which he had cleared and beheld the clump of pines on the summit reduced to charred branchless stabs.

"Even if the wolves came back, where would they hide to howl nocturnal defiance on the log cabin beneath!

"'It will be all right now,' said Bill, his oldest son, 'you'll surely have the valley all to yourself; people will soon forget there ever was such a place.' But the old man shook his head, saying that he would not be convinced until he heard a wolf call on the Knob.

"The next spring brought some signs of life to the valley. The oak and chestnut trees sprouted green leaves, even some of the pitch pines on the higher levels sent out shoots; fireweed, poke, and sour-grass were everywhere. One bright morning while plowing, a farmer residing near Aaronsburg saw a large black wolf trotting across his field in the direction of the Seven Mountains. That night Uncle Dan had retired at dark, but he awoke about nine o'clock, saying to his wife that he heard a wolf barking on the topmost crag of the Knob. She lit the lamp, and the old man dressed himself with trembling anxiety. Fastening his galluses with palsied fingers, he stumbled out on the back porch. His son Bill heard him and was soon out of bed and hurried after his father with a quilt. He got the old man to sit down on his favorite chair and threw the comforter about his shoulders.

"'Listen,' said the gaunt pioneer, holding his left hand behind his ear, 'there's a wolf calling on the Knob.' The son, and old Aunt Nancy, who were near, could hear the clear, distinct notes of wolfish anguish high up among the charred pines on the cone. Louder and fiercer and more heartrending it became until it died away in an inarticulate sob. Then all was still, save for the peepers in the marsh below the spring-house.

"'I'm afraid it's a token,' whispered Aunt Nancy to her boy. Scarcely had she uttered these words when Uncle Dan began breathing heavily.

"'Run quickly and get the lamp,' called the old lady. Before Bill could get back, the brave soul of the great gaunt patriarch of the Seven Mountains had departed for the unknown land."

III

THE GHOST

(The Story of an Old Academy)

IT was at the old Seminary in New Berlin that Douglass Clawaghter met Ettie Lucas. They were both pupils at this time-honored institution, though occupying very different stations in life. Even though they had been born and reared within twelve miles of each other, they had never laid eyes on one another until one dark afternoon in the natural history museum on the top floor of the seminary building. Both had gotten to the school a day before term opened, traveling by different routes. It was as if fate had sent them on one of her inscrutable errands. After making the necessary arrangements with the secretary, both had been assigned to rooms and had taken a stroll under the grand old maples and pines that completely embowered the campus. Walking in opposite directions, they had seen one another from a distance, each without a quickening interest. Then a September shower set in, cold and blowy, hurling down yellow leaves on the paths. Distant thunder rumbled. Jack's Mountain grew purple-black, and there were few patches of silver in the sky. Ettie was first to get indoors; she made a pretty figure clad in a clinging black dress, running before the storm. She ran upstairs and was in her room before Douglass entered the building. He paused for a minute in the hallway, reading the school announcements, which were tacked to a board on the wall. On a small slip of paper was written in neat, old-style script, "Natural History Museum, top floor." Douglass, who was of a studious turn of mind, rejoiced when he read this; it would be an ideal place to spend the time that intervened until the lamps were lit and supper was ready.

He recalled that his father had mentioned the existence of such a museum as one of the attractions of the academy. It had inclined him to his decision to matriculate, although he knew he would be isolated there by caste. Why his father was determined to send him to New Berlin, when there were so many more fashionable institutions, was an enigma. Perhaps he feared the boy might have temptations or acquire extravagant habits at the great New England preparatory schools. The elder Clawaghter was a typical Scotch-Irishman of the old-fashioned type. He had strong views on every subject and so on. Douglass climbed the three flights of stairs to the museum, leaning heavily on the walnut balustrades as he was in a thoughtful mood. The paint-faded walnut door was shut, but a key was stuck in it; evidently, it had just been opened for the semester. The young man entered the vast room; it was low ceilinged but occupied almost the entire top floor. The many windows were sloping; they were in the Mansart roof and commanded splendid views of the surrounding country; the sky was sun-silvered as the storm had ceased. The museum had a peculiar, musty, medicated odor, almost like stale pepper; it was close and needed ventilation. In long rows were the tall cases of white pine painted white with dusty glass lights. In them were collections of the birds, animals, insects, geology, and fossils, as well as many Indian relics of Central Pennsylvania. Brought together with great care by Professor A. E. Gobble and other scientists, they were worthy of metropolitan surroundings.

Almost the first object which greeted the young student's eyes was the stuffed effigy of the famous Dorman panther. This animal, one of the largest of its kind ever killed in the Seven Mountains and a splendid male, was mounted with mouth wide open, showing its dental development. Set up according to the custom of the time, it was stuffed with the bullet holes in full view; two gaping hollows, one in the jowl, below the eye, the other near the heart, showing where the great nimrod had ended the monster's life on that memorable Christmas Eve in 1868 on Shreiner Knob. Douglass' heart stood still as he gazed at the manikin; it was so typical of all that was noble and best in the wild mountain life of the region so fast passing away.

So wrapt was his attention that he was unaware of another's presence until a loose board in the bare floor creaked audibly. He turned around and beheld a wonderfully fair vision of young womanhood. She was of the blonde, or ash-brown coloring, above medium height. Slim and of graceful outlines—she was dressed in black—she was the girl who had hurried in before the storm half an hour earlier! Her face was most unusual, having a cast of features seldom seen in these times. The distance from the eyes to the upper lip was remarkably long; she recalled the familiar picture of Lady Janet Thraill. The lips were red and full and inclined to pout; the eyelids drooped, partly covering grey-blue eyes. Her color was rosy, the complexion of a healthy girl of seventeen; her fingers were very long and very white.

Douglass hesitated a moment before speaking; his nature was shy; then, he made bold to ask her if she was to be a pupil at the school. When she replied in the affirmative, she spoke in a decided Pennsylvania German intonation. It is delicious to those who are used to it; almost barbaric to strangers from the east. The young man knew this accent very well, though it was used by a class of people with whom his family and self rarely maintained social intercourse. The old Scotch-Irish families with their manor houses of herring-bone stone, with the family arms cut on slabs of granite inserted beneath the gables, their vast estates, political and social eminence, their ancestry running in unbroken lines far into the distant past in the old country, could feel little affinity for the German element, springing it was maintained, mostly from peasants. They were different in caste, in religion, in tastes; marriages or even friendships seldom occurred between them in the Seven Mountains' Country. But here was a girl, Pennsylvania German she might be, who was every inch a queen.

"My name is Douglass Clawaghter," said the young man to cement the introduction, "I live at Rossmere." Rossmere was the name of the manor house where the Clawaghters had resided for four generations. The girl looked at him in surprise.

"I am Ettie Lucas," she said simply, "my father is Simon Lucas, the lumber dealer at Abundance in Gregg Township." Douglass knew Simon Lucas by reputation; he was a worthy man but had risen from a plain pilot of a grain ark on Penn's Creek; he was a man of no social pretensions. There was no use pondering over the intricacies of caste on such an occasion; the girl was truly lovely; that was all there was to it. The young couple seemed to get along admirably; strangely enough, Ettie knew considerable about the fauna of the Seven Mountains, and they passed two hours blissfully in the dingy museum. It was dark, and the supper bell had rung when they descended. Besides three professors and the principal's wife, they were the only persons at the supper table. The bare, high-ceilinged room, meagerly lit by the single lamp which rested on the red table cloth, seemed very cold; the supper of ham and eggs, apple butter, homemade bread, coffee, and cake very good. The room was innocent of pictures; over one of the doors was a much-discolored bust of Simon Snyder, a resident of the nearby town of Selin's Grove, who was a great patron of education during his three terms as Governor of Pennsylvania; over the other door was a stuffed flying squirrel.

The professors and the principal's wife were very gracious. They talked glowingly of the prospects of the coming school year; it was to be the golden age of the old academy. They all seemed pleased that the two pupils acted so congenially together; it argued good fellowship. With "school spirit," the institution would have a new lease of life. The young couple were together all evening in the sitting room, laughing and chatting; Douglass was very entertaining, shyness and pride were nowhere, he became an immediate favorite. The next morning the body of pupils arrived; there were between sixty and seventy, mostly boys, and a sturdy, healthy-looking lot they were. Most were of the mountaineer type, black-haired and black-eyed, with high color and happy smiles.

Despite his wealth and station, Douglass mingled freely with all but kept his eye on Ettie. As for her, she seemed to have interest for no one else. In so many country schools, boys and girls pair off this way; in many cases, marriage results when school days are completed. The other lads, impressed as they were by Ettie's grace and beauty, observed Douglass' concern for her and kept aloof. The story was circulated that they had been friends for years and were engaged already. This gained credence from the fact that their homes were comparatively near together. In their simple hearts, they were unaware that social class is a wider barrier than miles. There was considerable snow in New Berlin that year—fully a month before the Christmas holidays, and the academy students organized several sleighing parties. Douglass always sat close to Ettie; on the way back, they invariably held hands and sometimes slyly kissed. Douglass wrote home enthusiastic accounts of the school, of his scholastic prospects. His parents were pleased, for they feared the place might be too quiet for him and the social status of his fellow pupils uncongenial. Ettie likewise wrote home how happy she was, but as her parents viewed the Academy as one of the greatest learning institutions on earth, this was to be expected. The sleighing parties paved the way for Douglass to invite Ettie to ride with him in a cutter he procured from a local livery stable while the rest of the young people rode in the big bobs. In some cases, this might have been frowned on by the faculty, but as the scholastic standing and general deportment of the young people were so excellent, they made every allowance for them. During the holidays, the young man drove across the ridge to Abundance and took supper with his sweetheart at her home.

He met her parents, who were assiduous in their attentions to him; he could easily see that they looked upon him as a most desirable suitor. He never mentioned her name at his home; often, he asked himself if this was right since, in the depth of his heart, he vowed he would make her his wife. He knew his family's proud spirit; how they would rebel at any idea of his even being attentive to a person who was not bred as he was, who did not belong to the same church. Undoubtedly the fair Ettie loved the young man to a certain extent; she would have been head over heels in love with him had she been older and able to appreciate his noble qualities. As it was, she thought more of his position than his personality. But here, let it be said, she would not marry any man for money; she was not at all grasping; besides, her father was in very comfortable circumstances. Unknown to her aristocratic lover, she was carrying on a correspondence with a young fellow of her own class who had formerly been a telegraph operator at Abundance but now worked somewhere on the Pittsburgh division. Maybe she secretly mistrusted her ability to live happily with a scion of the "old stock," the operator she could have any time. He might come in handy to soothe her in case she broke with Douglass. After the holidays, the young aristocrat and his sweetheart were as often together as previously. They were leaders of school life; they seemed of one mind and heart. No one suspected that the boy was hiding the affair from his family, that the girl was carrying on a secret intrigue with another lad. As good weather ensued, Douglass obtained permission to take Ettie for an occasional buggy ride on Saturday afternoons. They always returned before dark; they never visited any but the most frequented highways.

Everything seemed running along happily until one day, the young man received a message saying that his mother was seriously ill and that he had better come home. He was shocked by such a bombshell in the midst of his happiness but kept a "stiff upper lip," as they say in the mountains. He read the timetables carefully, revealing that he had missed the last train from Derrstown that would get him home that night. The next day was Sunday, with no trains running. He might drive the thirty-eight miles, but conscience told him that he must see his sweetheart first. He first went to the principal, informing him of the sad news that he had missed the last train but was going to hire a team and drive there that night. Then he asked permission to take Miss Lucas, as he called her, for a little drive "around the square" before departing. Asked when he would be back to school, he said that it depended entirely on his mother's condition. But the strange intuitive voice within told him that he would never return. When he gave the telegram to Ettie, she did not seem as moved as he hoped she would be. She showed more interest when he asked her to go for the carriage drive. She said she would be ready in fifteen minutes, which would give him time to go to the livery barn back of the Golden Swan and have a team harnessed. Within half an hour, he was driving up the cinder road to the front door of the academy beneath the still leafless trees.

The sound of wheels drew most of the scholars to the windows, and they pressed against the panes as they watched Ettie getting into the buggy. She looked so very beautiful that afternoon that he forgot his anxiety and took her for a longer drive than intended. It was almost dark when, at the old fort at Kreamer, he tamed the horses' heads towards New Berlin. The animals were walking through the muddy road, switching their tails which had been tied short to keep them dry. Ettie was talking lightly about school matters; she would not become serious. He handed her the reins, leaned back in the seat, and began weeping.

HOME OF THE OLD WOLF HUNTER

(Photo by S. W. Smith)

"Oh, how can you take my going away so cooly," he demanded when he regained his composure. Ettie did not answer for a minute; apparently, she was planning a good answer.

"Because," she faltered, "I never take things that way. I feel your going deeply, but I realize you will soon be back; there is no use grieving."

"You believe then in the certainty of human wishes," sobbed the heartsick youth. "Wait awhile; you will see we have no power to make our own destiny; we are like the seeds of the wild cotton."

"Nonsense," replied the girl, "you are coming back in a few days. If we are meant for each other, as you keep telling me, nothing can separate us permanently."

Then she began talking about her vacation plans, of some visits she wanted to make. She had failed her lover when he needed her most, but loving her to distraction, he was blind to her cruelty. She left him at the gate to the seminary grounds, her last words a promise to write him every day he was gone. He picked up the driver at the barn and commenced the lonely journey, mostly through pine forests.

It was nearly daylight when he drove into the park at Rossmere, with its swift running brook. Lights gleamed from behind the shades of the high windows of the manse, showing that the household was wide awake. His father, raw-boned, bearded, with keen grey eyes, met him at the door, giving him the details of his mother's condition. She might die any minute or linger for weeks.

For several days letters came from Ettie. They consoled him, though they were really stiff and formal. He tried to answer them, but as they were lifeless, he could put no life into his replies. He had reached home on the morning of May 4th, only a month and a half remained of the term, so he informed his father he would not go back. The old gentleman seemed pleased, especially as he agreed to renew his studies in the autumn. At the end of two weeks, Ettie's letters ceased, though, in epistles from some of his boy friends at the school, she was evidently still there and in good health. They urged him to come to the school for commencement day, and devoured as he was with love for the false girl, he foolishly decided to go. His visit surprised her as she entertained the young telegrapher as her commencement guest. His blood boiled within him when he discovered this. It was the story of water seeking its level. She had felt uncomfortable with her high-born admirer; she secretly longed for the freedom she could experience with one of her own class. He left abruptly a few hours after he had arrived; his fellow pupils thought it was because he was jealous. They were not penetrating enough to see that his pride as a gentleman was wounded.

Douglass was very unhappy all summer. He was deeply hurt but could not evict Ettie from his heart. He dreamed of her every night. He saw her image in every dark nook and corner in the woods. In the fall, as his mother was somewhat improved, he entered a preparatory school in Germantown, near Philadelphia. When he came home at Christmas, he learned that his former sweetheart had eloped from New Berlin with the telegrapher. They had located somewhere in West Virginia. She was now physically out of his life, but he could not exorcise her psychically. With all her cruelty, her base deceptions, he found that he still loved her. His dreams and visions continued. He vowed that he would never marry anyone else. Outwardly he was bright and cheerful, but in secret, his soul burned and twisted in misery. At the end of the school year, he returned home permanently and took up the management of the two-thousand-acre farm as assistant to his father. He attended to his work well; he rarely took a vacation, and he never noticed any women. He hated to see women, as in every one he saw was reflected the features of Ettie, who was not for him. As he was good-looking and winning, people wondered why he should be such a recluse. As fate does things, his father died first; the mother, overcome by the bereavement, passed away in twelve months.

Douglass Clawaghter, last of his people, became the master of Ross-mere. When he was thirty, he yielded to his loneliness and married. His bride was Dora McClenaghan, daughter of a wealthy landowner in Huntingdon County. She was straight-laced, older than himself, but a member of the same proud caste. Physically she was anything but good-looking. There was general rejoicing among the "old stock" whose very clannishness was causing their disappearance. Their unwritten law was that they must marry among themselves; many remained single rather than marry outside; there were not enough eligibles to go around. The young bridegroom took his sedate spouse to the old manor house, built in the Georgian style of architecture during the first decade of the last century. True to the Irish custom, a swift brook flowed through the grounds, terminating in an ice pond, which had suggested the word "mere" in naming the manse. Ross was a family name of which the Clawaghters were very proud. Many large white pines, stag topped and decaying, grew in the park; some weeping willows along the brook. A few aged boxwoods and arborvitaes huddled about the side of the house which faced the road, giving out strong odors reminiscent of cemeteries. Summer cypress, foxglove, cosmos, and hollyhocks flourished in the flower beds.

The house, built of limestone, plastered and whitewashed outside, was a melancholy-looking pile. Inside, it was stiffly furnished with tall walnut sets; some badly painted ancestral portraits hung on the walls. On the first landing of the winding staircase, which was of no mean proportions, stood a high clock brought from Ireland in 1798. Above it hung the antlers of the last elk killed in the Seven Mountains, which had been shot by Douglass's grandfather. The barns and several small cottages for retainers were the only buildings in sight. Beyond the road was a bleak limestone hill used for pasture, cropped short save for mullein and milkweed. Back of the house—on the side of the main entrance, loomed the Seven Mountains, crowned by the culminating dome of Milliken's High Top. Most women would have felt lonesome coming to such a place, at least after the first novelty wore off, but not so with the dignified bride.

She was so engrossed thinking about her own importance as lady of the manor that she could have felt like a queen in the Sahara. All she could talk about, think about, dream about, was class, caste, birth, ancestry, superiority, exclusiveness. She could not conceive of a paradise peopled by persons not of her strict ancestral lines. One must have the blood of Robert Bruce, an aide-de-camp to William of Orange, and not less than two early Judges of the Pennsylvania Supreme Court to be eligible for eternal bliss.

Whenever Douglass was with her, he could not keep his thought from the absent Ettie. It was a horrible obsession and became all the more repugnant to him as he absorbed his wife's aristocratic ideas and realized the mean position in the earthly scale that his former love had held. When he went out riding, there was a town several miles distant; he saw Ettie's face in every woman he met. When he kept to his estate, he still imagined he saw her coming out from behind the old trees, the rocks, bushes, sheds. Literally, since the girl had camped out in his soul, he could have no peace. He was a complexly organized, hypersensitive representative of a dying people. Providence wisely pays with extinction the over-refinement of race or individual. The gloomier and more solemn he became, the better his wife was suited. She perhaps liked men of the mold of John Knox or Edward Irving. If so, the moodier he became, the more his nature conformed with her ideal. But he felt he must have some relaxation.

He had been married a year, and since the brief honeymoon had been nowhere. There was to be a great fair at the county seat in October; it would make a nice drive for his wife and self. One of his friends, Findlay Chambers, had his horse, Harold the Dauntless, a son of the great Rayon d' Or, entered in the running race. Douglass's wife was not particularly interested in horses, but her clannish spirit was aroused at the thought of a racer belonging to one of her husband's friends competing, so she consented to go. Douglass was fond of horses and all the way was in high spirits. The crisp October air made the naturally lethargic team travel briskly; their dull coats actually glistened in the clear autumnal sunlight.

The magnificent weather had brought an immense crowd to the fair. Douglass and his wife, arriving somewhat late, were compelled to tie their team nearly a mile from the gate. Every livery stable and hitching post in town was doing full duty. The exhibition of cattle, fruits, vegetables, and farming machinery was of a high order, and the side-shows exciting as well as splendidly patronized. The harness and running races drew out big fields of fair-class horses. There were eight entries in the running race, at half a mile and repeat.

Douglass's wife, being stout, was not fond of walking, so most of the afternoon was spent on the grandstand. Just before the running race was called, the young husband asked permission to visit the stables and take a look at his friend's horse. As it was several years before the time of auto-mobiles, there was a vast concourse about the animals, so that Douglass had considerable trouble in elbowing to where Harold the Dauntless was being saddled. The animal was a big, slashing chestnut, a five-year-old entire horse, and just as Douglass arrived, the small colored rider wearing the green shirt with orange cap was being hoisted into the saddle by owner Chambers. Douglass shook his friend warmly by the hand and wished him luck; then, he followed the horse to the gate and patted his flank as he bounded through to the hard dirt course. The two young men walked together in the direction of the stand, chatting amiably.

Somewhere on the lawn, Douglass felt a pressure as if a person had brushed against him. He looked around, seeing the tall slim figure, dressed all in black, of Ettie Lucas. Their eyes met. For a moment, he was undecided and took a step or two further with his friend. Then he stopped, saying he wanted to go back to see someone, that he would meet him later on the stand. He turned and hurried toward where the girl had disappeared through the crowd. He looked in every direction, was actually rude in the way in which he jostled men, women, and children, but she was nowhere to be found. The grounds were not so big that such a well-groomed figure could hide herself completely, so he moved hither and thither for fully ten minutes. When he, at length, white as a sheet, with heart palpitating, gave up the search, Harold the Dauntless, winner of the heat, was being led through the gate. He thought of his wife on the stand, how she must wonder at the cause of his long absence, but he could not go back just yet. Earlier in the afternoon, he had seen a business partner of Ettie's father, who also lived at Abundance; he would seek out this man and learn where the girl was. He hated to humiliate himself to do so, as it was well known that he had a wife, but passion got the better of prudence, conscience. He had some difficulty locating this man, Luther Geise. The lumberman was glad to see him, and they both expressed pleasure at the victory of Harold the Dauntless, hoping that he would win the next heat. As quickly as politeness permitted, he asked him if he had seen Ettie Lucas. The fat lumberman looked at him in mild surprise. Then he replied, saying that the girl had not been home for a year, that she was hardly expected that winter.

"I was sure I saw her here a few minutes ago," gasped the young man.

"You must have been mistaken," replied Geise, beginning anew the munching of his cigar. The constant ghost of his life had come again, this time to mar his happy afternoon at the fair. He almost ran back to the stand, bounded up the rickety steps, and rejoined his wife. Just as he did so, the crowd yelled as Harold the Dauntless led his field under the wire in the second heat.

"My, but you look pale; what ails you?" said the wife, with tones of unusual concern.

Douglass was at first prompted to say "oh, nothing," but on second thought, replied that he had eaten an oyster sandwich which had made him very ill.

"You must be more careful in the future," said the wife gently. But what care could the young man exercise to rid his spirit of its awful possession? He tried to be agreeable and interested, but his mind was full of strange memories and forebodings. During the most thrilling finishes, he kept thinking of that late afternoon in the old museum at New Berlin, of the silvery light coming through the sloping panes; of the musty cases filled with the effigies of the wildlife of the Seven Mountains, of the unconventional beginning of his romance with the fair, false girl.

Then his pride of race rose uppermost; dreams of his ancestors who ruled Donegal, who fought and bled at the Boyne, who graced the Supreme Court of Pennsylvania, the Senate of the United States. All this was his punishment for loving outside his caste, the first who had done so in five hundred years. He was now married within the fold, ought not the penalty be ended now? When he was distressed, his wife had tried to comfort him; he should be grateful. But at his shoulder came a queer thrill, the spiritual presence of the German girl. Of what a warfare, his soul had become the battleground; nature striving to overcome caste; the human victim dwindling in the struggle. Beads of perspiration stood out on his brow; his eyes were glassy. His wife looked at him with compassion.

"Douglass, you poor boy," she said soothingly, "you look more like a person who has seen a ghost than one who ate a stale sandwich. I think we had better be starting home."

IV

THE CANOE

(A Story of Penn's Creek)

"I guess the young man's going to make a die of it," said old David Frantz, the wolf hunter. "I saw the canoe go under the bridge last night." We were leaning over the railing of the old bridge on a rainy morning in March, gazing at the surging, gray waters of Penn's Creek, when the ancient nimrod began his strange narrative. It was in 1901, and I had come by the morning train to Coburn, hiring a team at a livery and driving three miles west along the creek to where the old man resided. I had long wanted to meet this quaint character and fortunately found him in a communicative mood. After a pleasant chat by his stove, we had gone outside, as he wanted to show me where he had seen a pair of Otters the previous September. Then his conversation turned to local gossip and the supernatural, each word being interesting.

"Every time when a member of the Clawaghter family dies, a canoe, manned by the first settler of that name in this region, goes down the creek at dusk, to goodness alone knows where. You probably know young Douglass Clawaghter, the present head of the family; he is a very fine young man, common, sociable, square dealing; you would never think he had a dollar or lived in the biggest house in the Seven Mountains. He's been laid up with typhoid fever for the past seven weeks, but everybody thought on account of his youth, he's only thirty-one, he would pull through. But when I saw the canoe last night, I feared for the worst. I walked up to Cyrus Orndorf's later in the evening, he lives at the next bridge west, and he said that he had seen the canoe. That means it was no dream of mine, so I guess it's all off with the young gentleman. I'm terribly sorry, as everybody liked him in the mountains, and if he had cared to run for public office, both parties would have felt proud to nominate him. I'm watching to see if any rigs come along the creek road that have been past Rossmere, so I'll get the latest news. If you care to come indoors again, I'll tell you the story of the Clawaghter family and the 'token' which informs us whenever disaster overtakes them."

I was naturally interested, as folklore always had a deeper spell over me than researches into the vanishing fauna of Central Pennsylvania.

"You know the Clawaghters are one of the oldest families in the Seven Mountains. They were very different from the first from most of the mountaineers. The majority of us came from plain German stock, with only thoughts of hard work. The Clawaghters were true aristocrats. It is said that they came from the banks of a river of that name in the North of Ireland, but whether they took their name from the stream, or the stream took its name from them, is going back too far into ancient history for me. The first Clawaghters to come to Pennsylvania were two brothers named Michael and Desmond. They had been officers in the Irish rebellion in 1798 and barely escaped execution with Robert Emmet. They settled in Philadelphia, where they soon became favorites in society. Michael married a niece or cousin of James Douglass, the earl of Ross, for whom Douglassville, a town in Berks County, was named. They were always very proud of this connection with the nobility and called their estate Rossmere.

"Through his wife's relatives, Michael Clawaghter was able to purchase at a very low cost about twenty thousand acres of land in the Seven Mountains, and with his brother, Desmond, set out to develop the vast domain. They selected a site for a mansion and soon had a big force of Indians and white men clearing a space for a park. Skilled workmen were brought from Philadelphia, and a handsome manor house rose in the wilderness. Although the brothers seemed harmonious at the start, the fact that the property all belonged to Michael or his wife probably caused some discontent in Desmond's mind. He was younger than Michael by three years but lacked his good disposition and common sense. He had been much petted by women as he was extremely handsome, which made him vain and silly. He drank a great deal; it was to make him forget the loneliness of the mountains, so he confided to his German body servant. Some people thought he drank because his nature lacked resources; he never read; he cared nothing for fine scenery; he was too lazy to hunt or fish.

"Michael was vastly different. He was bubbling over with energy; when he wasn't working at his house or clearing new ground, he organized elk and wolf drives. Every night he sat up until past midnight reading or studying. The few pioneers in the surrounding mountains looked to him to settle their disputes, to read over their legal documents, to give them sound advice. He seemed anxious to accommodate, and soon he came to go under the name of 'the squire.' He liked the title, though, from all I can hear, he deserved a higher one. He was very anxious to get the manse roofed before winter set in.

"'As soon as it's under cover,' he said, 'I'm going after my wife; my real happiness will begin when we are together in this beautiful home.' His plan was to go by canoe to Selin's Grove, where he could pick up a likely boatman to carry him down the Susquehanna to Harrisburg or else travel that far with the mail carrier. At Harrisburg, or as many still called it, Harris Ferry, several fast stage lines ran to Philadelphia. He intended to buy some horses in the Quaker City and would probably drive his beloved wife to her domain with a coach and six!

He had considerable trouble with labor. One by one the stonemasons, plasterers, and carpenters, whom he had brought from Philadelphia, became homesick and quit. The Indians were uncertain workmen; the German farmers from the neighborhood had their own duties to attend to; they could only help him during spare hours. Some days very little work went on, and on these occasions 'Squire' Michael would go hunting. Desmond would get roaring drunk and lay in his bunk in the shanty, which stood in the lea of the unfinished mansion. As a big game hunter, the squire bid fair to obtain a permanent reputation in the Seven Mountains. In the nine or ten months he had lived at his projected manor, he had slain brown and black bears, wolves, mountain cats, elks, deer, fishers, and wolverines. He had been a member of hunting parties that had killed panthers, but he apparently had no luck bringing down a 'Pennsylvania lion.' Once when he was out alone, he surprised a huge 'painter' sleeping on a branch of a rock oak that hung over his path. He shot the brute in the shoulder, his aim had been for the heart, but the vital organ was not touched. Infuriated with pain and half asleep, the monster tumbled from the tree and hurled himself against the hunter. In the tussle, the squire got his hand in the panther's mouth and tried to break his jaw. I have read that 'Oom' Paul Kruger once did this with a South African lion, but Michael Clawaghter was of more delicate constitution. The effort was a failure; the panther closed his jaws, amputating the squire's left hand at the wrist. Then he thought wisdom was flight, so he disappeared up the mountainside, leaving the master of Rossmere wallowing in a pool of blood.

"As soon as he recovered from the shock, with the aid of his right hand and his teeth, he adjusted a tourniquet above his elbow, made from his belt, and staggered back to his clearing. Then he broke down and wept like a child. First of all, he had been beaten in a contest with a dumb brute; secondly, a ring which his wife had given him was on the little finger of the hand that the panther swallowed; thirdly, he would not be able to 'paddle his own canoe' downstream when the manse was roofed. Desmond was in his cups at the time and called his brother a 'baby' for crying; everyone present was surprised at the meek way in which he accepted the insult. Twenty years later, this same panther was killed at New Lancaster. After skinning him, the ring was found in his stomach and eventually restored to its rightful owners. I believe young Douglass Clawaghter wears it now. Panthers are surely long-lived animals!

"After the 'squire recovered from his mishap, his entire nature changed. He took to drinking, and it was hard to say which of the two brothers imbibed more freely. Both would lay in their bunks, dead to the world for days at a time. The work on the house languished; the Indians who, when not employed, skulked about the premises, stole great quantities of materials. This angered the squire, and he had several wordy arguments with certain redmen whom he accused of the thefts. He also had several quarrels with his brother and once, it was rumored, tried to shoot him. One morning Michael was found dead in the woods; it was in the gap, not twenty feet from where he had been worsted by the panther. There was a bullet hole in his head; he had clearly met with foul play. Desmond let on that he felt the catastrophe keenly and loudly blamed it on the

Indians. He talked so much that ill feeling was engendered against the savages. The Indians, anxious to remain in the locality, marched to the shanty in a body and demanded that the Irishman exhibit his proofs, and if he had any, they would all willingly submit to arrest. Desmond showed the 'white feather,' he had nothing to say, and public opinion veered around to the natives. This clinched the suspicion that Desmond was the slayer, but the simple farmers were too busy with their own labors to bother further about it.

"Leaving the shanty, the unfinished manse, and the materials in charge of his body servant, Desmond started east on horseback. He was gone fully a year. When he came back, he brought a wife and baby and the long-looked-for coach and six. Then it transpired that he had married his brother's widow, the real owner of the property. This change of fortune sobered him, for he was never known to drink again and worked harder than his brother had ever done to develop the property. The house was finished and became known as the Folly. He had signs nailed up along the roads which read 'To Rossmere,' but during his lifetime, the natives always referred to the place as 'Clawaghter's Folly.'

"Desmond Clawaghter did not enjoy his prosperity long. He caught pneumonia while at the county seat prosecuting some cattle thieves, and died there in a public house. He is buried in the graveyard of the Calvinists on the hill. I have often heard my father tell that he was out on the banks of the creek the night before the rich man died, not far from where we are standing now, and saw a canoe coming downstream guided by a one-handed individual. Half a dozen reputable persons saw it between here and the big river. The next evening came the word that Desmond had died in the 'White Horse' at Jacobsburg. You may think it strange that canoes could travel in this creek, the water is deep enough today, as you can see, but in the old days, before the watershed was destroyed, canoes, rafts, and arks regularly ran the creek from source to mouth—excepting in the very dry spells.

"Desmond's son William grew to manhood and managed the estate for his mother, being succeeded in turn by his son, Michael Ross Clawaghter, the father of the boy who is now lying so ill at the manse. The night before William died, the canoe, run by a one-handed man, came down the creek at dusk. A hundred people saw it and had it not been raining, some would have waded out and tried to stop it. Ross Clawaghter, as we called him, was a very high-strung man and hated all the legends that had grown up around the family. He particularly disliked the canoe story; said it was a lie invented by a lot of jealous yokels. This talk did not add to his popularity, but he gained some of it back by sending his son to the old academy at New Berlin. The night before he died, the canoe swept down the creek.

"That evening, I happened to be at the water's edge, putting the finishing touches on a raft. I had seen Ross that same morning; he seemed in perfect health and had just completed a deal with him to run half a million feet of logs for him off Volkenburg Mountain. He had said he would help me on the job, that he was as good as any of the lumberjacks. I was working away at the raft, with my head down, when my dogs began barking. I looked up suddenly and beheld the canoe with its one-handed steersman. I determined to lay the ghost if possible, so I yelled to it to stop, that I wanted a lift to the Coburn narrows; the Volkenburg rises straight up there from the creek. The ghostly figure neither turned to the right nor left but worked its paddle harder, so it seemed to me. I had boots on, so I plunged into the water, but it was gone under the bridge and out of sight in the gloom before I got halfway to midstream. Next morning a huckster told me that Ross had dropped dead from heart failure just after he had finished his supper. I inquired of my neighbors gradually so as not to make them suspicious, and everyone who happened to be out had seen the canoe. One of Jake Confer's boys wanted to shoot at it, but old Granny Confer, who was over ninety, wouldn't let him, said it was the worst kind of luck to shoot at a ghost. That was just thirteen years ago, and I had forgotten all about the 'token' until I saw it sweep under the bridge last night. I don't know what made me come out, except that the kitchen was a little stuffy, and I wanted a breath of air before going to bed. I was here, leaning on this cable rail, when I saw the skiff come out of the dusk. I could hardly believe my eyes because if it were Douglass Clawaghter that was to go, the whole county would sustain a big loss. I took off my hat and stood bare-headed until after the apparition had passed under me. Everybody had been telling me that the boy was going to get well; it certainly was a great shock to me. I do hope it was all a dream or some mistake. It is queer, but the Clawaghters have all been a short-lived stock so far. They had everything to live for, but paradise had designs on them early. Michael, they said, was thirty-two when killed so mysteriously; Desmond died at the age of thirty-five. William was within a month of his fiftieth birthday; Ross was about his father's age when he passed away. Young Douglass was only thirty-one when he took sick, but I do hope that he will recover. They were not a popular family, all except Douglass, as they kept by themselves and never lost a chance to show their superiority. But there are a score of families like them in this and adjoining counties; a funny lot are the 'old stock.' I wouldn't change places with them; my father died at ninety; I am full of work at seventy-nine."

When the old man concluded his story, we were soaking wet, as we were both so absorbed that we had forgotten to leave the bridge and go indoors. We were about to do so when the keen eyes of the aged wolf-killer noted a huckster's wagon coming down the road; it was still a quarter of a mile away, about on a line with Jonas Hartzell's hillside walnut farm. We waited on the bridge until it came near; it was a bizarre-looking outfit, a closed box-like vehicle drawn by two hay-bellied calico mares. Box and wheels were encrusted with mud, the accumulation of many winter and early spring rains. Old David Frantz called to the driver to stop, and the fellow did so, leaning out his head above his rubber apron.

"How's young Clawaghter?" called the old man in breathless excitement.

There was a pause, and the huckster whispered: "Why do you ask me? You know as well as I do."

"No, I don't," said the old wolf-killer impatiently.

"Well then, he died last evening about dark. They all feel powerfully blue up at the manse."

Then regarding me, he said jocosely: "Uncle David asks me if the young fellow died after knowing it since the minute after it occurred. You ask him if he saw a canoe run by a man with only one hand go under the bridge a little before dark last night. I know he'll tell you he doesn't

THE RESTLESS OAKS

(Photo by S. W. Smith)

believe in ghosts, but he saw that one all right enough, and more than once."

He then slapped the reins on the mares' broad, spotted backs, and the heavy mud-smeared vehicle began to flounder along the road towards Coburn. Just as he got almost beyond earshot, he stuck his fat head around the corner of the wagon, shouting, "Oh, you sly old fox, you don't believe in ghosts!"

The old hunter turned to me sadly, saying, "That young man deserved more respectful talk after he was dead, but I suppose he's paying up for the unpopularity of his ancestors."

Silently we wended our way over the bridge, looking down at the turbulent grey waters that flung themselves over rocks and submerged roots, and swept under the bridge, the waters that had carried to eternity the mystery of the Clawaghters. It was a sealed book now; the ghost had carried away the death message for the last time; the proud house ended with the young man who had just passed away. We were soon in the old hunter's cozy kitchen, where on a big old-fashioned settle by the stove, he began to tell of his experiences with the wolves of the Seven Mountains. The stories were positively refreshing and bright after the doleful chronicle of the successive masters of Rossmere. When each was finished, I asked for another; old Uncle David seemed to have an inexhaustible supply. When I started to go, I told him how glad I was to have met a man who had experienced so much; he had lived more vividly than many dwellers in a metropolis. And to this day, when I pass the little log cabin on my mountain trips, I point it out to my companions, saying, "In that little forest encircled house lived a man whose experiences were far more varied than almost anyone I have ever met," Then my thoughts always turn to that wet morning in March, when I arrived on the scene, so soon after the final passing of the house of Rossmere.

V

THE LOGAN BROTHERS

(Story of Two Indian Chieftains)

THE lamented Elihu Jones, in his fascinating work on the Juniata Valley, intimates that there were two Indian chiefs named Logan. Although the book obtained a wide circulation and has become a classic, most people have labored under the impression that but one chief of this name existed. While the two braves were brothers, they were decided individualities, as different as brothers could possibly be. James Logan, the high-minded orator whose wrongs have echoed in the ears of the multitude, was the elder of the two. In personality, he was the more aggressive, and consequently, he has been given credit for all the places which now bear the name. The younger brother, John Logan, was more identified with the Seven Mountains, and his career is more closely allied to the purposes of this work. For him, the Logan Spring near Reedsville was named, also the Logan Valley, Logan Township, also that historic old hotel in Altoona, the Logan House. It was for the older brother, James Logan, that Loganton and Logan Mills in Clinton County were named. The Logan brothers were both born on the beautiful Isle of Que, near Selin's Grove, which afterward belonged to the celebrated Colonel Conrad Weiser.

Shikellamy, their father, was a famous chief of the Mingoes, or, as the French called them, the Iroquois. He was said to be a half-breed. He had met and conceived a violent admiration for James Logan, the private secretary to William Penn, naming a son, who was born soon afterward in honor of the provincial official. He liked the sound of the name so well that another boy born fourteen months later was also named Logan, with a John as the first name so that they could be distinguished from one another. Shikellamy had four sons older than James Logan and John Logan. They were given Indian names and probably died before attaining manhood. At any rate, James Logan soon appeared as the head of the family, and his handsome face and figure, his oratorical and war-like powers, gave him a pre-eminence occupied by few of his people. John Logan, whom William Maclay described as one of the handsomest men he had ever seen, was of a retiring nature. He seldom spoke, was essentially a "family man." At the death of Shikellamy, the rulership of his territory passed to James Logan, whether because of his seniority or aggressiveness, is not known. He lived for a time on the plains in Middle Creek Valley and then passed further west, making his headquarters at the Sulphur Spring, a short distance from the present town of Loganton. He was extremely fond of drinking sulfur water, saying that it stimulated the warlike qualities he intuitively felt that his tribe must eventually use against the whites. He compelled his warriors to drink the water, each brave having his private gourd. These cups hung about the spring attached to the limbs of trees so that it resembled a European watering resort. His superior courage, intelligence, and strategy made him a marked man from the first with a certain element in the government. To these men, every clever Indian chief was a menace as long as he lived. The natives could not be robbed of their lands, their wives and daughters, and all their rights, and be shoved further west with impunity while they had leaders who were conscious of these injustices and demanded redress.

Teedyuscung had paid the death penalty; his murder was certainly arranged by the whites, as he told too many truths about the robberies perpetrated against his people. Shikellamy, by his complaisance, escaped a similar fate; by constantly yielding, he was allowed to live. Bald Eagle, early soured by an unhappy love affair with a white girl, Mary Wolford, vented his unhappy feelings by murdering the leading settlers, so his purpose in opposing white encroachments was not altogether prompted by unselfish motives. Cornplant was bitter in his denunciation of the Indians' treatment by the whites and was a marked man for years. James Logan, who bid fair to be the boldest champion of the Indian's rights, had a price set on his head before he was twenty.

A renegade white man, his name is known, but as his family is prominent in Central Pennsylvania, it is best not to publish it, who had helped Bald Eagle in his dastardly murder of James Q. Brady, the "Young Captain of the Susquehanna" in 1778, reported to James Logan that he had seen a letter from a prominent Quaker in Philadelphia which read, "Young Logan is a dangerous man. His rare oratorical gifts make him a vital force in inciting his people against the interests in control; he should be removed from the scene before he accomplishes any harm." After this, the sagacious Indian accepted *cum grana salis* all the protestations of friendship which the whites showered on him. It was sarcasm when he alluded to the "white man's honor."

Look on the pages of history, and you will find none of this. The same "inside ring" who made fortunes exploiting the lands of inland Pennsylvania before the revolution survived its vicissitudes and maintained their grip until the last acre was apportioned. The Indians were a thorn in their sides; they silenced them whenever they could and subsidized history to make it conform to their side of the case. A few fragments of Teedyuscung's bitter denunciations of the whites are preserved; still fewer of James Logan's remarks on the same subject. When Logan's words came near forcing their way into history, the story was started that he did not compose his speeches, that they were the flowery productions of some white man. But Chief James Logan did all he could to safeguard the Indians' rights, although he knew every time he spoke, his chances of dying a natural death were lessened.

His brother John took more after the sycophantic Shikellamy. He was always giving way to the whites; if they left him enough ground for his cabin and corn patch, provided it contained a good, sweet spring, they could have all the rest. Gradually he was forced in a westerly direction, far from the beautiful isle where he was born. When on a hunting expedition with his father, he had spent a night at the big spring near Reedsville, which became so indelibly associated with his name. Of all places visited, the memory of this idyllic spot lingered longest. When he realized that he must make a final stand somewhere, his mind traveled to the beautiful spring, to the tranquil valley in which it was situated. He resolved to go there and stay, come what may, until the end of his days. He had never resisted the whites in any form, their secret agents knew this, and the "powers that be" were willing to grant a favor to a "good Indian."

Consequently, when he moved with his family to the "Logan" spring, it looked as if he would live there in peace and quiet. In this, he was correct, as no efforts were made to disturb him. It is true that the spot was envied by numerous settlers, some of whom made furious protests against "a nest of Indians in their midst." But the peaceable chieftain held his ground, working in his beloved cornfield, fishing in Jack's Creek, Honey Creek, and Laurel Run, occasionally netting heath-hens or wild pigeons on Sample Knob. The more solid citizens respected him; he was on friendly terms with many of them. He was often a guest at the homes of the Hershbergers and McVeys. And yet, in the minds of most people of today, the Logan Valley derived its name from the unhappy, discontented, suspicious James Logan, whose gloomy life seemed to forbode his tragic taking off.

James Logan was not a hypocrite. He despised his brother for his truculent attitude, urging him to give up his one hundred acres and security for the broader field of maintaining the rights of the vanishing people. "The same people who let you live here are not your friends; I have seen papers that prove it," he entreated, "If someone influential enough wanted your log cabin, or your cornfield, or your wife, they would put poison in your spring; they would not hesitate for a minute."

But John Logan shook his closely-cropped head. "I believe most of the white folks are honest, that they will not molest me nor my family. I feel that I will always be allowed to live here."

In this world, events are mainly a matter of "how a man thinks." James Logan, distrustful, unhappy, vengeful, prophesied a tragic end for himself and got it. John Logan imagined the white people to be his friends that he would live and die at his spring, and so it came to pass. The only pity of it is that the identity of the two chieftains became confused in history. In almost any historical work on the early days in Pennsylvania, we read accounts of the "famous Mingo chief Logan"—but which one? The multiplicity of places, events, and unreconcilable dates caused investigators to doubt how one man could have done so much, been so many places at the same time. The peaceful, silent Logan tilling his cornfield and living humbly by his spring seemed a very different being from the errant, defiant, eloquent Logan who was so cruelly murdered in Ohio. Elihu Jones gives the true story, but as yet, it has not been generally incorporated in the school histories. It is stated that the final reason for James Logan's resentment against the whites was based on their refusal to allow his family to remain in Pennsylvania. It was intimated to him that he must move west; he was willing to go, but he feared the perils of a long journey on his family. When he had comfortably settled on the banks of the Muskingum, a company of regulars swooped down on the harmless family circle, butchering them in cold blood.

When Logan, absent at the time, returned, finding his people destroyed, he dropped to the ground, lying unconscious for three days. As he came out of his stupor, he raved in delirium. He begged to be taken back to the Susquehanna, to the beautiful Isle of Que where he had spent such a happy boyhood. His appeals were heartrending, and some attendants were almost moved to construct a litter and bear him to his old home. The general dislike felt by the white settlers for Logan and his followers was such that it was deemed best not to venture on such a pilgrimage.

As the bereaved warrior regained his strength, he was firm in his determination to revisit Central Pennsylvania. The longings of his sub-conscious self, as expressed in his delirious moments, were echoed by his vital personality. He would have made the journey attired in full warrior's regalia and attended by a faithful bodyguard, but some of the older braves counseled against it. The temper of the people, inflamed by false reports, sent broadcast to counteract any protest against the wanton murder of James Logan's family, had made it unsafe for any Indian chief to travel openly. There was no use being waylaid and shot or lodged in some filthy jail just to satisfy a craving of the spirit. But the heartbroken Indian demanded some change of thought currents to divert his mind from his murdered family. The old men argued together and decided that as the chief's health required the trip, it might be taken in perfect safety incognito. Logan was so emaciated from his long illness that his best friends would have trouble recognizing him, but other disguises were deemed necessary. He was garbed like a German emigrant, and a false beard made from horse hair almost covered his aquiline face. Armed with a German rifle and unattended, he started on foot for the scenes of his youth. He carried a pack of provisions on his back, as was the custom with many foot travelers. The country was full of restless Germans, many sunburned as dark as Indians, who were moving from place to place, looking for satisfactory spots to locate; one more or less added to this unkempt horde might not be noticed. As an extra precaution, he decided to travel by night, sleeping in dense thickets by daylight. Like all Indians, he could "see like an owl;" the Indian people were nocturnal by habit if the matter was carefully investigated. With a heart full of mingled regrets and hopes, James Logan started on the first night of the dark of the moon. His first stopping place was to be his brother's home near Reedsville. Here he had planned to remain a month, enjoying the society of his relatives. As he neared the familiar hunting grounds of the Seven Mountains, his wounded heart leaped with joy. Thrilling elk and buffalo drives were recalled; with them came memories of his grand old father and his brothers, most of whom were now dead. He saw some big game on the way, but in sadly diminished numbers. He met three bull elks on one occasion, five cows on another. He only encountered one buffalo, a great, rangy, nervous brute with sad, bloodshot eyes. He was afraid to fire his rifle lest someone hear him and perhaps penetrate his disguise. It was far easier to sleep all day than to run any risks—six months amid familiar scenes would warrant all the forbearance exercised in getting there. John Logan did not expect him; he was sitting under a linden tree, smoking his long pipe, when the prodigal brother tramped up the lane. He, of course, thought him to be a German tramp and greeted him with a cheery "*Wie gehts?*" James Logan, whose stern face had not relaxed in many months, ripped off his wig and beard and laughed heartily. The brothers embraced, and both shed tears. While they had never been very congenial in the past, they needed one another now. John Logan had heard vague, distorted reports of the massacre of the Muskingum and now was told the awful tale from the lips of the chief sufferer. Always ready to forgive and condone the white men's faults, it was a severe tax to John Logan's amiability to hear this frightful recital. Women, including the aged mother of the two chieftains, old men, and children cut to pieces in cold blood by United States regular troops, were beyond the imagination of the blood-thirstiest savage!

"For this, *I* will have revenge before I die," concluded the stricken chieftain.

"For once in my life, I concur with you in your wish," said John Logan under his breath. Then he looked about furtively to see if any eavesdropper was near.

"Forget about it for the time being, my brave brother, and pay us a good long visit," said brother John, placing his arm about the now sobbing form of the once greatest warrior of the Mingoes. James Logan would have undoubtedly enjoyed his sojourn at the hospitable cabin had it not developed that someone on the way recognized him. The story was brought to the neighborhood that the murderous chief James Logan had appeared, deeply disguised; evidently, he was bent on mischief. Within twenty-four hours, the rumor became distorted into the form that the noted Indian had killed a peaceable German on the road and had disguised himself to escape justice. Some newly-arrived Germans, with all the old world prejudices, became alarmed lest they be implicated for allowing an Indian warrior in the neighborhood. They were used as a foil by some of James Logan's old enemies to oust him from his brother's cabin. A committee of settlers sent a messenger to the little cabin, summoning John Logan to appear before them; they were to meet on the hill, underneath which the turbulent waters of Laurel Run suddenly sink out of sight. The old Indian concealed the cause of his departure, as he hated to worry James with this fresh trouble. He made haste to the meeting ground, where most of the settlers in the valley were assembled, whom he had counted as his friends. He told them he was unaware that his brother had committed any wrong or was wanted in any part of the country on criminal charges. He had lately suffered a crushing bereavement in the massacre of his entire family, that he had come to the "big spring" to spend a few months in peace and quiet with his relatives. There seemed no reason why he should be driven from the locality.

John Logan, generally so taciturn, quite surpassed himself in the eloquence of his appeal for his persecuted brother. Those who were disinterested favored allowing James Logan to remain as his brother's words bore the stamp of truth. But others more influential, who were obeying secret orders from the "league of land-grabbers," objected loudly; said the Germans would leave the valley; their will prevailed. John Logan asked one more favor of the assemblage; it was that if his brother was compelled to quit his roof, he could continue his journey across the mountains to the scenes of his childhood at the Isle of Que and drink once again from Molly Bullion's spring. The same parties objected to this; if James Logan wished to keep out of jail, he should return to Ohio. If he persisted in touring in the east, some charges could be brought against him, which would cause him to end his days in prison. John Logan again denied any charges, but his words were drowned in an angry uproar raised by the representatives of the predatory class. Crestfallen and disappointed, the old Indian slowly wended his way back to his plantation. There he had to break the news to James Logan, to tell him why he was called to "council hill" and the result of the conference. The persecuted warrior bowed his head sorrowfully.

"It is ever thus," he muttered, "no resting place exists for me in this world. I have been a marked man ever since I uttered my first public words against the robbers of my birthright. My lands are stolen, my family murdered, and my tribal organization broken up. I am a wanderer on the face of the earth."

Then he took his pack from its hook on the wall and began unstrapping it. He asked his brother's family to fill it with provisions for a long journey. Logan's wife and children were grieved to think their noble uncle must leave them so soon, yet his brief stay was destined to be remembered for the rest of their lives. The entire family accompanied him down the lane under the shady arch of acacia trees. The brothers embraced as they parted. It is always "as a man thinks." James Logan's last words to the family were: "This will be my final trip. Once back in Ohio, away from any friendly influences, my enemies will kill me."

They watched the bent and melancholy figure going down the road in the clear light of the golden hour, for he intended to tramp all night. "Farewell, brother," cried out John Logan as he was lost to view. Not long afterward, in 1780, came the news of his dastardly murder on the Ohio.

VI

DORMAN PANTHER

(The Life Story of a Noted Hunter)

THE stage from Lewistown was three hours late; darkness had set in, all the windows in Bannerville were ablaze with light. The peepers sang vociferously in the stream and marshes; otherwise, there was an oppressive stillness in the little town, the stillness of expectancy. The reason for this was that a dozen young men, natives of the village and surrounding country, who had been soldiers in the bloody war with the Southern States, which had lately come to a close, were due to arrive after their years of active service at the front. As reported by the county newspapers and letters home, their valorous deeds had already made them local heroes, superseding the grey-haired, middle-aged veterans of the conflict with Mexico. These old soldiers were in uniform tonight, anxious to do homage to the younger boys in blue. Fully a thousand persons had gathered in the little community, crowding around the porch of the general store and post office as there the stage would come to a halt. It was hoped that it would arrive on schedule so that the young veterans could see the decorations. Three large flags hung from poles over the post office porch, and the posts and roof of the porch were draped with bunting. Every little home along the hillside street displayed a flag, and some had the paling fences of their front yards festooned with colors. Lamps were placed in every window so that the illumination would atone for the darkness which eclipsed the display of red, white, and blue. Many young girls were dressed for the great occasion; they wore blue and white muslin gowns, red sashes, and some even had on red stockings. They wore tiny flags in their hats, and those who had donned coats, for the May night was a trifle chilly, had rosettes of colors in the lapels or carried small flags. Many horses were tied along the side alleys, munching the bark off the shade trees, as it was before the days of civic associations. All had their harness decked in colors; even the heavy farm wagons to which most were attached bore patriotic emblems. A few town boys had tried to organize a band; they had five or six instruments, and were ready to strike up the only piece they knew, "Ring the Bells of Heaven" when the stage was in sight.

It was conjectured that the train at Lewistown must have been delayed, as when it was late, the stage was always behind time. But the crowd was patient, and as the event was to be the greatest one in their lives, all were awed into silence. It was nine-thirty when the shout went up that the stage had been sighted. Fully fifty small boys ran up the hill along the ridge that the highway followed to obtain an advance view of the important caravan. The few persons who lived along the road, who had not made up their minds to come to the celebration, could not resist the sight of the stage crowded with soldier boys and dropped in behind it, forming an irregular guard of honor. The big driver, who himself had been a soldier for six months, had put on his uniform for the occasion and kept cracking his long whip, which was draped with patriotic streamers. The old lantern on the dashboard sent a light ahead on the road and gave notice of the cavalcade's appearance. When it turned the corner at the beginning of Bannerville Street leading down to the post office, it was sighted by all, and a mighty cheer arose. The crowd surged towards the oncoming conveyance, and the horses could scarcely travel. So slow was their gait that a hundred stalwart youths fairly pushed the animals from the traces, brushed them aside, and seizing the pole, drew the big stage to the post office. When it stopped, the young soldiers were dragged out bodily. They were embraced by parents, brothers, sisters, sweethearts, cries of joy mingled with hurrahs and songs. In the midst of this, the tall leader of the band climbed to the post office porch and, adjusting his pine torch, started his aggregation to play "Ring the Bells of Heaven." After having been half kissed and hugged to death by their relatives and sweethearts, the soldier boys were now congratulated by the Mexican War veterans and admiring friends. An old blind man bent almost double, a survivor of the war of 1812, was helped through the throng by two of his grandsons and shook hands with every young soldier. When the band ceased playing, there was another cheer, and then a big dark-complexioned Lutheran preacher rapped on the post office porch floor with a broom handle and asked a prayer of thanks for the safe restoration of the local soldiers. After this, the district attorney, who was also a congressional aspirant, who had come over from Swinefordstown for the occasion, delivered an oration. It was full of patriotic fervor and was frequently interrupted by applause. After the speechmaking, the young and old veterans were escorted into the storehouse, where an elaborate supper awaited them.

A table of pine boards stretched the entire length of the long room, from the front door clear to the letter boxes in the rear. Muslin flags served as cloths. Among the many delicacies served was ice cream, a great rarity in the Seven Mountains in those days.

One of the first of the young soldiers to alight from the coach was Lewis Dorman, the son of Widow Dorman of Dormantown, a village about three miles west of Bannerville. He was a handsome youth of medium height and athletic build. He had clear-cut aquiline features, and his straight black hair, worn parted on both sides, was brought down over his ears. He had piercing black eyes and wore a small black mustache, of the style which has become so popular with young men in the big cities nowadays. His mother was the first to greet him when he emerged from the vehicle, and the scene between the two was affecting. On three occasions, he had been reported missing after important battles but wounded though he was, he had been able to creep back through the enemies' lines to his own regiment. Happy as he was to see his beloved parent, the young cavalryman kept casting his dark eyes about the crowd as if looking for someone else. The fitful light of lamps and pine torches was dim enough, but the congratulatory throng crowding about him made it difficult to see very far. When he was able to climb on the post office porch, he obtained a good view of the assemblage; he presented a picturesque figure with his wide military trousers and blouse, his chevroned sleeves, cap in hand. After he had stood the suspense as long as he could, he turned to an aunt, to whom he had always confided his troubles, asking the whereabouts of Letty Lenoble. The good lady gazed at him in silence for a minute.

"Haven't you heard," she whispered apologetically, "she ran off with that Yankee who worked on Berkheiser's mill,"

"When," said Lewis, turning deadly pale and letting his cap drop from his hands. "Why I only got a letter from her two weeks ago."

"It's been about two weeks since she went away," replied the aunt.

His rosy color gone, the young soldier moved among the merrymakers like a ghost. Clammy-handed, he accepted their congratulations; he was the only person at the long table who did not eat; he was the only one in the throng of one thousand who was glad when the homeward pilgrimage began. He who had served his country well, had been promoted to be a first sergeant for general efficiency, was a good and dutiful son, had been marked by fate for this sore trial.

"The Lord chasteneth whom He loveth," whispered his aunt to him as the little family party drove silently homeward. The young sergeant's mother was aware of his disappointment; she did not need to tell him. She had hoped that he would not notice his sweetheart's absence, but this silence told her that he knew all. Thus the homecoming was robbed of much of its gaiety; shadow instead of sunshine prevailed. When Lewis reached his little bedroom, which he had quit three years before, he found it just as he had left it; his favorite violin rested on the dresser. The room was lit with candles, and the bed was draped with an American flag. In these remote mountains, patriotism lived in its purest form; there were no copperheads or anglophobes to make it unpopular. He took out his leather wallet, which he had worn over his heart all through his enlistments, and re-read the date on his sweetheart's last letter. It was April 14th, just three weeks before. The letter had taken a week to reach him; probably on the very day of its arrival, Letty had eloped with the ill-favored Yankee. It was full of love, of hopes of his speedy return; the entire affair was a mystery. He remembered the Yankee well. He had come to Dormantown as a common tramper.

Ike Berkheiser had taken pity on him, washed him up, and given him work. The fellow abandoned liquor and worked faithfully but was unsociable and taciturn. He was a small man with a big, broad head, popped eyes, and when Lewis last saw him, wore a stubby tramp's beard. What the cameo-faced Letty, who was elegance itself, her skin was fine to the point of transparency, her nature sensitive and elevated, could have seen in this sodden individual was beyond comprehension. In a transport of grief, he held her letters one by one over a candle, reducing them to ashes. Then he took out a tiny tintype, looked at it fondly, kissed it once, and held it over the flame until the likeness was obliterated. The room smelled strongly of chemicals when he blew out the last candle.

Lewis Dorman's nature at twenty-one became warped by his crushing disappointment. He lost ambition, willpower, and above all, self-esteem. He placed himself lower than the brute who had run off with his sweetheart. He never touched his violin, an instrument for which he had seemed to possess much talent. He only did such work as was absolutely necessary around the little place; the farm had been sold at his father's death five years earlier, and he spent most of his time in the woods with his favorite bull terriers.

The November of the year of his disappointment, it was in 1865, he killed an enormous brown bear in the "sink," a rocky desert in the White Mountains. This determined him to adopt the career of a hunter, to secure specimens of the fierce animals which were then making their last stand in the Seven Mountains. During the winter, he trapped a dozen wildcats, a Canada lynx or catamount, thirty grey foxes, a pine marten, and several opossums. His record was the envy of the boys of the neighborhood. His relatives encouraged him, saying among themselves that he would forget his unfortunate love affair in the forests.

During 1866 he spent most of his time in the mountains. He went away in the spring, fishing and shooting water-fowl, exploring the least known streams and climbing the rugged peaks of each of the Seven Mountains. When he returned home in August, he looked, so the neighbors said, "like a wildman." He had let his hair and beard grow; at twenty-two, he could have passed for a man of forty.

That fall, he killed a brown bear, three black bears, one of the latter weighing "hog dressed," 542 pounds. It was the "record" black bear in the Seven Mountains for many years to come. He also killed a magnificent stag, with a wide spread and nine points on each horn, which was also a record head for a time. He engaged in several unsuccessful panther hunts, others ranging over the same territory, notably Dan Treaster, Eph. Zerby,

Johnny Swartzelland Calvin Wagner, killed magnificent specimens the same year. Otherwise, 1866 was a great twelve months for the young nimrod, Lewis Dorman.

That winter, he resumed his trapping operations, capturing in one month five Canada lynxes, the largest number ever caught by one hunter in so short a period in the Seven Mountains.

He spent Christmas at home, seeming in better spirits than usual; once or twice he even played on his violin. He had built himself a log cabin near the "sink," adorned with hunting trophies; the array of heads, claws, and horns was so formidable that two visitors from McVeytown were afraid to sleep in the shanty. There was a good market for the hides, and above what he needed for ammunition and provisions, he gave to his mother.

He fished and hunted during the spring of 1867 but spent most of the summer at home. He shaved his cheeks, wearing only a chin beard, and trimmed his hair; his family had hopes that he would soon become "his old self."

That autumn, he left home early in September, telling his relatives that he had located several panthers and would devote his entire energy to this form of hunting until successful. On Little Panther Creek, he killed his first black wolf and was so elated that he sent word home with Indian Joe, another love-sick soul, who for years wandered aimlessly among the mountains. That was the last that was heard of the young hunter, directly or indirectly, until the following April. The secret of his silence was that he had the misfortune to see Letty Lenoble. He had trailed a panther to the headwaters of Rapid Run in Centre County and, while looking for traces, came to a footpath that led close to the creek.

It was in the evening, and while thus engaged, he saw his former sweetheart walking along the path carrying a small pail of milk. They looked at one another, but neither spoke. Lewis lurked in the neighborhood for several days, ascertaining that the Yankee to whom Letty was married was running a steam sawmill on the south branch of White Deer Creek. He must have prospered, as he was working in some grand timber, had the latest machinery, a big crew of helpers, good horses in his barn. The house the family lived in was a model of neatness and convenience.

All these evidences of happiness and success were too much for the discarded lover, so he wandered out of the country into the North. He gave up hunting temporarily, working all winter at a logging camp on Little Pine Creek near Waterville.

He arrived home unexpectedly in the latter part of April 1868, unkempt and dejected. He confided to his mother and aunt the cause of his long silence and received much loving sympathy and interest. His family tried to rouse him by saying that he must secure a panther, that the animals were being rigorously hunted for the $12 bounty which was paid in most of the mountainous counties; there was no time to be lost.

In September, he consented to go on another hunt but affirmed with a laugh that he would not return until he killed his panther. He carried his violin with him as a sign he intended to stay a good while. He amused himself shooting wild pigeons, turkeys, and grouse until there came a tracking snow, which occurred the first week in November. At the headwaters of Pine Hollow Creek, near the extreme eastern end of Centre County, Lewis's bulldogs located four panthers; by their tracks, two were enormous males, two females. Their keen senses appraised them of the danger, and they separated, two traveling east in the direction of the divide above the head of Rapid Run, two moving west, along the ridge above Pine Hollow. The pair, which moved west, on account of the tracks of the male being the largest, the young hunter elected to follow. He kept them within half a day for three days when a warm spell set in, followed by a week of rain, and the tracking was spoiled. He could not believe they would cross his "line" and travel east, so he kept beating about in the vast pineries, gradually moving his position west. A week of good weather, Indian Summer, followed the rain, but despite the dreamy allurement of the atmosphere, the hunter never relaxed his purpose. The weather again turned cold, and another tracking snow fell about December first. He found the trail again on Round Top Mountain, following it along the ridges to Mount Stromberg, near Coburn. There, a blizzard set in, and the crafty brutes, during its fiercest moments, doubled on their tracks and started east. A thaw delayed his progress, but conditions soon righted themselves so that he again took up the trail which led over Paddy Mountain and along the ridges to Round Top. There the female left her mate, who moved northeast, across the Union County line towards Big Laurel Run. The hunt had now lasted nearly two months, the dogs were tired and restless, but Lewis Dorman was indefatigable. The male panther, evidently tired of his solitary life, for on the night of the 23d of December, he roared loudly and long from the topmost pinnacle of Shreiner Knob.

Dorman, who with his dogs had bivouacked on a nearby ridge, had never heard anything like this before and sat awake all night by his fire, awed by the savage love song. He unstrapped his violin, trying to catch the weird notes on his bow. It could only be likened to the music of the spheres. He had often heard about panthers wailing and screaming, but there was a majestic melody to the awful sound which seemed to be the very voice of the wilderness. At the same time, the panther is naturally a silent animal, rarely making an outcry except at its mating season.

Just as the morning star grew dim, far in the distance came what at first seemed to be an echo in a minor key; it was the answering notes of the female. Something in Dorman's blood told him that he would soon bring his quarry to bay. Muzzling his dogs and placing them on a leash, he crept on hands and knees through the snow. He descended the ridge, crossed the draft, and assumed a good location on the north slope of Shreiner. At dusk, he found the trail of the female and followed it to where she had hidden herself in an inaccessible position in the rocks, evidently waiting for her fulvous-coated master. The full moon, which had been entirely obscured the night before, now rose and shone at intervals. Across its face swept sooty colored clouds, the tips of the giant white pines soughed and murmured in the night wind. Dorman was certain that the male panther was in hiding near the summit but would visit his mate that night.

About ten o'clock, he heard several short howls and moans, and then, perhaps fifteen minutes later, the two panthers emerged from the rocks. For a minute, the moon-rays disclosed them; the male with blazing eyes was licking the female's tawny coat and stroking her with his tail in passionate ecstasy. Then clouds hid the light; the chase was not yet ended. In the darkness came several fierce roars of wild rapture. Suddenly the moon became clear, revealing the male panther alone, stalking along the trunk of a fallen pine with head erect. Dorman's chance had come; he fired; there

MILES TO WANDER (Photo by S. W. Smith)

was a hideous shriek of pain, echoed in treble key high up among the rocks. Again he fired; the wounded panther leaped twenty feet into the air and, with a resounding thud, fell in a lifeless heap in the snow. The hunter and his dogs hurried to the spot, and a cozy fire was soon crackling by the steaming carcass. While he was skinning it, far up on the rock-crested summit, came a sound like a woman's sobbing. Was it the pantheress, conscious of her bereavement, or a banshee wailing of dead sorrows?

That summer Eph. Zerby met a female panther with three cubs on the mountain west of Cobum; probably, it was this same brute. There were panthers in the Seven Mountains for the next fifteen years. Lewis Dorman finished his task and, after resting until daylight, started across the mountains to the Forest House, the nearest habitation, to enjoy a much-deserved Christmas dinner. Azariah Banks, the Yankee proprietor, was delighted when he saw the hunter with his violin and his trophy, which had the skull with it.

"There have been several panthers around here lately, but by the size of the head, the teeth, and the length of the skin, you must have killed the old daddy of them all." The shrewd Vermonter knew how to make business out of his distinguished guest. He quickly sent out his two hostlers on horseback to notify the mountaineers that there would be a Christmas night dance at the hotel, telling them to be sure to add that Lewis Dorman, a veteran of the 7th Cavalry, had brought a giant panther to the hotel and would furnish the music with his fiddle.

Before sundown, the lumbermen and shack dwellers, old and young, came flocking to the hotel with their women folks. By this time, Dorman and the landlord had stuffed the hide with sawdust; Mabelle Banks, the landlord's pretty daughter, sewing it together so that it looked as natural as life. Big black buttons were inserted as eyes, and a skewer was put in the maw so as to reveal the fierce teeth. It was set up on the shelf above the big fireplace and garlanded with ground pine. The dance began at eight o'clock, and the big room never held so many people before. Lewis Dorman, flushed with triumph, seemed to have forgotten his troubles. The dance music fairly flowed from his soul. During the first pause, a slender, blue-eyed girl with curly chestnut brown hair elbowed her way to the young fiddler's side. "Mr. Lewis Dorman, don't you remember me; I'm

Stella Berly, who used to work at Carskaddon's camp on Little Pine; I want to congratulate you for killing the panther and for your beautiful music."

The young man looked at her with pleasure beaming from his eyes; he held out his hand and clasped hers tightly. It was a joy to be appreciated. Instantly all the woes of his previous life vanished into the clouds of tobacco smoke which hung above him; he was born again and in love. Stella did not dance anymore that evening but sat close to the young man, fanning him.

When an intermission was granted at midnight, they walked together out into the frosty night, under the cloud-swept moon and the stars. "I have always liked you," she said, taking his arm. "I almost died of grief when you left the camp that Saturday night without saying goodbye to anyone and never returned. I dreamed of you nearly every night. I never ceased feeling that we would sometime meet again. You can imagine how my heart leaped for joy when news came to our camp out on Spruce Run that you were at the Forest House with a big panther you had killed and would furnish music for a dance. Christmas had started in very dull for us. I said it was the dreariest one of my life. Your coming has made it the happiest."

They were standing on the bridge which crosses Buffalo Creek, watching the foaming, surging torrent. The girl's sincere words, her beauty, and sprightliness awoke an emotion in Lewis Dorman's nature such as he had never felt before. The blood coursed through his veins; he was supremely happy when he took her in his arms.

"We will be married any day you say, dearest," he whispered as they strolled back to the dancing room. "We have a nice double house at Dormantown in Mifflin County. I had an aunt who lived in one-half of it until my father died; then, she moved in with mother; we can live there and be supremely happy.

"I know we will," said the girl, whose life had been lonely ever since she had been left an orphan seven years before. "We can go after the preacher tomorrow; the sooner, the better."

When the music struck up again, and Stella still sat by the violinist, the wife of the boss at the camp where she was employed whispered to her, "I thought you were crazy for a dance tonight?"

"I was," answered the girl, smilingly, "but I met my old friend, Mr. Lewis Dorman, and we are going to get married tomorrow."

The young man smiled his acquiescence, and the buxom woman shook hands with them both. Others in the room noticed this, and soon the news was known to everyone. There was a scramble to congratulate the happy couple, which was so lengthy that it almost broke up the dance. As soon as possible, Dorman struck up the "Log Cabin;" placing it with more feeling than ever before, as he was thinking of a cottage where he hoped to live in peace and happiness with the girl who loved and appreciated him.

Next morning the young couple were driven to New Berlin, where they were married, the happy bridegroom presenting the panther hide to the officiating clergyman. In that manner, it found its way into the Natural History Museum of the old academy. When the Swinefordstown stage reached Bannerville on New Year's Eve, several of Lewis Dorman's one-time army comrades were standing on the post office porch. When they saw the erstwhile "wild man of the woods" cleanshaven, save for his little dark mustache and dapper and jaunty looking, climb out, assisting a very pretty young girl, one of them remarked: "What sights one sees when he hasn't got a gun."

That night the young hunter presented his bride to his family circle; it was a happy occasion. Within a week soft yellow lights were gleaming in the windows of the side of the little house in Dormantown that had been dark for so long.

VII

THE TOKEN

(A Story of Poe Creek)

ABSALOM PLANKENHORN was pretty thoroughly tired after the day's threshing and spent half an hour after supper trying to wash the chaff and dust off his head and face. When he climbed the winding stairs to his little bedroom under the roof, he was ready for a good night's sleep. The one window was a considerable distance from the floor, the sill was very broad, and through the open sash, while he lay in bed, he could watch the stars blinking. The late summer air was cool, and the din of the crickets and katydids seemed to shake the roof with their reverberations. He had expected to fall asleep immediately, but he was over-tired, and it was an hour before he was in dreamland. The katydids all but drowned the methodical snoring of Farmer Rhinehart, who occupied the room directly beneath.

Absalom, whose father had died several years before, had been sent into the Seven Mountains to work for the farmer, and he liked the crude life on the upland farm better than in the more modernized regions of Ferguson's Valley. He lay awake thinking of the busy day just passed, of the happy prospects that the crops would yield more than expected, of the many scenes incident to the arrival of the traction engine which pulled the thresher and separator. He had worked all day in the mow; it was a lively task, but he had found time to laugh and joke with the other boys; it was the great event of the year on the lonely farm.

On three sides of the farmhouse and barns loomed the steep mountains. Very little timber of any value stood on them; here and there, a punky original white pine reared its stag-topped head above the tangle of saplings; there was a brown streak across the face of one of the mountains where a spring fire had traveled; it looked lavender colored at sunset; in the golden hour the white barkless trunks of dead pines near the summits stood out as distinctly as skeletons. Far away in the brushwood could be heard the cries of the jaybirds, the cawing of crows. On certain dark nights, foxes barked along the foot of the mountains. After heavy rains, Poe Creek roared, but in dry weather was inaudible.

All these familiar scenes and sounds rose in the hired boy's vision as he lay awake. Then his thoughts turned to the morrow, with the continuation of the same work; he saw himself breathing chaff, sweltering in the mow; he fell fast asleep. It was probably midnight when he awoke with a start. A misty veil or curtain hung over the window. It sparkled as raindrops do on a spider's web. He looked more closely; it was the stars shining through the veil. It seemed to be rolling and coiling itself together in the form of a waterspout. Head and arms appeared, but the figure, human as it was in outline, was veiled, unrecognizable, transparent. After assembling itself, it swept across the room, so close to the bed that the awe-stricken boy might have seized it. Though overcome with terror, he could not keep his eyes off the apparition. While it floated about the room, he could not bring his senses to tell him what it was; his faculties were in a state of suspension. It could not have been present more than two minutes all told; soon, it was by the window again, completely welling the aperture with filmy vapor. Then as if struck by a gust of night wind, it disappeared completely. As its last vestige vanished, the boy gave way to a paroxysm of fright, sitting up in bed crying, "it's the token, the token, the token." Then he buried his frowsy head under the patchwork comforts and cried himself to sleep.

In his family, before any member had died, this filmy ghost always appeared; his mother had seen it before his father's death, before the deaths of his youngest brother and sister. He had heard his father talk about it often in his lifetime; he who had seen it when he lost his parents, brothers, sisters, and grandparents. The old folks had come from Berks County; the "token" was omnipresent in the family then; they had a tradition that it had appeared to the family for centuries before that in Switzerland. It was probably as old as the family itself; it was a visible expression of their intuitive sense, their gift of second sight. On other subjects besides impending deaths, they could have looked into the future had they but trained their souls, but this was first developed as it was the most important happening in their prosaic lives.

There is one old Pennsylvania family where a bird flies in the window a few nights previous to a disaster, with another, it is the appearance in the yard of a strange black dog, which barks all night hideously. With still another, it was a canoe in the nearby creek, manned by a one-handed being, which swept downstream the night the bereavement was to occur. When Absalom Plankenhorn awoke, as was his custom, before daybreak, his heart was heavy, his head ached and throbbed. Despite the starlight of the evening, the morning was overcast and damp. His first thought was that having seen the "token," he should go home at once. Perhaps his mother was dying, or another of his little brothers or sisters. He had no letter to show to Farmer Rhinehart, he was afraid of the big fellow anyway, yet he must pluck up courage somehow and tell him he was going to quit at sundown.

All day long, he worked faithfully but unsmilingly. The other boys were in rare humor; their high spirits advanced with each day of the threshing. The engine spouted black smoke; it worked with a will; the straw stack grew as high as the barn; it was a day full of energy and progress. The distant summits were a peculiar bluish grey, which always indicated rain in the Seven Mountains; every effort was made to finish the work before a storm. Several times gusts of wind blew down clusters of yellow leaves from the old chestnut trees back of the barn, giving an almost autumnal aspect to the scene. The golden rod along the road was well advanced. At dinner time, Absalom tried to pluck up the courage to speak to the farmer, but he seemed in an impatient humor; it would be best to wait until the thresher "blew off" for the night. With all the added energy and extra hands, a small jag was still to be threshed when the engine slowed down at dusk. Although it had run an hour and a half after the stave mill across the narrow valley had given its goodnight whistle, the morrow would witness some more of it. Farmer Rhinehart was in a disgruntled frame of mind. He kept saying that if he had realized the extent of the crop, he would have gotten twice the number of extra hands, and he hated to thresh in the storm which was sure to come.

"Look at them mountains," he kept saying as he tramped up the path to the farmhouse, "they never was like that and no rain."

Clearly, this was no time to approach the farmer about leaving when he regretted not having hired more helpers. The flannel-cake supper did not unbend him; he was moody when he sat on the kitchen porch afterward; it was foolish to think of expecting consideration from such an overly tired person. But the boy was determined to quit; he had seen his "token," death was nigh in his family; he must be on the scene. He recalled that one of his uncles traveled in from Freeport, Illinois, after seeing the banshee, arriving in Ferguson's Valley just an hour before his mother, Absalom's grandmother, passed away. As he sat on the porch while the farmers and threshers mopped their brows and smoked, he conceived the idea of slipping away during the night. All he could expect of Farmer Rhinehart would be "no;" there was not an hour to be lost. Had he been older and possessed of more willpower, he reasoned that he should have left for home that very morning. He had no baggage except a little tin trunk, which he could easily carry on his shoulders. If he got away at midnight, he would be home by the following noon. He ought to be able to steal out of the house unnoticed as all of the family were heavy sleepers. Still, Zack, the watchdog, would be a force to be reckoned with. As family tradition stated, this dog was the descendant of a shepherd bitch and a giant black wolf, one of the last to linger in the wilds of Poe Creek.

Before going upstairs, Absalom slipped out to the smokehouse where he knew were kept some stout pieces of rope; they hung on a set of stag horns. He selected a piece long enough to drop his little trunk out of the window; he was afraid he might hit it against the walls and arouse the family if he carried it down the narrow stairs. The family and the hired help went to bed at about the same time. All were so exhausted that they forgot to bid one another goodnight. When Absalom reached his tiny room, he took off his shoes and packed them with the rest of his belongings in the trunk. When everything was in it, he bound the rope around it and sat down on the bed to wait.

The snoring in the room below soon began, but the boy waited until his silver watch told him that it was midnight, exactly twenty-four hours had passed since he had seen the "token." Then he carefully lifted the trunk to the window sill and climbed up after it. The window was scarcely large enough to push the trunk through, but he accomplished it and dropped it slowly to the yard. Zack heard it nevertheless, barking loudly and, with his crest bristling, sniffed at it suspiciously as it rested among the hollyhocks. All was quiet again; Absalom waited until an hour had passed. Then he stole downstairs as noiselessly as possible. The hinges of the door at the foot of the stairs creaked as he pushed it open; he knocked against the dough tray as he passed through the kitchen, he had some difficulty in turning the lock in the door. In a moment, he was out in the yard, only to be espied by Zack. Though the wolf-dog knew him well, he knew his duty better and began his low, wingeing bark, so reminiscent of the ancient wolves of the Seven Mountains. As he always barked when a prowling wildcat or fox was about, the family, if they heard him, paid no attention. He followed the boy to the front gate, alternately barking and snapping at his heels. Absalom kept whispering to him, "Zack, Zack, be a good boy, be still." He slammed the gate on the dog and started out on the path which led across the mountains on the south side of the valley. At the foot of the first ridge, close to the creek, he had to pass the tie-camp where a contractor from Coburn was demolishing one of the finest white oak forests in the commonwealth. Here three ugly-looking dogs rushed at him. Had he not found a handspike on the road, he might have been bitten. On the way up the mountain, the promised rain began to fall. By the time he had reached the summit, it was coming down in torrents. Several times he lost his way, stumbling about among the rocks and briars. His feet were cut and torn; he became drenched to the skin. The darkness was profound; the footpath became hopelessly lost among the tangles of vines and underbrush. Halfway down the mountain, the face of the cliff was serrated with huge rocks and crevices. Some of these formed caverns, the openings of which seemed logical as resting places until the daylight would set in. It seemed useless to flounder about in the tempest; a few hours and all would be clear. The tired lad crept into one of these apertures and sat down on his trunk. His back was sore; his feet hurt terribly. He took off his cap to let the water run off it. He leaned against the wall of the cave; he might have some comfort until daylight.

Just as he sank into a doze, he felt some shaggy object brush heavily against him. He sat up, looking about him in dismay. A huge female wolf, whose home he had pre-empted, had come in from the storm, was trying to oust the intruder. Perhaps she had young ones further back in the recess, was fearful for their safety. Absalom could feel her hot, fetid breath in his face. She might become angered and spring at him if he did not depart quickly. He had heard that wolves were ugliest when they had young.

Swinging the trunk on his shoulder, he scrambled from the cave into the drenching rain. The she-wolf had proved an instrument in the hands of the "token," which was urging him onward. Down the mountain, he struggled; once, he fell on his face in a patch of brambles. He knew he was far from the path, but once off the mountain, he would be all right—besides, it would then be dawn. As he worked along, he imagined seeing a slight greyness in the sky. It had seemed like an eternity getting off that mountain; it was due to get brighter. But the rain drove into his face fiercely; it confused his sense of direction. He fancied he saw a building ahead; it looked like a great barn; near it seemed to be a roadway. He was getting out of the woods, sure enough! He scrambled forward, filled with fresh energy. He even jumped over logs and stabs. A giant grapevine heavily intertwined with a hickory tree impeded his path. He pushed his way through it; on the other side surely was the road. He lunged through; he stumbled; he turned head over heels, still clinging to his precious tin trunk; he uttered a cry of fear as he felt himself in swift running, cold water. He had fallen into a mill race; he must struggle for his life. The trunk submerged him; like many mountain boys, he was unable to swim; in his frenzy, he held on to his belongings more tightly. The sweeping current carried him forward; almost instantly, he was tangled in the water wheels. There, in the awful place, he could only have one thought; the "token" of the night before had been for him; the storm and the she-wolf had been partners in his fate. The volume of water engulfed him; he was helpless and dead within a short space of time.

For several days, Miller Ratgebber did not visit his mill buildings; he sat indoors by the stove until the dismal coal rain had ceased. When the Keewaydin blew again and fleecy white clouds circled above the points of the Seven Mountains, he was willing to resume his work. Something seemed to be choking the wheels; it might be drift from the three days and three nights of rain. All the creeks in the valley were badly swollen; some bridges had been carried away. With his hired man, Sammy Grubb, he investigated the trouble. To their horror, they found the remains of a young boy and a small tin trunk, almost inextricably tangled in the paddles. They took out the impediments and then drove to Abundance to inquire if anybody was missing. It was only when the coroner held his inquest that the dead boy's identity was learned.

"I can't imagine why he should have quit so suddenly; he was a good boy and always wrote that he was perfectly satisfied," said his mother, "except that he came of an old line family that had a ghost or 'token.'"

VIII

PIPSISSEWAY'S PINE

(A Story of Paddy Mountain)

WE were crossing Paddy Mountain on a bright morning in the latter part of April, experiencing that wonderful sense of being born anew, which comes to everyone in the spring-time who is fortunate enough to be in the mountains. We frequently stopped to gaze at endless ranges of brown hills, looking like the furrows of a freshly plowed field, with the peaks of the Seven Mountains rising from them like sharp rocks upturned by the celestial plowman. Here and there, we stopped to pluck a violet or to enjoy the sweet-scented loveliness of the arbutus or mayflower.

The timber had been cut in the region we were traversing, and here and there, we crossed the abandoned routes of the branches of the prop-timber railways which had gridironed the mountains to carry away to the mines the last of the forest monarchs. The mountains had grown up in hardwoods, mostly white oaks, and the buff-colored autumn leaves still lingered on many of these. In our five-mile walk, we did not see or hear a single bird; the warblers and the game birds were hidden in the tracts of original forest which remained; they would not bemean themselves by living in a slashing. We could not help wondering when the last patch of primeval trees was cut would mean the final extinction of the more picturesque forms of bird life.

The heath-hen which had lived in the Indians' cornfields was destroyed when the white men seized the fields, the paroquets which rested in aged lindens and elms by the inland creeks vanished when the big trees fell, the wild pigeons lessened as the beechwoods were demolished. The hemlock warblers will doubtless sing their requiems in the last of the giant evergreens.

It was a bleak region, this vast upland, when the sun went under a cloud; it was like nature denuded of all her make-up, standing before us in bare ugliness. But fortunately, the sun shone most of the time, coaxing forth the fresh spring odors and now and then encouraging to burst into love rhapsody, some amorous peepers in a bog. It was nearly noon when we came in sight of the modest cabin of Peter McNarney, one of the hermits of the Seven Mountains. When we reached it, we saw nobody but soon located the quaint old man in his back-kitchen stewing milkweed shoots. The savory odor of this delicious delicacy sharpened our already keen appetites.

The little old man, with his long grey beard, resembling one of the gnomes in the stage presentations of *Rip Van Winkle* came forward to greet us, smiling with his bright Irish blue eyes. He was in his shirt sleeves and wore a battered black derby hat on the back of his head. Peter was not a hermit of the ordinary stripe; no unrequited love affairs, no religious asceticism, no hatred of the shams of the world had driven him into the wilderness. He had moved up on the high plateau about fifty years before, was a pioneer lumberman in that section. He never married because he was never able to find a woman pretty enough to suit him, who would be happy in the lonely forest, he said. When the timber was all gone, he found himself stranded with his cottage on the bare mountaintop like the proverbial clam at low tide. He was of a cheerful disposition and lived with his dogs and cats on the little which he had saved in the prosperous lumbering days.

He always had a good potful on the stove around meal times, and many travelers went out of their way to stop at his cabin for a toothsome repast. Like many Irishmen, he was strong in his likes and dislikes. If he fancied people's looks, he would invite them to remain for dinner; if not, even though they might ask for accommodations, they would be told that they had better go on to Abundance or Indianville, that his larder was empty. One thing in his favor was that he liked most persons; few suffered the unpleasantness of being turned away. He never asked for pay, but like the monks of St. Bernard, travelers were expected to hand him the value of the meals. My companion had known Peter for many years; consequently, we were invited to remain to sample the milkweed shoots, "the first mess of the season." They were truly delicious, served with a white cream sauce, more tender and richly flavored than asparagus; they fairly melted in our mouths. We left nothing in the pot, which pleased the old man, as milkweed shoots were the dish for which his cuisine was noted. The persimmon wine he gave us was also very good.

After the feast, we sat outside the door on a little wooden bench, surveying the limitless landscape and planning our journey for the afternoon. Across the ravine from the cabin, near the top of the opposite ridge, stood a gigantic white pine. It was fully one hundred feet high, green at the top, and shrouded in heavy, healthy foliage. It did not seem to be punky; it looked so thrifty and vigorous that it was strange it should have been left by the rapacious loggers. We scanned the ridges in every direction; this was the only living original pine in sight. Perhaps it was an ancient "corner" or line tree, marked by the colonial surveyors, and had an interesting history—at least it was well worth asking about. Peter laughed heartily when we pointed to the huge pine and inquired of him its lineage.

"Well, you may wonder that it is standing there; I expected it to go a dozen times when the lumbermen swept over these mountains, but it survived every crew. I've gone out myself a dozen times to slash it down, but I was never able to phase it. I don't believe that it is a line tree, but it has an old and a queer story attached to it; the queerest that I've heard in all my years in the Seven Mountains. It goes back about five hundred years to Indian times; still, I have every reason to believe that every word of it is true. Indian Joe told it to me when he was boss of the first crew which lumbered off the mountain where it stands; he knew all the old legends, and with all his other faults, I don't think he ever told an untruth intentionally.

"No doubt you have heard of the great chief of the Susquehannas, Pipsisseway; he had his royal lodge house in your country in the Bald Eagle Mountains. He conquered most of the tribes in this region; his greatest victory was near Rock Springs in Spruce Creek Valley, over the Lenni Lenape, who came across the Indian Steps on the Tussey Mountains in an effort to capture all the northern valleys. Historians say that was in the year 1635. Pipsisseway annihilated them, making himself the greatest figure in Indian history. After this sweeping victory, the famous warrior came to this mountain to pay his respects to a venerable wise man who lived, so Indian Joe told me, right where my house now stands. From the sound of it all, Pipsisseway was so pleased with himself and this world that he aspired to have the inevitable approaches of old age and death put off indefinitely.

"Of the many wise men who lived in his domain, the one on this hill was the greatest. Most of them had flocked around the victorious king, but this one remained on his mountain. It whetted Pipsisseway's curiosity to see him; he could not return to his home on the banks of the Susquehanna until he had indulged in a thorough talk with this indifferent soothsayer. Furthermore, he had heard that the wise man was a hundred years old, yet straight as an arrow, keen-eyed and vigorous. If he could stay the hand of time for himself, perhaps he would place a like spell on the mighty monarch.

"It was a great day when the king arrived with his army of retainers. He fully expected to awe the ancient wise man, to get anything he wanted from him. The soothsayer emerged from his hut at the approach of the royal party and advanced boldly. He was a splendid-looking man, erect like an original pine, and looked hardly a day over thirty-five.

After king and wise man exchanged formal greetings, Pipsisseway's herald recited a lengthy address to the soothsayer. It went on to say that his majesty was conferring a great favor, a condescension, in fact, to go so far out of the way to visit an obscure wizard on his lonely mountain top; that most of his kind would be overjoyed to be granted even a brief audience at the royal headquarters; that he should feel highly honored, and be willing to perform anything which the famous warrior and king might request of him. Throughout the harangue, which lasted over an hour, the wise man remained unmoved; his lip curled disdainfully, and he was clearly unmoved in the presence of royalty or its satellites.

"With dignified reserve, the wise man responded that he would be pleased to do all in his power for the great king, that his sole purpose in life was to alleviate the wants of humanity. Then the royal stewards spread a carpet made of a hundred panther skins, and a sumptuous repast was served. The wise man was seated on the king's right hand, an unprecedented honor. During the meal, Pipsisseway constantly talked about himself and his victories, of how he would perpetuate his name in the regions over which he ruled. He said he believed that he was the greatest man who had ever lived, that he was made of different material from the ordinary mortals. He explained that when he cut himself, blood of a purple color flowed; other beings had red blood. He could not understand why he sometimes suffered from bad health like common people. He should have been allowed to escape the ills of the flesh; they should belong to the plainly born. He never allowed the wise man to get in a word 'edgewise,' as we say in the mountains. It was so sickening that the soothsayer's desire to eat was destroyed. He had to force down the food and drink, as it was a crime punishable by death for a king's dinner guest not to empty his dishes and drinking vessels.

"After the meal, the king suggested to the wise man that they take a walk together, as he had some subjects he wished to discuss privately with him. They strolled down the mountain, across the ravine, and up the face of the opposite ridge. The vainglorious king did not mince words. He said he realized that he was indispensable to the welfare of his people, to the entire Indian people for that matter; it would be an irreparable calamity if he should grow old or die. It would confer a lasting favor on humanity if such a rare being could be conserved to this life. In their stroll, they paused under an enormous white pine, which towered above its fellows. It was of the variety we call a "cork" or Michigan pine; the bark was smooth and a golden brown, the needles very thickly clustered and shining bottle green in hue. The branches grew far down on the trunk, the lower ones wide, gradually narrowing towards the top into a delicate tuft or crest. It is the lone pine you see yonder.

"'I noted with pleasure your answer to my herald's address that you would do all in your power on my behalf,' said Pipsisseway. 'I knew this; else, I would not have traveled so far to see you.' He placed his hand on the wise man's shoulder and said with emphasis: 'I would like you to bestow on me the gift of immortal life, also of immortal youth.' The wise man looked at his king dumbfounded.

HERE THE REDMEN RESTED   (Photo by S. W. Smith)

"'Sire,' he answered, 'I would love to do anything in my power to aid you, but the things you ask I am unable to perform; I possess a certain wisdom, but I do not rank with the gods.'

"Pipsisseway's heavy jaw dropped. 'I am astounded,' he gasped, 'I was told that you could do *everything*, that you are a hundred years old but have miraculously preserved your youth. I will turn over to you one-quarter of my domain if you will give me immortal life.' Even in this extremity, Pipsisseway sought to drive a hard bargain.

"'I do not believe I am a hundred years old,' replied the wise man respectfully. 'I am quite old, that is true, but I do not know my exact age. The couple who reared me found me floating on a large piece of hemlock bark on the Juniata, not far above its confluence with the Susquehanna. They never knew to which tribe I belonged or my age. I was probably one or two years old when they discovered me; to the best of my knowledge, I am only in my eightieth year.'

"Pipsisseway gazed at the soothsayer in speechless wonder. He could scarcely realize that the erect, clear-skinned, black-haired figure before him was nearly half a century older than himself. He, a king of aristocratic blood, must grow old; this foundling had conquered time.

"'How have you retained your own youth if you cannot preserve it for others?' he demanded impatiently.

"'By simple living, by loving my fellow beings, trees, flowers, birds, and animals, by peace and calm, by purity, by lofty thoughts.'

"'Do not I live the same way?' snapped the king.

"'You have a fine intellect, sire, but you have had every wish gratified. You have loved no one but yourself; you have persecuted many. Change your nature, and you will stay young. It is not within my gifts to aid you.'

"'What *can* you do then?' said Pipsisseway, 'you are nothing but an overrated person, a recluse with a halo of unreality.'

"The wise man kept his temper and replied softly, 'I can put the spell of immortal life on this tree under which we are now standing; it will be here five hundred years after you and I are both gone.'

"'If you can do that,' growled the king, 'why can't you help me?'

"'This tree lives righteously, calmly; it has pure thoughts, lofty ideals. It harms no one; it only seeks the sun, its god; it will reap its reward.'

"The wise man's mysticism was too much for Pipsisseway, so he snapped that they had better return to the camp; the hour was late. Very little was spoken on the way, and king and wise man parted cooly. The soothsayer was kindly disposed, but Pipsisseway was in an ugly mood. He had met his match; he had found that special privilege has no place in the infinite.

"Gitche Manitou, the god of the Indians, evidently heard the words uttered under the majestic pine. Within a few years, Pipsisseway the mighty was stricken with swamp fever, passing away despite all human efforts to save him. He died so completely that even his name was forgotten. The wise man lived a score of years longer, dying as the old saying goes 'full of years and honors.'

"The grand old pine which had heard the expressed opinions of both men was blessed from that minute. It was given the greatest of gifts, immortality. When Indians built campfires beneath it, the bark never became scorched; when they ventured to drive a peg in it on which to hang their kettles, their hands were seized with sudden weakness. They could not hold it long enough to strike with a mallet. When the first English surveyors visited these mountains, they noticed the tree as a likely corner because of its conspicious height. When they tried to mark it with their axes, the bits flew off the handles; they could not strike it, try as they might. The first lumbermen came here about 1862 to cut the choicest pines for spars in the navy. They selected the giant pine as the first to fall. When the axe-men drew near it, they were attacked by a strange giddiness; their strokes went wide, they fell to the ground deadly sick and had to be carried back to camp. As there were so many other fine trees, they made no second attempt to fell it. A fierce forest fire came through here in the spring of '64, the year after I built my first shanty. I was burned out, most of the green timber was killed, but the old pine escaped without even so much as getting its bark blackened. I tried my hand at cutting the tree many times just to see if I could do it; I lost enough bits to start an axe factory; I never was able to even nick it. I always became so sick, besides, that I had to lay up for a day or two after every essay. I said to myself, 'old man, that pine isn't for you; treat it well, and you will be happy; molest it, and you will never have any luck.'

"In the fall of 1890, some parties from Derrstown bought all the timber left on the mountains about here. That winter, they took off the original pines. They tried to get Pipsisseway's pine, as I called it, but the axe-men fell about like a lot of steers at a slaughterhouse every time they went to slash it down. The following summer, they cleared the hemlocks but kept away from the big pine. The next three or four years were spent cutting the yellow pines for props and the oaks for ties; every axe-man took a look at the big pine; they seemed to know it was 'not for all markets.' After the prop-timber and tie men left, several hot fires swept over the slashings, burning tops and branches to a crisp. The old pine came through them all without a mark; it is a regular old fireweed; I intend to be on friendly terms with that tree; it's going to give me some of its vitality; I think it has already, for I'm pretty spry for one who is going on to eighty."

There was a pause; we took our eyes off the old hermit and gazed at the sky, which was fast darkening. We gave him a present "to buy some tobacco," thanking him for the story and the dinner, and said goodbye. As we started on our way, we looked across the ravine. The giant Michigan pine outlined against the coming storm was swaying its deep green branches, crooning softly and happily in the fitful April wind!

IX

UNCLE JOB

(A Story of Two Comets)

UNCLE Job Conley was a good-sized boy of fifteen when in 1835, he first saw Halley's Comet. The sight of the superb silver aureole tearing its way through the eastern sky made a profound impression on his awakening mind. An old German who was standing near him on the steps of the country store at the same time excitedly exclaimed, "that means another terrible war, or if it doesn't mean that we are due for another cholera epidemic." After most of the crowd had looked at the silvery orb until long past their bedtimes and one by one had ambled out the tree-hooded lanes to their quiet little candle-lit homes, young Conley stood speechless and alone in admiration.

Colonel Ezra McCann, who lived at the manor house, happened to be engaged in a business transaction with storekeeper Durst that night, and when at ten o'clock he emerged from the cozy office, he noticed the boy gazing intently at the superb constellation. He knew the lad slightly and spoke to him in a pleasant manner, referring to the magnificence of the heavens and how the comet had lessened the dignity of all the stars. The boy's replies were so intelligent and interested that the colonel, the leading man in the neighborhood, asked him if he would care to ride with him as far as the gate of Kildarry, which was on the road to young Conley's modest home. The boy accepted with marked alacrity. He did not mind the walk; he took it every clear night, but he wanted a chance to continue the delightful conversation about the heavenly bodies.

Colonel McCann let the horse walk most of the way, especially when they came to open spaces with no trees to obstruct a view of the spangled sky. The Colonel explained various theories of the beginning of the universe, which were at variance with what Job had learned at Sunday School; they set his mental forces tingling. He told the boy the names of the leading constellations and stars, the story of the moon and the tide, but above all, recited the thrilling history of the comet and its periodical re-appearances.

"Scientists have calculated," he said impressively, "that the comet reappears in this latitude at regular intervals of seventy-five years. It will be back again as sure as mathematics can make it in the spring of 1910. How old are you, young man?" he said suddenly, to which the boy replied that he had passed his fifteenth birthday the previous November.

"I will not be here in 1910," said the Colonel Badly, "it will be another case of 'Caesar turned to clay,' but you, with your strong physique and clean life, ought surely to, *barring accidents*. I wish I knew where I would be in seventy years or *seven!*"

It was not long before they reached the iron gate which led into Kildarry, and here the young man alighted, thanking the colonel and wishing him good night. As he headed his Morgan horse towards the drive, the fine old gentleman called back, "Don't forget, the comet will be back in just seventy-five years; live by that fact and set your hopes on seeing it again. When you do, give a thought to this night and to me, floating somewhere in the 'great perhaps.'" Then he cracked his whip and was gone up the darkened roadway.

The boy was deeply impressed by the words of this educated free-thinker. For years it was hinted in the neighborhood that Colonel McCann was a skeptic, but he had never met anyone to whom the colonel had expressed his views. Outwardly he was a professing Presbyterian of the old school. Previous to this conversation, he had considered free-thinkers as queer; heaven as a certainty. Now, as he walked along the silent road, he seemed to have suddenly lost the key to the golden streets; the universe loomed vaster and colder than ever before. Above him, the superb comet swept in its conquering way, illuminating all the heavens but adding to their mystery. How strange he reasoned that scientists can calculate just when this comet will return, yet cannot tell what it is or the universe of which it is a part.

"I wonder *can* they calculate it; do they know as much as Colonel McCann thinks they do; the only way to find out is for me to live seventy-five years until Halley's comet is due to reappear. If it doesn't, I will say that faith alone is real; if it does, it must share its place with mystery—our two companions through existence. It is something to live for, and to use the colonel's words, 'barring accidents,' I will see that comet in 1910, and I will surely think of this night."

Before he retired, he pushed open the wooden shutters of his room to take another look at the wonderful constellation, shedding its radiance upon the cone of the Petersburg, and which was to be his star of hope through life. That was the last night the comet was seen in the early evening, and the dwellers in the Seven Mountains did not feel sufficient interest to lose their sleep to sit up to watch its reappearances. Whenever Job met the aged Germans on the road, they always said, "get ready for war," or "prepare to fight cholera." They were satisfied with their primitive beliefs.

Several times he saw Colonel McCann driving in his elegant carriages; the old gentleman was a lover of fine horses, his pet scheme was to introduce the Morgan breed into the Seven Mountains, as he believed they were particularly adapted for the uneven, hilly roads. The colonel always bowed pleasantly to the young man, though conscious of his position, he would have been totally ignorant of the word "snob," an appelation that characterizes most of the "dollar aristocracy" of today. The boy felt a debt of gratitude to him that he never could repay; he had given him an ideal to live for, a concrete reason to hold a tight grip on life for the next seventy-five years.

A little more than a year after the comet's appearance, Colonel McCann died, aged sixty-three years. It transpired that he had been in failing health for several years, that he was a doomed man. Job reasoned from this the cause of his melancholy outlook on life; his uncertainty about the future state when prematurely brought so close to it. The young man attended the funeral held at the stately brick church of the Calvinists at Jacobsburg. The edifice was packed to the doors, and the clergyman eulogistically preached the dead man's beautiful faith for two hours. Evidently, he had not revealed to his family the doubts which lurked "in his heart of hearts," which everyone else knew, had passed away ostensibly redeemed. He was laid to rest in the nearby graveyard on the hill among the Irish junipers and arborvitaes. It was expected that an imposing monument would be soon erected over the remains of one who had represented the district for twelve years in the State Senate and been ever a public-spirited citizen and a power for good. Five years passed, and not even a marker was put up. Wild roses formed a frowzled covering to the mound. Then the Colonel's widow died at her son's home in Philadelphia, and her remains were brought to Jacobsburg for interment. A monument was erected to her; undoubtedly, she deserved it, but the worthy colonel's name was cut on it in smaller letters and below hers. In five years, he had been totally forgotten. No wonder that with his keen perceptions, he looked into the future years as a black, blank waste insofar as the perpetuation of his own personality was concerned. But his name and spirit lived on in the heart of the young farmer boy whom he had encouraged and befriended.

On several occasions, he visited the graveyard and pulled up the weeds, which now threatened to choke and obliterate his last resting place. The young man married early in life and brought numerous progeny into the world. He succeeded his father on the old family farm, and while he got along well, he never became wealthy nor desired to be. He had a firm grip on life upon his soul; "barring accidents," he would see the great comet reappear in seventy-five years. In the spring of 1883, he was already past middle life, and his friends and relatives had begun to call him "Uncle Job." He was erect, worked as hard as any of the boys on the farm and in the lumber woods, but his silvery hair and chin beard made his new appellation seem suitable.

One evening after supper, he heard one of his sons read aloud from the county paper that a great comet was due to appear above the Seven Mountains within the next few weeks, that some of the older people had believed comets to be portents of war, famine, or pestilence. The article concluded that astronomers believed that the same comets returned to localities at regular intervals. Uncle Job was deeply interested in the article and spoke about the comet he had seen in 1835, forty-eight years before.

"Colonel McCann, who used to be a prominent man in this part of the country, told me that it would return in exactly seventy-five years." One of Uncle Job's grandsons who were present—a pert lad who had attended high school for a term in Jacobsburg—spoke up.

"I guess this is the comet you saw, all right, only it's coming back in forty-eight instead of seventy-five years. Those old-timers thought they knew it all, but their notions are getting exploded."

The old man was crestfallen; perhaps his hope for all these years was coming to pass within a few weeks, his firm belief in Colonel McCann sustained a moment of eclipse. He said nothing more, but about ten days later, when the Lutheran preacher came in for supper, he brought up the subject at the table. Uncle Job had married a Lutheran, and while he himself had joined the Calvinists early in life, he had not attended services in many years.

"I don't take any stock in what scientists say," said the preacher positively. "I never believed that man is descended from a monkey, and I refuse to believe that any astronomer can figure out the exact date for the return of a celestial body. It is all buncombe. My opinion is that the comet we will see very shortly is the same one you looked at forty-eight years ago."

This delivered before the assembled family knocked the props from under the old man's beliefs. He felt very downcast that night, but fresh faith came to him the next morning. He would not discredit Colonel McCann's words until he had seen this new comet; he could remember exactly what the other one looked like. A picture of it in every detail had burned itself into his soul. The new comet came, and the family and the preacher, who happened to be spending the night at the house, witnessed the phenomenon from the front yard.

"That's not the comet I saw in 1835," said Uncle Job, clapping his hands.

"How do you know, gran'pap," chirped the pert grandson, "you're pretty apt to forget what it looked like after all these years."

It was now the preacher's chance to follow up this advantage. "This is probably the same comet that was here forty-eight years ago; there is no man living who could remember exactly what he saw at such a distance so long ago."

As the reverend gentleman was on the eve of his thirty-third birthday, his experience with long vistas of memory was limited. Uncle Job was too wise to enter into an argument with the assembled party, so he said no more. But he went to bed happy; the comet now in the heavens, though vivid and imposing, was not the one he had seen in 1835. The next evening his wife, who had felt badly at seeing the old gentleman "sat on" the night previously, took particular pleasure in reading aloud an article from the county paper. "It said that the comet now to be seen had not been in this hemisphere in over a hundred years. In 1835 Halley's Comet had appeared over the Seven Mountains; its return was predicted for 1910."

"What did I tell you all," said the old man gleefully; "Halley's Comet is yet to appear."

"I wouldn't believe everything those country newspapers say," remarked the pert grandson.

Uncle Job was satisfied; furthermore, "barring accidents," he was going to see Halley's Comet when it reappeared. Years passed, and most of the old man's friends passed away; he became the patriarch of his community. He had the misfortune to bury his wife five years before the expected revisit of the comet. The old couple had often talked about the coming event and how they would see the comet together; it cast a deep shadow over his anticipations. On New Year's Eve, he sat up with his descendants to welcome in 1910, the year of the comet's expected appearance. He was in fine spirits and talked with almost the enthusiasm of youth about the days of 1835, of the changes that had occurred between then and 1910.

"I wish Preacher Fishback was alive; he insisted that the comet we saw in 1883 was Halley's; I guess he died thinking that way."

During the spring months, the county papers and the Philadelphia papers took up the subject of the expected comet. They described the looks of the comet minutely in 1835; it verified Uncle Job's recollections exactly. Whenever he could obtain a listener, he would tell about having seen the great comet seventy-five years before; some foolishly kept away from him, like the un-enlightened shun old soldiers' war stories. He was probably the only person in the county who had been reasonably mature before it appeared; his views on the subject should have been reported in the county newspapers. During seventy years, the habits of the country people had changed; they were willing to sit up to see the comet on the first night of its appearance and not, as in the old days, wait until it came into view early in the evening. Surrounded by his family, the old man waited for the great sight. Even the grandson, who had scoffed twenty-seven years before, had been "converted" and wanted to be present to witness the genial patriarch's triumph. It was a wonderfully clear night; myriads of stars illuminated the heavens, and their light was sufficient to cast a silvery aureole over the cone of the Petersburg mountain. Early in the evening, the whippoorwills sang shrilly; the peepers chorused in the low grounds about Shaver's Run, crickets were fiddling everywhere. The air was sweet and calm; there was a rich odor of pine and damp leaves.

When the hour approached, the party went out in the yard, the old man leading the way, walking steadily, but carrying his favorite gold-headed cane. His family noticed that he did not step off the high rickety porch steps as lightly as of yore. The sight which met their eyes was beyond expectations; the superb, luminous ball, with its spangled trail of light, bisected the heavens with its majestic presence. It dimmed the stars; it made the summit of the Petersburg glisten like a peak in some land of eternal snows. Uncle Job stamped his cane on the ground and laughed like a boy.

"What did I tell you all? I said, ' barring accidents,' I'd be here to see the comet again and prove that it wasn't the one that visited us in 1883."

The entire family congratulated him upon his good fortune, wishing him many more days of health and happiness.

"I have only one regret," he said quietly, "and that is that mother (meaning his late wife) isn't here to see this with me."

When all had seen the comet to their hearts' content, the family party went indoors; most of them scurried away to bed as they had worked hard all day and were sleepy after this unusual dissipation. Uncle Job and his two eldest sons sat in the kitchen for a few minutes discussing the wonderful visitation. When one of them made the sign to go upstairs, the old man remarked that he thought he would go out on the porch to get another look at the comet before retiring.

"This is like Colonel McCann's voice from the tomb; he certainly predicted everything just as it has happened," he said.

As he went to the door, one of the sons moved to follow him.

"Better not go with him, Josiah," said the other, "he wants to look at the comet by himself, to think about mother and the old days."

The door slammed, and they heard the aged man's cane striking on the porch floor; they resumed their smoking about the empty stove. Fifteen minutes passed; why did the old man remain outside so long; the air was chilly; he had better be in bed. The men went out on the porch, expecting to find their father sitting on his homemade rocker, which an ancient German had given him on his eighty-fifth birthday. He was nowhere to be found. They ran to the far edge of the piazza, where they heard a groan. Looking down, they saw the old man lying in the flowerbed; in the darkness, caused by the thick growth of vines, he had stumbled off the porch and was evidently seriously injured. They picked him up and carried him tenderly to the kitchen, laying him on a lounge. His lips moved, and he said distinctly, "Well, I've seen the comet after seventy-five years. Colonel McCann said I would, 'barring accidents.'" Then he lapsed into an unconscious state and died soon after the doctor arrived.

X

SWARTZELL PANTHER

(A Story of Hayvice Valley)

IT was Saturday afternoon in Siglerville, and residents in the country surrounding this quaint little mountain community had driven in according to custom to execute their week's shopping. Nearly a score of teams were tied to the long, badly chewed rails in front of the general store. Other wagons, buggies, and a couple of saddle horses were fastened to trees or posts on the opposite side of the road. The mud was "hub deep" as it was in the early spring, indicating that it must have taken some of the heavy farm wagons many hours to drag their way from the distant farmsteads to the little trading village. The boardwalks were thronged with happy-faced mountaineers, for the day was sunshiny and balmy, who seemed to utilize the afternoon in town as a social rendezvous. Some of the old men with their long curly beards, coonskin caps, and high boots presented a most picturesque appearance.

There was one turnout, a dilapidated carryall drawn by two long-haired plow horses, which had stopped in the middle of the street, that especially attracted my attention. A great rangy wolfish-looking dog stood under the high box; his tongue hung out, his tail was between his legs, he was mud-spattered, evidently had traveled from some distant point in the mountains. An old man and woman sat in the carryall; they conversed with a tall mountaineer standing near, bearded, booted, and capped like the rest. He carried a shotgun and was so tall that his eyes seemed to be on a level with those of the persons in the wagon. The old man in the carryall was well worth glancing at a second time; lean and eagle-nosed, his wide-brimmed soft hat and flowing grey side whiskers gave him a decidedly clerical expression; his companion, a woman past middle age, was pleasant-faced, spectacled, and neatly dressed in black, in the style of about 1893. I asked my companion who these interesting persons might be. He replied that the couple in the carriage were Jimmy Shattuck and his wife.

"Jim used to be a Methodist preacher," he stated, "until he married a daughter of old John Swartzell, the famous panther hunter of Hayvice Valley; the man they are talking to is old Cal. Wagner from Germany Valley, who has killed his share of big game in his day." Then he pointed to the wagon box on which the elderly couple was seated. "Look, do you see they are sitting on a panther hide now; it was the last one that old man Swartzell killed. No greater hunter than he ever lived in the Seven Mountains, not even Dan Treaster."

I had been so interested in the physiognomies that I had almost missed seeing the panther relic, so now I gazed at it carefully. It seemed to be an enormously long one, as it stretched over both ends of the seat, but it was badly faded, and the hair was worn off in several places from hard usage in all kinds of weather. I looked at the hide, rooted to the spot, for it brought back a flood of memories, which always thrill me when I see a souvenir of pioneer days. My companion, knowing my interest, said he would tell me the story of Swartzell's last panther.

"The old man killed this one fully ten years after the animals had ceased to be common in the Seven Mountains; as near as I can recollect, it was about 1882. They hung on much longer than that; there may be one or two wandering through these regions yet. They come all the way from West Virginia now when the 'coast is clear'—they are great travelers, but they ceased breeding here over thirty years ago. Johnny Swartzell was an antic sort of chap; life in a lonely forested valley did not make him solemn; he laughed at everything and seemed to regard existence as a huge joke. When his buckwheat was a failure, he said he could do just as well trapping; when hunting got poor, he said he'd live by farming. He was a famous pigeon trapper. I have always heard it said that his were the best-constructed bough-houses in the Seven Mountains. He used to salt a hundred or two barrels of pigeons every spring; these he sold in the lumber camps so that the 'lumber-jacks' hereabouts feasted on fat squabs all winter. When they stopped nesting in these mountains, he barrelled the choicest young birds he caught in the fall; they surely made excellent eating. Lumbermen make better wages now, but they don't live as well as in the 'good old days,' when they got a dollar a day and grub.

"Johnny had traveled about a great deal in his youth, although he was born in the Seven Mountains. He had spent considerable time among the Indians in the 'northern tier' and had many of their mannerisms and expressions. He liked to tell the story about one young buck who drank too much alcohol and, digging up his tomahawk, attacked a peaceable home on the Genessee one midnight, killing half the household before they got awake.

"'You can never trust an Indian,' he often said, 'not even Indian Joe.' This made old Joe, who was the only Indian in these parts, real angry when it was carried to him. He hadn't any sense of humor at all. He said he felt that he had lived among the white folks long enough to have lost all of his native cussedness, that he was a white man in everything save in his color.

"Hayvice Valley was the last region in the Seven Mountains inhabited by the Indians; it was likewise the last habitation of the panthers. Even now, it retains a wild atmosphere; there is a tract of original white pine in the south end, which was secluded enough to have afforded a nesting place for a colony of great blue herons. When the milliners had the protection taken off these useful, snake-eating birds in 1909, it has since been restored; a party of 'bark-savages' from the north end of the valley made a carnival one Sunday afternoon, destroying them with shotguns and clubs.

"But to return to Johnny Swartzell, he was very fond of telling Indian stories; they were so exciting that they would have been good enough to collect into book form. He always liked to plague his daughter Maggie, who you see in the carryall, by telling her that some night she would find a wild Indian under her bed. The old homestead was a one-story structure, consequently, all the bedrooms were on the ground floor. Maggie was never scared by the joke, even when she was a wee bit of a girl. She always laughed and said she would run and get her father and have him shoot the savage.

"'You'd act very differently,' he said, 'if you really saw one. You would be so scared you'd drop in your tracks.'

"'Wait and see,' she would answer, and then the whole family would indulge in a good spell of laughter. There were few girls in the mountains as fearless as she; at sundown, she would go after the cattle, tracing them by the tinkle of the cowbell. Sometimes they would be hidden deep among the original timber; at others, they would be near the crests of the lonely hills where wolves were known to congregate. It was no rare thing to have a calf killed by wild animals, but Maggie and her faithful dog, it was the grandmother of that animal standing under the carryall, never had an adventure. Wild animals know *what* they can attack and *who* they can't!

"Scarcely a night passed when she started for her room, which was on the far side of the kitchen but that the old man would caution her about the 'wild Indian.' Subjects of conversation were few in the secluded valley; repetitions, if they were at all humorous, were tolerated. On very rare occasions, peddlers or traveling preachers penetrated into Hayvice, where they were sure to find a genial welcome in the Swartzell home. No matter how bedraggled or dirty, they were put between the clean sheets in the spare room. Maggie would laugh to herself after showing some of these individuals to their rooms; they looked a great deal more outlandish than the wildest Indian. The only real native she ever saw was Indian Joe; he was always scrupulously attired when he was sober.

"Maggie was fond of fresh air and, in winter and summer, slept with her windows open, the wooden shutters ajar. She kept them fastened together by stout cords to prevent them from banging in windstorms, but a would-be intruder could have cut them and come in easily. The Swartzell family felt safer in the wilderness with windows open and unlocked doors than persons in cities where there is a multiplicity of bolts, chains, gratings, and police protection.

"One evening in September, a Russian Jew peddler named Benny Kaplan, he afterward became the leading storekeeper in Jacobsburg and built the Kaplan House, arrived at the Swartzell home. He was in a state of great perturbation; his stiff red hair was literally on end, and his fingers trembled so violently that he could scarcely unloose the buckles of his pack. He said he had been followed for five miles by an animal that looked like a big grey cat; it kept a hundred yards behind, ran when he

PENNSYLVANIA MOUNTAIN WAGON OF 1840   (Photo by Rev. W. W. Soll)

ran, stopped when he stopped, and walked at exactly his gate when he walked. He had been for a night at the Swartzells' the week previously; he had not intended coming so soon again, he said, but the afternoon was waning, and he dreaded the seven-mile walk across the mountains to Abundance—followed by the big grey cat. City people, especially foreigners, were gifted with eyes that magnified; that was old Johnny's private opinion, but nevertheless, he soothed the peddler's fears. It was terrible to have been followed by a panther; he must remain all night and forget about it in a comfortable sleep. Before retiring, the old pioneer gave the Russian a good jorum of Troxelville whiskey so that he heard no more from him until breakfast time. Benny rested well, and after a plentiful breakfast of buckwheat cakes and wild honey, his genial host accompanied him as far as the top of the mountain. When he got back, in time for dinner, he jested about the peddler's adventure.

"'I don't believe he was followed by any *painter*. It might have been a rabbit, a fox, or at most a bob eat; I haven't seen painter tracks in Hayvice since the twenty-seventh of February, 1872." The matter was dismissed as a joke; nothing more was thought about it. 'If it had been a wild Indian, I wouldn't have been more surprised,' was his final remark on the subject.

"There were some very cold nights after Kaplan's visit. On one of them, a light skiff of snow fell. 'If this keeps up, I'll have all my trapping done by Christmas; there are a couple of wolves and a big lynx that live too near here to suit my taste,' said the old man as he pitched the chunks of beechwood into the big stove. Before going to their cold rooms for the night, the family always roasted some chestnuts on the top of the stove. The old man, his wife, the youngest boy, Oscar, and the daughter, Maggie, were home at the time.

"The night of the thirtieth of September was remembered as being particularly frigid. There was no moon, but the stars glistened like frozen crystals above the tops of the tall pines. Oscar had walked to Siglerville that day to buy some groceries, taking the dogs with him. He usually remained for supper at the Bald Faced Stag Hotel; it was his only dissipation so that he could see the mail stage arrive from Milroy, getting back home before midnight. He knew the 'shortcuts' across the mountains; he could walk the distance that way quicker than it could be driven.

"Maggie retired about nine-thirty, her father giving her his usual thrust about the wild Indian. The girl took her tallow dip and dashed for the cold room. She looked under the bed as usual but, of course, saw nothing. The shutters were ajar as usual; it seemed so bitterly cold that she thought she would close them tightly. As she drew near, she saw what seemed to be two golden stars shining through the narrow opening. They couldn't be stars, for, on second glance, she saw the evening star above, a frosty quicksilver color. The thought flashed through her mind that the yellow stars were the eyes of an intruder, possibly the wild Indian. Quick as a flash, she seized the candle from the chair where she had left it and, leaving the door ajar, darted into the kitchen. The old pioneer was in his stocking feet, sitting by the stove.

"'Father, father,' she whispered, 'you are right at last; the wild Indian has come; he isn't under my bed, but he's looking in at the window.' The old man had called 'wolf' so often that he appeared incredulous. He made no move to get up or reach for his rifle, which hung beside the corner cupboard.

"'Get your gun quick, or else I will,' said the girl. Her voice indicated she was in earnest, that this was no time for joking. Her tones rekindled the old love of the chase, and he arose, grabbing the rifle which Maggie handed to him. No panther ever sprang more quickly than he in covering the distance from the kitchen to the bedroom. With his trained eyes, he recognized the interloper outside the window—if it was an Indian, he was bent on manslaughter, so he fired. Outside came a howl of pain; it sounded human, yet so horrible that it was like the cry of a fiend. The 'golden stars' no longer appeared. Striking the cord which bound the shutters with the butt of the rifle, the pioneer broke it. The shutters flew back, and he leaped through the opening. Outside was a pile of shingles, on which he stumbled and rolled over the gun to the grass. He was quickly on his feet; he fired again, and the aim was true, as the horrible cry of pain seemed to echo among the cold, lofty stars.

"Old mother Swartzell and Maggie were out in the yard by this time, too surprised to even guess what was going on in the pasture lot. All became silent except for the tremulous tinkling of the cow and sheep bells, huddled away in one corner of the field. Pretty soon, the gaunt figure of Johnny Swartzell appeared in sight beyond the yard fence. He waved his rifle; his long beard blew in the frosty breezes.

"'I got him, hooray, I got him good,' he shouted triumphantly.

"'Who is he, for heaven's sake? I hope you haven't killed an Indian,' called out Maggie, half seriously, half in fun.

"'He was a wild Indian, but not the kind you mean; he's an old socker of a *painter*. I'll bet he's nine feet long.'

"Mother Swartzell recovered her presence of mind and with Maggie ran to the house, returning with a smoking lantern. By this time, the happy pioneer had opened the gate which led to the pasture field, where he stood mopping his brow with his sleeve. Just as the women appeared with the light, the ruddy gleam of a cigar appeared in the darkness, and then the shrill barking of dogs—it was Oscar back from Siglerville.

"'What's all the commotion?' yelled the young man.

"'Father's just killed a nine-foot panther that was trying to get in my window,' answered Maggie.

"'Get out, you're foolin',' said the lad, quickening his pace.

"When all had assembled at the gate, the old man led the way across the rocky stumpy, mullein-grown field, pastured close as only sheep can do it. When they reached a clump of scrubby red hemlocks, with bark worn smooth by cattle rubbing against them, he held his lantern aloft. Lying in a limp mass across the exposed roots was the sooty-grey-colored form of a mammoth male panther. It may not have been nine feet long, but it was at least seven from 'tip to tip.' The old hunter stooped down and turned over the creature's big round head with his hand. The first bullet had gone through the muzzle and emerged below the ear; it had not caused death. The second pierced the breast and entered the heart.

"'That second shot was fired at random,' he said with elation, 'pretty good firing in the dark, eh?'

Then the old man and his son skinned the carcass, which was very fat. Evidently, the panther had found plenty of sickly fawns, diseased grouse, and droopy wild turkeys along the way from Clearfield County.

"'Say, pop,' said Oscar before they returned to the house, 'don't you think that this was the big grey cat that followed Benny Kaplan the other day?'

"'It might have been,' said the old man slyly, 'but surely he doesn't look like a fawn, or a grouse, or a turkey; *painters* don't eat Russian sables.'

"The panther hide became a prominent ornament to the lounge in the kitchen, and it is related that the famous hunter spent his declining days on it. In his last illness, it was used to cover his feet on nights when the room was icy cold. After his death and that of his wife, young Oscar married, which threatened to leave Maggie alone in Hayvice. Then Preacher Shattuck came to the rescue and married the girl; the match turned out very well; Jimmy Shattuck handles the rake as well as he did the scriptures. They say that the farm is the garden spot in Hayvice. The devoted husband thinks a lot of the panther relic, and you ought to hear him tell the part his wife played in securing it. It seems as if she did the killing, with old Johnny merely looking on."

As we talked, the ex-preacher cracked his whip, waving farewell to Cal Wagner, and the hairy team started the old carryall in motion. As they plowed up the hill, I could see the ends of the panther skin flapping out from each side of the driver's seat. It was truly the spirit of Hayvice!

XI

A MODERN PETRARCH

(A Story of Alexander's Stream)

WHEN the youthful poet Edgar A. Poe left Poe Valley after his unsuccessful quest for an inheritance and his equally unsuccessful love affair with the daughter of a leading farmer in that valley, he started in the direction of Lewistown, there to take the stage for Philadelphia. He was suffering the first poignancy of his disappointment; his heart was so sad that he neither looked to the right nor the left. It was useless to do so, as the beautiful world appeared a blur and a blank. With characteristic improvidence, he made only a half-hearted effort to trace his share in the ownership of the valley after he had met the beautiful Helena Walters. When after his brief and tempestuous courting, he found that she loved another and his inferior, he was too anxious to quit the region to consider further the possible possession of some of its real estate.

His claim of kinship to Daniel Poh, the frontiersman, was a good one, but as ever in his life, he sacrificed all to the recklessness of lore. By what path he left the secluded Talley is not known, but he first reappeared in civilization at Potter's Bank, where he rested aimlessly at the hotel for several days. He appeared to have plenty of money, for he hired a carrier to return to Poe Valley to get his knapsack which he had left at the Walters' home. He left the hotel unexpectedly one evening, and nothing more can be traced of his wanderings until he reached Milroy a week later. There he became communicative with the landlord at the Raven Hotel, telling him the story of his woes and how he would like to return to Poe Valley to press his claim for the property were it not that he hated to face the fair being who had refused to give up her unworthy lover for him. He learned the names of several lawyers in Lewistown, saying that he would engage one of them to press the case. He had the chance to go by stage to Lewistown, and several teamsters who liked the attractive youth invited him to accompany them. But he said that he had something he wanted to write; the sentences formed themselves better when he walked than when he rode.

The weather was good; perhaps it would arouse his love for the beautiful, remove the haze that was before his eyes since his disappointment. Everything in the young man's life went by extremes; he enjoyed as keenly as he suffered. A period of misery was always followed by one of elevation; in his darkest hour, he could look with certainty to a happy tomorrow. Without these alternating currents of experience, he might have desired to die of grief. He left the Raven Hotel—by the way, a strange prophetic name—one fine morning, strolling along the highway toward Reedsville. On the road, he became acquainted with a German drover, who told him about the wonderful cave with the petrified infant in it on the old Naginey farm. The poet expressed a wish to see the interior, seconded by the drover, who said he hadn't been in the cavern in seven years. He found an accommodating boy who agreed to watch the stock for a shilling, so he entered the cave with young Poe.

The entrance, which had never been large, was completely choked by leaves; after these had been removed, the explorers had to lie on their backs and slide into the aperture like serpents. The interior thrilled the impressionable poet, who was not above scraping on the bush-hammered walls—"Edgar A. Poe. 1838" —with the aid of his case knife. After leaving the quaint labyrinth, they visited Winegardner's Cove, which they found filled with ice in August. Then the men parted, the drover moving in the direction of Yeagertown, the poet departing in search of Alexander's Stream. The hotel proprietor at Milroy had told him of this wonderful fountain that gushed out of the rocks below the old manse; its volume of water was scarcely less than that of the famous fountain of Vaucluse in Provence. It was at Vaucluse that the unhappy poet Francesco Petrarch wrote so many of his impassioned verses to Laura Sade, who, as the wife of another, was beyond his reach. It was there a couple of centuries later that the greatest of modern Italian poets, Victor Alfieri, mingled his tears with the fountain and composed a dozen sonnets to the Countess of Albany, also the wife of another.

When Edgar Poe came in sight of Alexander's Stream, his heart leaped with sublime rapture. In all his travels, he had never seen a spot so marvelously beautiful. Out of a dark chasm in the limestone rocks swept a great jet of crystal water, so immense that it formed the torrent or river called after the Alexanders, which empties into Honey Creek about a quarter of a mile below. Above the hundred-foot cliff from beneath which the cataract burst forth stood a noble grove of primeval walnut, hickory, and white oak trees, many of which are standing today. Further to the north, on the extreme crest of the hill, commanding a superb view of the Seven Mountains, was the ancient manse of the Alexander family. The Alexanders were among the earliest Scotch-Irish pioneers in Central Pennsylvania; they were noted as owners of vast estates and occupied a high position, socially and politically. Their blood flows in the veins of many of the famous leaders in art, literature, and finance all over the United States.

Below the fountain, the shores of the stream were lined with ancient elms and willows. Beyond the banks were several wooded knolls covered with hickory and cedar trees. It was a classic spot, a fit abode for the gods. It was to one of these knolls that the young poet hied himself that bright morning. He seated himself on an old log at the foot of a giant shellbark. This tree was broken down by a storm in 1911. From where he sat, he could watch the fierce torrent of water belching forth from the fissure in the high cliff, the foaming stream which flowed from it running towards the tranquil, dreamy Honey Creek. He could admire the many varieties of primeval trees and watch the kingfishers and the big woodpeckers or "rosenspechts" darting about. He could faintly hear the cawing of ravens in the tops of the tall oaks on the apex of the cliff which overhung the fountain. It was an ideal spot to compose, to feel divine melodies, a sequestered nook where one would have to admit that nature like woman was, despite her inconsistencies, very beautiful.

The young man took his notebook, ink bottle, and quill from his knapsack and began to write: the first dozen lines had been running in his head for the past twenty-four hours. Transferred to paper surcharged with the *atmosphere* of the wondrous fountain, they seemed the most beautiful that had ever flowed from his facile pen. He took off his broad-brimmed hat, leaned his head of curly, light-brown hair—Venetian blonde, some called it—against the trunk of the tree. He closed his eyes for a minute while fresh images adjusted themselves in the portals of his consciousness. He made a pretty picture, with his slender, intellectual face, with features so refined and delicate, the gentle breeze playing with his golden curls.

While meditating with eyes closed, he was unaware that a love-ly-looking, dark-haired, dark-eyed girl, erect and slender, carrying a small tin pail, passed along the footpath within five feet of him on her way to the mansion. She was lost to view among the giant trees when he opened his eyes. Perhaps the passing of the beautiful unseen spirit was the cause; at any rate, his exquisite piece called "To Iolanthe" was instantly completed to the final syllable. With his copperplate hand, he transcribed it in his copybook, rather pleased with the effort. It told of a sad, unrequited romance; it described a fair but false goddess with ash-blonde hair and drooping eyes. The unseen inspiration had cast a golden shadow through his closed lids; the face and form of "Iolanthe" were hers in every particular, except the coloring. By intentionally refraining from describing Helena Walters, he had unintentionally portrayed someone else. Poets are always clairvoyant.

Consequently, when fifteen minutes later he saw a slim, youthful figure coming toward him, he felt sure that he had seen her before. He did not possess the power to describe women he had never met, but where had the rare vision crossed his path before? He had tried to dis-guise Helena's personality in the poem; to his surprise, he had been able to see mentally an entirely different person. He felt such a sense of old acquaintanceship for the girl coming towards him, and his heart was so frightfully lonely that he clambered to his feet and bowed to her. She spoke to him the same moment; the recognition seemed mutual. The young girl's blood had been tingling ever since she had seen the young poet resting against the tree with his eyes closed. She had never seen such a handsome man before; his east of countenance was entirely different from anybody except her ideal. Though country raised and used to hard work, she possessed a refined soul; within her was the spring of spiritual progress. People gifted thus can attain any position in life; they are the real elect of the Calvinistic doctrine; those born without it must always flounder in the sphere in which they are born. He spoke about the beauties of the fountain, saying that he had come many miles expressly to see it. He had never seen anything so wonderful in nature before, not even the Natural Bridge in Virginia, His home was in Baltimore, but he had been doing literary work recently in Philadelphia. The girl opened her black eyes wide; this was the kind of man she had dreamed about but never expected to meet.

The poet asked her to sit down for a minute; perhaps she would care to read a poem he had just finished. She seated herself gracefully on the log, and he handed her his copybook. He leaned against an ancient white oak that stood nearby, watching her intently as she read. She was about eighteen years of age, rather tall, with the slim lines of a nymph. Her face was pale, the arched nose turning up just a trifle at the end. The upper lip was short, but the lips themselves were colorless and pitifully thin. They were the mouthpiece of a starved soul. The line of the chin and throat was particularly graceful. Her old black dress adjusted itself to her graceful form. As she continued to read, her smile grew less; a shadow fell across her expressive face. When she laid it in her lap, she did not utter a single word of approval.

The young poet, hungry for kindness or praise, endured the silence for a moment. He spoke to her gently, asking what she thought of the poem. For some reason, he valued her opinion more than that of anyone in the world whom he had met. She looked up at him, their eyes meeting in sympathetic confidence.

"I don't like it at all," she said.

"Why not?" asked the poet, piqued by her blunt criticism yet secretly divining the reason.

"You know very well," she replied, but then, reflecting a second, she added, "but I am foolish to care; you are a stranger to me; you may be a married man for aught I know."

As Poe fancied himself still bound to eternity to Helena Walters, it would be violating the proprieties of romance to admit a fondness for another quickly. He longed to tell her that he regretted the poem, that it meant nothing anymore, but in the coldness of his intellectual pride, held his tongue. The girl, having made all the advances she wished and finding them not reciprocated, that the poet stood by his guns, so to speak, turned the conversation into impersonal channels. The young writer came over to where she sat and seated himself beside her. He felt a strangely sympathetic atmosphere in her; he seemed to have found one who could *understand*. He began telling her about his troubles, which seemed uppermost in his mind. He could talk more freely with her than with the stolid Pennsylvania German landlords at Potter's Bank and Milroy. His nature required confidences, sympathy, love. He was feminine in the intimacy of his nature. He told her his name; recited about his trip from Philadelphia, of his high hopes at becoming a landowner in the Seven Mountains how it had all been upset by his falling in love with Helena Walters.

At the mention of this name, the young girl's pale face grew paler; the year before, she had been loved by Abram Halit, the fiancé of Helena; she had been deserted by him for this fair blonde girl from Berks County. It was a strange complication; the poet meeting and loving Helena, who refused to give up her lover for him, his coming to the fountain and meeting and being admired by the rejected sweetheart of Helena's lover. The poet laid especial emphasis on his failure to understand why Helena should prefer a coarse fellow like Abram to himself; the girl could not understand this either, as she had known the young man in question. As the conversation progressed, and the girl's sympathy was so pronounced and her personality so attractive, he felt his artistic pose slipping away and the force of his affection for his new friend engulfing him. His desire to leave it a chance acquaintance vanished; he asked the girl her name, saying that he had been deeply benefitted by the meeting. She said that her name was Anne Savidge, her father was the overseer for the Alexander estate, that she lived in the little white cottage a short distance below the mighty fountain.

Her frankness added to her other charms quite won the young poet's heart. He longed to tell her he loved her but feared to do so as the change might seem too sudden after his attitude earlier in the interview. Looking into his heart, he understood now that he loved her from the first moment he laid eyes on her; it was the suddenness of the change of heart as much as his pose as the unhappy lover of the girl in Poe Valley that had caused him to miss his opportunity. If he told her that since they began talking, he had changed, she would regard him as inconsistent; she could never respect him properly. All these thoughts flashed through his mind as he gazed at his sympathetic companion and talked in as commonplace a vein as was possible for one of his vast mental attainments. Used to inferior women, he underestimated the bigness of Anne Sividge's nature. Had he told her his true feelings, she would have forgiven the past in an overpowering and lasting love. He saw the tender look in her eyes but feared to destroy it by an apparent confession of fickleness. He would go his way, adding one more complex experience to his vivid career.

The afternoon proved even balmier than the morning; the bright sun rays revealed yellow leaves among the green on the giant trees. A flock of black ducks alighted on the stream and were toyed about by the current. Grey squirrels lost their shyness and dug out last season's nuts from knot holes in the old shellbark, cracking the brittle shells with their tiny invincible teeth. The poet had been so confidential; he had confessed to loving and losing that Anne allowed the conversation to veer about to the story of her own brief life. It had been entirely free from love affairs until two years before, she said. Then Abram Halit had come to break colts for the Alexanders. At first, she had disliked him; he was so vain and boastful and selfish. But other girls admired him; she had heard it said that he could have any girl he wanted in the Seven Mountains. He had begun to show her little attentions, which greatly flattered her, as there were several other girls in the neighborhood to whom he had previously exhibited a preference. He returned to his home in Poe Valley for a few days at Christmas.

While there, he met Helena Walters, who had moved there with her parents that autumn from Berks County. She was a German girl but had captivated young Halit completely. He told her about meeting this fair charmer when he returned. He said she was pretty but that he cared little for her. All went well until he dropped a letter from his pocket one night. It fell back of a chair; she said nothing. After he had gone, she recovered and read it. It was from Helena Walters and addressed to Halit. In it, she mentioned having received a letter from him the day before; it was couched in passionate language; the girl was clearly madly in love with him. The next night she mentioned Helena Walters to the unstable lover; he said he had not heard from her since his return. She produced the letter; he was unable to fence; he broke down and confessed that he loved her better than Anne. They parted then and there; she had never seen him again. He did not stay much longer on the Alexander estate; he was back in Poe Valley if the poet had met him there. She hated the thought of him; she wished she had never seen him. She was not surprised to hear that he was engaged to Helena. She strongly believed that he would treat her as he had other girls. A girl was silly to pin her faith on such a man. She thought Helena was foolish to have kept on with him when she was loved by a stranger of manifestly finer character. Since she had been disappointed in Abram Halit, she had never felt any interest in another man, at least up to that morning. She did not think that she ever really loved the fellow; she was infatuated with him, that was all. She was happy that she had found him out when she did; it was a useful experience. She had been very contented for the past year; she had never thought of him, would not have mentioned his name had not her new-found friend fallen afoul of him.

The young poet listened attentively to this long recital, never interrupting her. As it advanced, he felt his head growing hot, his hands becoming cold. He had gotten up and sat down several times, twitched nervously, but Anne had kept straight ahead. When she had finished, there was a silence so lengthy that it became oppressive. The poet edged closer to her, taking one of her hands; it was colder than his own. Looking into her face intently, his soul ablaze with jealous fury, he said that he believed she still loved Halit. The girl quickly drew her hand away, getting up with tears streaming from her eyes.

"How could you say that?" she gulped. "I thought you were so *different*—I—I wish he was dead, I wish I was dead; it was nothing, only an idiotic infatuation."

The poet proved himself to be neither tactful nor considerate, further wounding her by saying that whenever a woman talked incessantly about a man, she still felt an interest in him.

"I hate him, I hate him," said the girl, clenching her fists and leaning against the shellbark defiantly.

"No, no, you don't," said Poe; "the reason I talked about Helena Walters so much was because I loved her; you told me about that cursed Halit because you liked to hear the mention of his name."

"Oh, Mr. Poe," sobbed the girl, "why do you treat me this way; why do I stand here and permit myself to be abused by a stranger."

"I don't know why you do," said the poet, who, despite his bravado, was the unhappier of the two.

"I know why I do," she cried, "it is because I love you; you knew I did from the minute our eyes met. I loved you when I saw you sitting with your eyes shut, composing that poem before you even saw me."

"I feel that you love me," Poe answered, "but not as I want to be loved. I crave, and I require a woman heart-whole. No one with the image of another man lurking somewhere in the inner recesses of her soul can fill my want. If I had met you before you knew that low-bred Halit, all would have been well. It is too late

The girl was over her weeping and was smoothing her disheveled dark hair. She looked the poet full in the eyes and then replied, "If you have such a want, why did you love Helena Walters after she told you of her betrothal to Halit?"

"It was because I did not believe that she really loved him; I suspected the sincerity of her affection in a hundred ways. With you, I am sure of it."

Anne made no effort to argue further. She held out her grimy cold hand; the poet took it, placing it to his lips and kissing it.

"I'm afraid that big as I am, my mother will trounce me for being away so long," said the girl; "she always is scolding me for spending so much time at the manse. I'll have to tell her I was there all this time instead of barely a hundred yards from home."

"Come down to the pool and bathe your eyes before you return, else your mother will think that you have been crying about Abram Halit," said the poet with cruel emphasis.

"I will wash my eyes or do anything to please you," said the girl, "but if she asks me what I was crying about, I will say it was about you, a stranger."

They climbed down the soft bank, where the poet bathed her eyes with a clean white handkerchief. The water, fresh from the pure heart of Mother Earth, freshened her appearance; no one could have guessed a recent tragic episode. The poet, with his arm around her waist, helped her up the bank, back to the shade of the ancient shellbark, where their hands clasped in a farewell.

"Won't you give me one kiss?" said the girl, "I love you, even though you doubt me; I will always feel the same."

Poe caught her in his arms and kissed her long and tenderly; each was loathe to break away. Finally, the girl recovered herself and, with a smiling face, turned on her heel and scampered down the path towards the little white cottage. When she was gone, it was the poet's turn for tears. Seating himself on the moss-grown log beneath the aged shellbark, he gave way to a lifetime's pent-up emotion.

"I do not understand myself," he murmured. "I expect everything but can give so little myself. I can never be happy."

Like Petrarch at the Fountain of Vaucluse, he must wish for the unattainable. Then he smoothed back his light brown curls, put on his hat, and started towards the high road. At the gateway, he paused long enough to take out his copybook. He ripped out the leaf containing the poem "To Iolanthe," which he had finished that morning, tearing it into four pieces. These he tossed into the air. The next morning when Anne, after a sharp scolding from her mother and a sleepless night, started for the manse with her tiny bucket of cream, she found one of the fragments; it was the one from the lower right-hand corner. On it, she deciphered *"never to forget, . . ." "losing thee" . . . "yet will love thee always."* Clasping it in her hand against her heart, she hurried on her way, so excited that she could not attempt to search for the other pieces. All her life and her hopes were contained in those few words. To the end of her days, she wore them in a silver locket; they were buried with her when she died, a respected spinster of sixty years.

XII

THE THREAD
(A Story of the Wild Pigeons)

THERE were signs of an early autumn in New Lancaster. By the second week of September, the maples and tupelos on the ridge which formed the northern wall of the valley were tinged with scarlet. Quite a few yellow leaves had been blown from the sturdy chestnut trees which lined the pastures; several hoar frosts had developed the nuts. The nights were very cold, so much so that the foxes barked from sheer discomfort. The dogs, shivering in their kennels, were glad to have an excuse to howl in answer. The days were wonderfully clear, with not a trace of clouds, the blue dome being the color of southern azure. There was no humidity; the darkness of the pines and hemlocks, "the black tops," as the woodsmen called them, were clearly differentiated from their fainter-tinted fellows. The rich, juicy green leaves of the corn stalks had shriveled, revealing the darkening ears; the giant red and green pumpkins which grew on shrunken stems at their feet. The wild morning glories had gone to sleep for good. In the early mornings, one could see the breath of the sheep and the cattle. Weather like this always aroused the latent energies of old Adam Johnsonbauch; he seemed like a different man when the first bright tints were noticeable on the upland maples.

"These are the days that send the pigeons south," he would say gleefully. "I have kept track of their habits every fall for over fifty years; I know them like a book. They haven't been through here, except a scattering bird or two since 1881; it's over thirty years ago, but that's nothing. I mind very well my grandfather, the old revolutionary veteran, telling me that on Powell's Creek in Dauphin County, they skipped coming from 1803 to 1833. When they did come, he declared that they had to feed them to the hogs, and when the hogs got tired of them, they used them to fertilize the gardens. They say the sweet peas were colored like the male birds' breasts the next season. Every man and boy killed all he could; what was the use of letting them fly south, others killed them there, and they might cause a pestilence if they increased too quickly. I am sure they are in Canada now breeding like flies far away from molestation. Some day a party of Indians will locate them, and once scared up, they will start south. When they come, they will stretch from mountain to mountain, covering this valley like a canopy, darkening the sun. I have a feeling that they will come back this fall. It's all foolishness to say they are extinct. "When I read talk of that kind in the Pittsburgh papers, I throw them in the stove. People can't wait, that's all. I know they didn't fly over Powell's Creek between 1803 and 1833; it will be the same in New Lancaster; we'll get our pigeons back—more than we want.

"I can recall the day well when the women folks would get down on their knees and pray for the abatement of the pigeon nuisance; they complained that it kept everybody from working, even the little children got sore gums from biting off too many squabs' heads. You couldn't get a soul in this valley to eat a wild pigeon at one time; it was too common an article of food. We shipped what we could to Jacobsburg or Lewistown; what we couldn't ship, we dumped in the gardens and turned them under. The women vowed the only good thing the pigeons ever did was to give the richer color to the sweet peas. But they couldn't discourage us; we kept on trapping, and I am sure we got our share.

"Old Zenas Kline trapped four thousand in one day; he had his whole family out biting off the heads; when they were done, the pile of dead birds was as high as his corncrib. You should have seen his hogs that fall; they were the fattest in the valley; everybody envied them. I'm going to get all I can, even if they make me work day and night if they come back this fall. When the last big flight came through here, I was busy with my buckwheat; I don't believe I got more than a couple of thousand all told. I recall I got a dozen fine stool pigeons that fall, young cock birds with breasts as red as winter sunsets. I kept them four years; they did very well. Although there were no flights, I declared I'd feed them until another flight came; but man can't control his own wishes.

"Just about this time of the year, preacher Swope came with his wife to spend the day. We were busy raising potatoes, so we left it to the women to entertain them. The preacher put his horse in the barn, where he got kicked by my stud colt. He left his dog running loose; the mongrel got in my pigeon coop and tore to pieces all my stool pigeons. As I didn't want him to complain on my colt, which all my women were scared of, I didn't dare say anything about his dog destroying my valuable pigeons. I knew that when the birds came back, I would have to be provided with stool pigeons, so I looked about carefully the next Spring.

"Early in April, I noticed a flock of six yearling birds roosting on the big buckeye tree back of the orchard. I set a spring trap for them, but I only got one. Luckily this one was a cock-bird, and a beauty. The others were very shy, and when I caught my bird, they were so scared that they flew away, never to return. I watched for them below their roost with my shotgun every evening, declaring that if I could not get them alive, I would have them dead. But I did not get them either way. That was in the spring of 1887, just twenty-five years ago. I'm very careful of that pigeon; I keep him in a nice roomy coop on the back porch, and I shoot every cat that sets foot in the yard. I have tried to get other pigeons since then, but they were smart enough to keep out of reach.

"I well recollect that in the late seventies, when I worked in a lumber camp in Clarion County, the pigeons were nesting at the headwaters of Little Tionesta. That was the greatest carnival of pigeon slaughter I ever witnessed or even heard of. The mountaineers moved into the vicinity of the nesting grounds, bringing with them their horses and cattle, prepared to remain all summer. Hundreds of Indians swarmed to the spot, drinking and carousing when not gathering squabs. The Indians would fell the giant hemlocks containing the nests. When a cheer went up, we always knew that they had found a quantity of fat squabs. When there was silence, we realized that it had been a slim find. An old man from Tionesta set up a drinking booth in a quiet corner in the woods. He sold hard cider for five cents a tinful and did a rushing business.

"When the pigeons started south in September, I don't believe that they brought a single young bird with them. A hundred acres of magnificent timberland were destroyed by the hunters, the trees being left to

(Photo by S. W. Smith)

THE ROAD TO POE VALLEY

rot on the ground. I believe two hundred thousand pigeons were killed that season. It demoralized the whole upper end of the county, as no one could be found to stick to his work in the lumber camps while there were pigeons to be killed. I believe the pigeons were very useful birds. They ate the beetles and grubs, which destroy the pine and hemlock trees. Since they are gone, I have seen whole sides of mountains in the northern counties brown with dead hemlock trees, killed by the beetles. It was this way: when the squabs were first hatched, the old birds fed them with a pap, which we called 'pigeon's milk.' When they grew older, the mother birds would go into the big timber and catch a hemlock beetle or pine grub. This they would force down the squabs' throats, and it was sufficient to nourish them until they were able to fly. As the grub was absorbed, the squabs became thinner until, finally, they were forced by sheer hunger to take to their wings and fly from the nests. The nests were made from a very few sticks, resting lightly on the hemlock boughs. They were marvels of equilibrium, for, despite their flatness, the eggs or squabs rarely rolled from them in the fiercest windstorms. Though the pigeons sometimes ate off a whole field of buckwheat, they did so much good in destroying insect life in the big timber that they deserved the little buckwheat they got. But I'm sure they will come back; their absence is merely another incident like happened on Powell's Creek in the 'old days.'"

In this way, the old trapper would ramble on by the hour when he could find a listener. Though he had served in the Civil War, he would rather talk pigeons than Appomattox. In every man's life, there is one incident that overwhelms all the rest; with some, it is participation in a war, a great disaster, a love affair. With old Adam Johnsonbaugh, pigeons were the mastering thought; all else seemed inconsequential beside memories of flights that darkened the sun, of butcheries that ran up into the hundreds of thousands. Each spring, he would bring forth and mend his best net and repair the poles of his bough house, which still stood in the old-time buckwheat field. He would bring his pigeon basket made of thin hickory sticks from the attic, which had been used to carry the stool pigeons and flyers. He was on the alert for all rumors of the pigeons' return; his faith was unswerving. Strangers often told him that if a flight did occur, the state game protectors would forbid any wholesale trapping. At these statements, the old man would laugh until tears came to his eyes.

"Wait 'til they see a *real* flight, with a hundred million pigeons in the air—they won't begrudge us mountaineers a few hundred thousand."

But spring would quickly melt into summer, and then in due season, autumn would show its unmistakable portents on the ridges. Old Adam was always ready for the fall flights.

"They have the young birds with them then; three times as many go south in the fall as fly north in the spring."

To the younger residents in New Lancaster, the pigeon question was a thing of the past. The birds were extinct; the liberal rewards offered by Professor C. F. Hodge of Worcester, Massachusetts, and others, had found no claimants. The whole subject was tiresome to them. A few children, brighter than the average, who had heard their grandparents talk "wild pigeons" used to come on Sunday afternoons in summer to look at "Uncle" Johnsonbaugh's stool pigeon. The old man would cheerfully explain that when the great flights began, he would sew the bird's eyes shut and fasten it by a cord to a low perch. When the flocks were overhead, he would hide behind his bough-house and pull the cord, making the captive flap its wings as if alighting. It would have been better to also have "flyers" on long strings to attract the attention of the hungry myriads, but he would do his best with the one bird. When several hundred alighted on the "bait" of buckwheat, he would spring the trap, and the net would descend over them. Then he would kill the victims by pinching their heads or biting their necks, piling their bodies back of the bough-house, and begin the operation over again.

The stool pigeon was a magnificent-looking specimen. Though it was twenty-five years old or more, its plumage was as bright, its reddish eyes as clear, as if it was a "yearling." As it sat on its perch, scrutinizing inquisitive visitors, it was a picture of alertness and beauty. It was a large bird, measuring fully eighteen inches from bill to tail; its breast shone with all the vividness of a December sunset. Fully a dozen cats and twice as many rats and weasels had measured their lengths in the backyard riddled by the old man's shotgun after unsuccessful forays to the pigeon coop.

"I don't believe there are half a dozen stool pigeons in the state," the old man would say proudly. "I am sure I have the only one in the Seven Mountains. When next the flight begins, I will be able to make the first grand haul; I ought to get a thousand at the least calculation, the first day."

The children, awed by such big figures, would take another look at the patient bird and then edge away to their play.

One bright Sunday afternoon in mid-September; it was the year when there were such bountiful signs of early autumn; the old man, finding the time from dinner hour to supper time passing slowly, went for a walk to the top of the ridge back of his house. There was a good stand of thrifty white oaks and chestnuts that he intended "putting into ties" that winter; he wanted to look them over again to get a general estimate as to the numbers. As he counted and figured, he climbed higher and higher along the steep path. Almost before knowing it, he had reached the top of the ridge. A few hundred yards north of where the mountain dipped towards New Lancaster was a large open space; Andy Breon had taken ties from there the winter before. It afforded a magnificent view of the mountains in all directions. One could see clear to Milliken's High Top, to the Broad Face, to the Tussey Knob, to Round Top. Meanwhile, the old trapper's wife and daughters became tired of sitting on the front porch looking at the unchanging view across the road; it consisted mainly of underbrush, with a good-sized maple or two; all view of the ridge that formed the southern barrier to the valley was hidden by the foliage.

The women concluded that they would stroll up the road and visit the widow Glatfelter; she was ill, and a granddaughter had come to nurse her, bringing a huge house-cat; her little log cabin stood just half a mile west of the comfortable Johnsonbaugh farmstead. They took Nick, the faithful shepherd dog, with them, leaving the house unguarded, the precious stool pigeon without a protector. The old man on the mountain top had become very much interested in something which appeared far to the north. When he first saw it, it resembled a thin thread of smoke, as if someone was burning new ground on the northern slopes of Penn's Valley. While it apparently rose from the distant valleys, it deflected at a certain height and seemed to be sweeping in a southerly direction. It hardly looked like smoke; if it wasn't so copious, it might possibly be a huge flock of blackbirds. He climbed on a big chestnut stump; he strained his eyes to catch the meaning of the phenomenon. It wasn't smoke; it was birds of some kind, too big for blackbirds, not dark enough for crows. He gave a great shout of joy; the pigeons were coming! Already the vanguard was twenty miles away, but he felt sure that he could reach home, bring out the net and the stool pigeon, and trap a few hundred before sundown. Taking a final look to reassure himself, and with blood tingling in his veins, he started towards the valley. Cool as was the afternoon, he was in a heavy perspiration before he was halfway down. The sun was traveling rapidly westward; the valley was in shadow; the summits still were bathed in pale gold light. There was a chilliness to the atmosphere as he tramped over the soggy pasture-field back of his barn. He stooped to pick a wild lily of the valley; it was seared by the summer's sun, yet sadly beautiful. He had hot plucked a wild flower since his young manhood when he courted; the pigeons were coming back, bringing with them early sentiments. He climbed the barnyard fence, hurried across the reeking area, pushed open the garden gate, almost racing along the path, and was soon in the backyard. He moved rapidly Up the boardwalk, was up the three loose steps of the kitchen porch in one bound; he stood breathless beside the pigeon coop. To his surprise, one of the slats was broken; there was a strange stillness in the pen. He peered through the grating of laths; the bird lay motionless on the gravel floor. Many loose light colored feathers were strewn about. He saw a deep red patch on the back; the bird had been bleeding—why, it *was dead*. Pushing back the button, he opened the door and drew out the dead bird. The loose neck dropped over his hand; the ruby-colored feet had become a yellow pink.

The old man clutched the flabby bunch of feathers and sank down on the kitchen steps. His leonine head hung on his breast; tears trickled from his weather-beaten lids. He was in this abject position when his wife and daughters chatting gaily came around the comer of the house. "Why father, what ails you?" said the old woman, thoroughly alarmed. "Are you sick; what has happened?" chorused the girls. Nick, the dog, began to snarl piteously.

For a minute, the old man seemed unable to recover his self-possession; he gazed around him blankly. Then he clambered to his feet, holding out the dead pigeon for inspection. "What has happened," he said meekly, "all my hopes of years are knocked to pieces; while we were away, someone's cat got into the coop and killed my stool pigeon. I thought I had killed all the cats in the valley."

"What of that father," said one of the daughters, "there will never be another flight while any of *us* live."

"That's why I feel so badly," said the trapper, "the flight is on its way here now. I sighted them not over an hour ago from the top of the ridge. I wanted to be the first to capture a wagon load."

"Nonsense," said the girl, "you couldn't have seen any pigeons. The papers all say they are as extinct as the dodo bird."

Old Johnsonbaugh turned towards the northern mountain, pointing with his trembling knotted finger, "See, do you observe that thread away off there to the north; it's the pigeons, the pigeons."

The women looked the way indicated. They saw a dark blue trail rising high into the heavens, pouring south. "It's only blackbirds," snapped the oldest girl as she flounced into the kitchen, slamming the screen door after her.

XIII

ON THE LEDGE

(A Story of Jack's Mountain)

WHEN Faires Boyer moved to Unionville, Ohio, in the spring of 1896, he took with him an interesting collection of wild animal hides. The great hunter of the Seven Mountains wished to possess some tangible souvenirs of his early exploits while he spent his declining days with his son in the middle west. Chief of these mementos was the skin of a huge panther which he killed after a desperate hand-to-hand conflict on the very topmost ledge of Jack's Mountain, where it frowns down on the picturesque old town of New Berlin. The hide, one of the darkest colored ever procured in the Snyder County wilds, was a sooty brown in hue and measured from nose to tail seven feet, nine inches. It would be interesting, even at this late date, to prepare a list of the "record" heads and hides of the Seven Mountains. While not the largest, Faires Boyer's panther comes very close to holding the honors for that species.

Benjamin Frownfelter, a retired schoolmaster who resided at Centreville about 1880, wrote a very painstaking treatise on the fauna of Snyder County, expecting it to be embodied in a history of the county published within the next year or two. For some reason, perhaps the wealth of technical language, the volumes appeared minus Professor Frownfelter's article, although interesting chapters on the flora were included in the history. In the professor's treatise was a list of panthers killed in Snyder County and territory included in it before its separation from Union County, together with their measurements and individual characteristics. He made special reference to Faires Boyer's panther, stating that it was the darkest colored specimen ever secured in that region. He compared the coloring of panthers killed in the Adirondacks and in the northern counties of Pennsylvania with those taken in the Seven Mountains and in several Southern states, including Florida, showing that the tendency was to become darker as they were found further south. He considered the Boyer panther practically identical in color to a specimen secured in Manatee County in the everglades of Florida the same year, 1873. Unfortunately for students of Pennsylvania *Mammalia*, the Frownfelter manuscript has been lost, but those who have seen it unite in saying that it was a mine of information, condensed into a comparatively brief number of pages. While the Dorman panther killed in 1868 achieved a state-wide reputation, being mentioned in hundreds of newspapers at the time, the Boyer panther has barely been heard of. Killed amid unusual circumstances, it certainly deserved greater notoriety. Before leaving for Ohio, Old Boyer stated that the hide he took with him was the eighth he had killed in the Seven Mountains. Professor Frownfelter, it is said, gave Boyer's record as 1855, 1; 1856, 2; 1857, 2; 1862, 1; 1863, 1; 1873, 1. This shows the former prevalence of these animals and their gradual decrease as years went by.

There were always fewer panthers in the northern than in the southern counties. They were almost unknown by the first settlers in some counties in the "northern tier." They were never plentiful in Potter County, whereas, along the Juniata, hunters killed as many as seven or eight in a winter as late as the first third of the nineteenth century. Samuel Askey, a Centre County hunter, killed sixty-four panthers near Snow Shoe between 1820 and 1845. Boyer prized the dark-colored hide, partly because of its unusual shade, partly because it was his last kill, but most of all, on account of the thrilling battle he fought with the monster before killing it. The night before he left for his new home, he brought the giant hide to the Golden Plow Hotel and told the story of the hunt to a crowd of listeners who completely jammed the office and porches. After the marvelous recital, every man present filed past the venerable hunter, shaking him by the hand and wishing him a safe journey to the west. There are many living along Penn's Creek who heard the narrative that memorable evening or previously, so it will be possible to transcribe it—of course lacking "Uncle Faires" wealth of picturesque details. It seems that in the fall of 1873, several sheep were lost by farmers living along the southern slope of Jack's Mountain. At first, it was believed that it was the work of hunters or tramps, but the action of some of the dogs in the neighborhood gave rise to the theory that the thief was a panther. Like in most matter-of-fact communities, the story was ridiculed; Lewis Dorman had killed the last panther in the Seven Mountains, there could be no more. The papers resented the imputation that panthers still lurked in this region, quoting several alleged hunters to prove the contrary.

In December was the mating season of the fierce brutes, which made Faires Boyer, the most skilled hunter in Centreville, who for the past ten years had been spending most of his time trapping otters, assert that if there was a panther on Jack's Mountain, it would make itself heard at that time. That panthers wailed every night is incorrect; they were naturally silent animals—love alone made them sing their songs so weird and terrible which are inseparably linked with their story. Accordingly, the sagacious hunter moved out to a shack that stood at the head of Hemlock Hollow in one of the most inaccessible regions on the mountain. He took along provisions enough to remain two weeks. Before leaving, he told his friends that if there was a panther on the mountain, he would bring back its hide; he never found the trial that led to disappointment. He took one very small reddish dog with him, "just to aid finding the scent," he said. Boyer knew that as the panthers' love season drew near, they invariably, if not provided with mates, traveled along the summits of the highest ridges, uttering their love songs, but only at night. Like most of the cat family, they were nocturnal animals, sleeping principally by day. If he took up a good position every night on the mountain top, he could hear the panther's song, even if it was five miles away. If a male, the notes would be deep, akin to the roaring of a lion; if a female, it would be in a shriller key, almost like a housecat's caterwaul, but many times louder. Had it not been for their wailing, panthers would probablj^ be plentiful in the Seven Mountains today. They were very shrewd, were seldom caught in traps, but they betrayed their presence in a locality by their noisy love songs.

The panther of Jack's Mountain "gave himself away" the first night of Boyer's arrival at the shack. He had planned to go on watch on the comb of the ridge, but it was not necessary to stir from his door. Soon after dark, the familiar notes were heard far up on the topmost pinnacle. It was the voice of a male panther. At first, it sounded like wind soughing through the old pines; the next measure was louder, a song of strength and power. This was continued with variations for over half an hour. At the end, it died away into a wail of deepest anguish. No answering voice had come; the huge brute must lie down among the rhododendrons disappointed. Why this lone panther had traveled so far east puzzled the hunter. One theory was that it had been driven by dogs from its familiar haunts in the Beech Creek region, where these brutes hung on until the last original timber was gone; another that it was in search of a mate.

Between Jack's Mountain and the headwaters of the Lehigh, where a few panthers persistently lingered, stretched a wide area of inhabited territory, but love knows no limits. A female panther strayed into the Blue Mountains in Albany Township, Berks County, where it was killed by coal burners in August 1874. It was a lonely straggler from the upper Lehigh region and was probably trying to make its way west in time for the love season. As it was the last panther ever heard of in eastern Pennsylvania, this amply accounts for its presence in a settled region.

Boyer remained quietly in his shack all day. He slept most of the time so that he could feel fresh for his night's work. The sunset was a magnificent riot of cerise and gold; even the matter-of-fact hunter was impressed by its grandeur. At dusk, he shut the dog in the shanty and started alone up the hollow. When he reached the summit, he sat down among the ferns, resting his back against a gnarled Jack pine. It was comparatively quiet on the mountain's windswept comb. A few half-hearted crickets chirped among the weeds, their fiddling weakened as if by the high altitude. When it became completely dark, the love song of the panther began. It sounded as if it was about a mile west of where the hunter was seated. The night before, it had been a mile to the east, not far from where the mountain drops off abruptly to New Berlin. The hunter waited until the song, which on this occasion lasted more than an hour, came to an end. The final notes were so despairing that they made the bold hunter shudder with lonesomeness; evidently, the brute was losing hopes of finding a mate that season.

When all was still, Boyer moved cautiously along the ridge in the direction from whence the sounds had come. He knew that after a panther finished crying, it always lay down. His plan was to get as close to the approximate resting place of the brute as possible, to wait there until daybreak, and surprise and shoot it. He traveled fully a mile and then dropped down to await the dawn. When the crimson coronet appeared from behind the palisades along the Susquehanna, he began to search about carefully. He had not gotten far when he came upon a round open space, where the ferns and bushes were flattened, the monster's late resting place. The animal had been sleeping within a hundred yards of him but, scenting him, had gotten away before daylight would disclose it. Boyer now regretted having left the dog at the shanty; it would have apprised him of the panther's nearness. He had not brought the dog as he feared its barking might give the quarry too much of a start. It was hard to tell which course would have been the best. At any rate, the panther was gone. There was nothing to do but to return to the shack and take a good nap until sundown. He trusted that the panther's amorous propensities would make it pour forth its love song again; passion is generally stronger than the sense of self-preservation. He muzzled the little dog with cords, taking it with him that evening.

He took up the same position on the comb, waiting for the hunted brute to weep out its hungry soul to the wilderness. It was almost midnight, and the hunter was nodding with drowsiness when he heard a single sharp cry. It was nearly a mile to the east, not far from where he had noted it the first time. He waited an hour; he heard no more. The panther had intended to be still but had emitted one involuntary wail. Evidently, the crafty brute had doubled on its tracks and passed close by him that morning. Tucking the dog under his arm, he moved along the ridge, this time going less near than formerly to where he imagined the panther was resting. He sat among some huge rocks until the grey dawn and then resumed his tramp east. Just as he expected, he found where the panther had laid among the ferns. The monster preferred a soft bed in the open to a cranny in the rocks. Here, Boyer removed the muzzle and put the dog in the nest to catch the scent. The little beast scurried around in circles for a minute or so and then started on a trot eastward.

This time the panther had not doubled its course; it had headed towards the end of the mountain, to the ledge overhanging New Berlin. The dog had not proceeded far before he began exhibiting signs of terror. At first, when he imagined he was on the trail of an animal the size of a wildcat, he was bravery itself. Now some unseen power had told him that he was trailing something of enormous size; he fairly cowered in his tracks. The hunter patted the little animal's sides, urging him forward as best he could. At length, the dog refused to go any further, so he picked him up, tucking him under one of his arms, for he was a very tender-hearted man. Without the dog's assistance, there was always the danger of the panther having backtracked, perhaps passing within a few feet of him, but Boyer's instinct told him that the animal was near the ledge. He primed his rifle, setting the dog down a minute while he did so. He had to smile as he gazed at the little animal cringing and shivering between his legs. As he neared the end of the mountain, there was a "bald spot" where there were great flat rocks, grey and covered with lichens; the few stunted pitch pines were shattered and barely clinging to life.

The morning sun was shining through the misty clouds; he could look about him clearly. A hundred feet ahead, he saw what at first looked like a round rock resting on a flat one. He peered at it more carefully; it was the panther taking a bath in the early rays of the morning sun. Its heavy, round head was lowered and faced towards the east. It was in a difficult position to receive a mortal shot. Boyer decided to move no closer but stepped a dozen paces to the south to advance along another line to get a shot at the side of the monster's skull. The little dog made no sound; it had shaken violently when it saw the brute it had been trailing; it was rigid under his arm, literally "scared stiff." Just when the hunter was within a few feet of where he decided to fire, the panther got up, stretching his magnificent dark body and yawning like a huge cat. No time was to be lost, so he dropped the dog and fired his rifle. Whether it was a case of "buck fever" or not is hard to say; he only ridged the monster's belly. Looking about, the panther sighted his foe, stopped short, stretched himself, and yawned again. In all his thirty years of experience in the woods, Boyer had never seen such an exhibition of sublime insouciance. He fired again, this time piercing the animal's shoulder. For just one step, it limped, then it walked leisurely out on the ledge and lay down. The slab on which it rested jutted out over the valley; it was a perilous position for man or beast. The hunter fired a third time, the bullet piercing the victim's neck. The panther's head dropped; it looked like the mortal shot. Laughing with exultation, Boyer hurried over the rocks and windfalls in the direction of the ledge, the little dog, which seemed to divine there was to be no more danger, trotting closely behind.

When Boyer was within ten feet of the panther, he fired again to ensure the animal was dead before dragging it back on one of the flat rocks and skinning it. This bullet seemed to have the effect of re-animating the dying brute. It rose to its feet like a flash, its eyes blazing fire, its sturdy muscles twitching with fury. Turning about, it sprang at the hunter, who deftly sought to guard himself with his rifle. The weight of the two-hundred-pound monster was too much for him, and he fell on his back on the rocks. If he had pitched forward or sideways, he might have fallen over the precipice. Although downed, the hunter was by no means worsted; his hand was on his long hunting knife, and he ripped open the panther's bowels as it lay across him, snarling furiously. With a gasp of pain, as despairing as the last notes of its nocturnal love song, it expired. The little dog, hiding among some hog-berry bushes, reappeared and began biting at the carcass.

Boyer crawled out from his perilous position and dragged the bloody carcass by the tail to the biggest and flattest rock. Then he lit his corncob pipe and began the operation of skinning. Every minute or so, he would stop and stroke the soft dark fur; it was far and above the handsomest of any he had killed or even seen.

"I don't expect I'll ever shoot another panther in these mountains," he said nonchalantly as he peeled the last corner free from the flesh. "And it is fitting that this one should give me a tussle. Come what may, I'll never part with his hide."

He carried his trophy back to Centreville, going to his home on the shore of Penn's Creek by an unfrequented path. The first that the neighborhood knew that he had killed the panther was when they saw the hide drying on the back wall of his barn. The *New Berlin Sentinel* and the *Middleburg Post* barely made mention of the occurrence; it was speedily relegated to forgetfulness. Had Boyer told the details at the time, a great excitement would have resulted. But he almost lost the title of panther-slayer had it not been for his dramatic recital the night before his departure for the west; the description of his exploits in Professor Frownfelter's treatise on the Snyder County fauna, as stated previously, was never published. Thrilling as were many of the experiences of the old-time hunters of the Seven Mountains, none can equal the exciting moment when the wounded panther charged at Faires Boyer on the ledge.

XIV

THE INDIAN MOUND
(A Story of the Chieftain Viperine)

IN the center of a field of rich alluvial soil facing the public road, which runs from Hartleton to Middleburg, rises a large circular hillock. It is beautifully proportioned and smooth except at the bases, where it has been scarred by searchers after Indian relics and bones. Several corn crops were raised on it successfully; the stalks were of unusual height, some ten feet from tassel to root. As the mound seemed to require no fertilizers, the farmers concluded that it must have been an Indian burial ground. The young men of the neighborhood bored into its sides but found nothing. This seemed odd as arrowheads were plentiful in the surrounding fields and along the banks of the creek. A professor from a college in eastern Pennsylvania who was making a walking trip through the Seven Mountains in search of geological and botanical specimens heard of the mound and went out of his way half a dozen miles to look at it. He appeared on a Sunday afternoon when there were many farmers in their "store clothes" standing about the roads; his inquiry for the mound caused them all to follow him to the much-debated spot. One glance was sufficient to satisfy the learned man.

"That is no Indian mound," he declared with the emphasis of one who is uttering the last word on the subject. "It is a hillock caused simply by the erosion from that stream; what is its name?"

He was told that it was known locally as Wildcat Run. He unwrapped his geological map and, with a great flourish, drew on it the position of the stream and the mound. Below these marks, he wrote "hillock caused by ancient erosion from creek." The gaping farmers accepted the statement as final; the hillock was no longer called the Indian Mound. When they went home to supper, they told of the great man who, at a glance, had classified the natural wonder. The very old people shook their heads, refused to be convinced.

"It *is* an Indian mound; there's a story connected with it," they all contended.

But their descendants were unimaginative; they hated the legends because there was a possibility that they might not be true. That is the chief fault with the present-day dwellers in the Pennsylvania mountains, especially the wealthier classes; they are absolutely lacking in imagination. The older people were imaginative; it was their chief charm. The writer recalls an evening at an exclusive hunting club where the subject of the wild pigeons in Pennsylvania was brought up. Each man decisively declared, "they are extinct." The gamekeeper of the organization began to relate instances where reputable persons had seen them. The wealthy self-made men, rather *gauche*, would hear nothing of it; they had not seen the birds themselves; they had no imaginations to grasp that others might possibly have done so. They pronounced them "extinct," so the subject was dropped. But it was probably the best thing that could happen for the mound that the word "Indian" was removed from it. It effectually stopped burrowing into its sides; its symmetry remained unmarred. When strangers passing along the highway paused to marvel at it, there generally was a native handy to counteract their first impressions.

"It was caused by the water from that creek over yonder," the yokels would acclaim with the same gusto as had the professor a score of years earlier. They seemed to take perfect delight in ripping the spiritual fabric from the one point of interest in the township. As long as the very old people lived, the legend of the Indian mound was kept in existence, flowing like an underground stream. The unimaginative younger generations always frowned down attempts to tell the story. "The professor knows" was their favorite method to silence the tiresome romance. But sometimes, groups of the old people would get together on Sunday afternoon and refresh their memories; the story being synonymous with truth, would not die. Even the fact that such luxuriant corn grew from the mound, far taller and bigger eared than in the rest of the field, had no influence on the farmers. Their minds were made up; it was not an Indian mound; if good

PENN'S CREEK AND PINE CREEK, AT COBURN

(Photo by S. W. Smith)

corn grew there, it was because it grew there. Histories of the county and township were written, which ignored it; educated persons passed along the road but were unmoved by the sight of the mound. The say-so of an obscure professor whose name actually became lost shelved the publication of the story of the great Indian memento for over twenty years.

One bright blowy April afternoon, a stranger passed along the high road. He stopped to admire the wonderful mound, then looked eagerly about for someone to tell him the story. It was perhaps fortunate for him that no one was about. A quarter of a mile distant at the foot of the long hill, behind a clump of bare bleak walnut trees, stood a weather-scarred cabin. A trail of very blue smoke emerged from the chimney. It seemed to take the form of a beckoning Indian. The stranger made haste to visit the humble cottage; something told him that the mound's history could be obtained there. A very cross dog was in the yard, but it was worth running the risk to pass this snarling sentinel.

In response to a knock, a ponderous old man with a great shock of white hair, keen blue eyes, and an aquiline nose opened the door. On his bronzed face was a week's growth of beard; otherwise, he was very neat and tidy. He was a Civil War veteran, as he wore a bronze Grand Army button on the lapel of his vest. The stranger asked him if he could give some information about the mound in the field nearby. The old man looked at him half amused, half quizzically, saying, "a professor from somewhere in the eastern part of the state told us that it was caused by the water of the little creek which runs back of it." Then he paused, thinking that this stranger, like the rest, would be satisfied. There was something in the tone of the old man's voice which sounded as if he doubted the professor's story; it was worth delving deeper. The stranger asked if he could come inside for a few minutes; he wanted to ask some more questions concerning the mound. The old man asked him to enter with a great show of cordiality.

Once seated on easy chairs by the comfortable wood stove in the square whitewashed room, which was barren of pictures save for a newspaper calendar, the visitor asked the old veteran, who said his name was John Stoner, late of the 149th Pennsylvania Volunteers, if he didn't believe that the mound in question was of Indian origin.

"You are one of many persons who have asked me that question in the past twenty-five years," he said with candor. "I used to like to tell folks what it was, but after that professor was here, the old legend got 'knocked into a cocked hat.' Now I always tell them it was caused by erosion, and they appear to be satisfied. It's a big word and means a lot." Then he briefly outlined what the professor had said and how eager all the younger residents were to accept his statements.

"It may be all true," he continued, "but the Indian story dies hard, at least with me. An Indian named Hilltown Billy told it to my father; he believed it, and I believed it, though that professor *ought* to know. The story of that mound always reminded me of the account of the Tower of Babel; it made me think that the man who first said that the Indians were the lost tribes of Israel wasn't so far from wrong. Many Indian traditions remind me of what I have read in the Bible; I always pictured the Children of Israel to be dark and handsome like our first natives. The Indians five hundred years ago must have been a noble people. They had never seen the whites, and their intellects were pure Indian intellects.

"The later chiefs, like Canasatego, Teedyuscung, Shikellamy, James Logan, or Cornplant, had all absorbed ideas from the Europeans; they were neither one thing nor another. There were ancient dynasties that possessed as much power and culture as the Pharaohs of Egypt. The Indians remembered them by some distinctive name, as they had no written history. Thus the dynasty of which the great war chief Pipsisseway was the last was known as the 'Flower Dynasty' because so many of its kings were named after popular flowers. There was Pipsisseway; his son, who never ruled, was called Lupine, and the great chief's grandfather, old Viperine. Pipsisseway's father was named Ironwood, a tree that bears a pretty red blossom. Viperine was not a particularly warlike chieftain. He had inherited vast possessions and power and was more anxious to be remembered as an orator or a bard. He was probably little of either, but the storytellers of his day feared to mention him in any other way except as the greatest speaker and poet who ever lived. When Indians are vain, they are 'terrors.' That he wasn't proficient is proved by the fact that not a single word of his orations and songs have come down to us. He probably uttered high-sounding platitudes that go in one ear and come out the other. He was always calling his people together to give them 'speeches from the throne' or to hear his epics. He conceived the idea that he was the most intellectual man who had ever lived. So that there be no invidious comparisons, he had the tongues cut out of every Indian known to have any pretensions to oratory or poetry. This was a disastrous proceeding as much of the poetry and history from the past centuries was in the mouths of these same men. When they were silenced, the golden treasure of antiquity was lost. Only a few fragments of the period anterior to Viperine have come down to us. Less is known of the ancient history of the Indians of Central Pennsylvania than of those of any other part of the continent; the fault of this can all be laid on the vainglorious chieftain. But manufactured fame is ephemeral; probably only a dozen people in the Seven Mountains now living have ever heard that such a person existed.

"Viperine wasn't his real name; it was the Indian equivalent of that wonderful mid-summer flower; some call it blueweed, or viper's bugloss, but viperine is its prettiest name. The 'animal' and 'mountain' dynasties that succeeded were but faint reflections of the glories which went before. The still earlier 'rock' dynasty, about which very little is known, was said to be the strongest of all. After Viperine had ruled for nearly thirty years, he decided to utilize the occasion as a jubilee. He wanted to brand his greatness, so to speak, on the memory of everyone in his realm. He imagined that the best way to do this would be to erect a monument higher than the tallest mountain, which would serve as a ladder to the stars. It would be constructed of rocks and earth and be surmounted by a pavilion, in which the mighty monarch could reside in the exclusiveness befitting one of his rank and brilliancy; his sole company the sun, moon, and stars. No one was good enough to associate with him; he wanted to accentuate the positions by a difference in residence,

"According to his lofty ideas, it would take a year to climb to the top of the monument; mortals desiring converse with him would have time to become sufficiently impressed by his grandeur while they toiled onward to the starry apex. One of the many serious obstacles to the consummation of his fantastic scheme was that it first entered his head less than a year before the date of the jubilee. There was no time to be lost; all the Indians must appear on the scene and work until death relieved their exertions. Verbal invitations were broadcast, telling the unsuspecting subjects of the forthcoming jubilee, and bidding them assemble immediately at the royal encampment on Wildcat Run. No word was mentioned of any work being required of the guests, except that they bring all their housekeeping utensils for a lengthy stay. They were required to leave their weapons at home; it was to be an occasion of peace and thanksgiving. While they were traveling toward the vale of the Wildcat, the crafty king had his home guards burn off the forest for several miles on every side of the spot selected for the monument.

"When the horde of Indians arrived, they found a vast open plain provided for their residence. Viperine appeared to them personally when all had assembled, delivering one of his oratorical flights. He advised them to set to work building homes on the plain, that their presence in the neighborhood would last for some time. He congratulated them on their wondrous opportunity to see and hear the voice of the greatest human being that ever lived. His grandson, Pipsisseway, was given to just such manner of speeches! When all had erected shacks and lodge houses, he appeared before the multitude a second time, congratulating them on being able to live so near a mighty being like himself, and requested them to erect a stockade around the entire plain, which contained their homes. As no reason was assigned for this stupendous work, there was some grumbling, but all soon turned in, and the elaborate enclosure was constructed. When all were inside, the bodyguards of Viperine closed and bolted the gates. Then representatives of the vainglorious chieftain commanded men, women, and children to begin work on the royal pyramid, which was to be as tall as the stars. A few demurred, but they were promptly executed with great barbarity as a warning to the rest. As there was no use of further resistance, the cowed, unarmed savages submitted to the gigantic task. They were told off in companies of one hundred men each, under the leadership of one of the king's personal bodyguards. When thus subdivided, they were marched into the surrounding country. There they were put to quarrying blocks of stone, digging earth, or building sleds to convey materials.

"Viperine's orders were reckless of human life—*at first*. For the slightest insubordination or lagging, death was the sole punishment. The bodies were thrown into the excavations. Executions were so frequent that the women and children, who had been left inside the huge enclosure to cook and work for the men, were speedily drafted to do manual labor. Food was scarce, as no one could go hunting. It was a horrible spectacle to watch the heavily loaded sledges drawn by emaciated men, women, and children bringing rocks and earth to the site of the monument. A deep foundation of rocks had been constructed, and on this, the pyramid of earth, with its skeleton of stonework, was to rest. It was a boldly conceived plan but not practicable beyond a hundred feet in height. This the builders soon realized. The personal suite in charge of operations feared to tell the monarch, knowing that it would wound his colossal vanity. They knew a time would come when the edifice could go no higher; the foundations were not large enough to support such height and weight. The work progressed slowly, as it was feared that if it was done hastily, the whole thing would topple over before it had reached a hundred feet. Then every being connected with it would be executed to the last man—with only Viperine left to execute the official headsman. The personal suite trusted that the king would tire of his folly and call a halt before the inevitable catastrophe occurred. If he could cease the operations before the structure collapsed, it would be a great saving to his prestige. But Viperine was blind to the architectural defects and, with great outbursts of impatience, ordered the work to progress faster every day. He threatened to go on a war of conquest to a distant part of the continent to capture slaves to help expedite the work. Every morning he was carried on a litter to the vicinity of the work, where he would sit, watching the construction, garrulously giving the minutest instructions. If he noticed a workman pause for a moment's breath, he would have him removed from the structure and brought before him and beheaded. On some days, the bodies of a hundred victims would be piled in front of the royal palanquin.

"As time went on he became so irritable and disgruntled that he could scarcely restrain himself from taking part in the work himself. Were it not that he boasted of the indolent lives that his ancestors had led for centuries, he might have joined in the throng who carried deerskins filled with earth to dump on the top of the slowly growing mound. On one particularly hot day, no less than a thousand workmen were prostrated by the sun. The savage monarch ordered that all these unfortunates should be executed before the following sunrise. Just after he had promulgated this inhuman order, he noticed that two workmen had placed a huge block of stone an inch out of plumb. He sent orders that they straighten it under penalty of being tortured to death. The poor, half-starved wretches were so frightened at the approach of the king's messenger that they seemed unable to rectify their mistake. First, they would set it in too far, then moved it out too far; the awful punishment hanging over them numbed their senses.

"The king meanwhile watched the proceedings with growing wrath. He sent another messenger to say that if the work was not made right instantly, it meant death to the two workmen and the two messengers. The four victims worked with a will, but their hands trembled so much that they could not set the stone plumb. The king, seeing the confusion, could stand it no longer. Seizing a sword from one of his guards, he leaped from his throne and started for the monument. He swore horrible oaths, declaring that he would kill the four stupid brutes and finish the work himself. He shouted that every person employed that day on the monument must die before dark. The sun was frightfully hot, and a hundred-yard dash at full speed for a monarch who had never set his feet to the ground was too great an exertion. He covered the distance between his palanquin and the foot of the monument in record time in an attempt to climb up the vast mound. The workmen and bodyguards were transfixed where they stood; the picture of the indolent monarch running sword in hand was the most amazing sight of their lives. Wild with the fury he had been repressing for days, the king started to rush up the steep incline. He had not gone five steps before he was seen to froth at the mouth and drop his sword. He spun about like a dervish and fell to the earth, rolling down the incline like a log. The workmen dropped their tasks; the guards abandoned their posts or prisoners; the members of the royal family forgot their dignity, all hurrying to the side of the fallen ruler. When the first person reached his side, Viperine's eyeballs had already rolled up in his head; he was stone dead.

"The news caused a riot among the workmen. They rushed from the monument pell-mell; gathering their scanty belongings and families, they charged the gatekeepers and escaped from the stockade into the forest. When the sun set that night behind Shreiner Knob, the vast enclosure was depopulated, save for the royal family and bodyguards. There were hardly enough present to give the late king a stately funeral, such as he would have liked. At the suggestion of his twelve-year-old son and heir, Ironwood, the body was buried in the core of the monument, several feet above the level of the earth. Below rested the mutilated corpses of hundreds of murdered workmen. There were not enough workers to dig the tomb elsewhere. There the distorted body was laid to rest, and earth and boulders thrown over it. After five centuries, it rests undisturbed, its secret well guarded. The professor from the eastern part of the state helped to keep the grave inviolate by declaring that the mound was naught but the erosion of water in the olden time. Even though the body sleeps so well under its grassy covering, the soul must be as restless as the bounding surf. It must be undergoing erosion in its stormy passage to the calm land of shades."

XV

LYNX OF INDIANVILLE GAP

(A Story of Animal Sagacity)

THE calico pony which Lot Frankenberger had bought at the sale in Millheim and which previously had acted so docile was running away. He had taken fright at the road machine at the entrance to Indianville Gap, and there seemed no stopping him. He had been trotting along slowly, with his head hanging and the lines lying loosely on his back, when the "chug, chug, click" of the machinery sent his nose into the air, and off he went at a gallop. Old man Frankenberger had handled all kinds of horses for forty years and was not in the least disturbed when the animal bolted. The men in charge of the machine knew his ability as a horseman, consequently made no move to help him. They were sure he would see-saw the pony's mouth until it came down to a dog-trot again. It was late in an autumn afternoon when the adventure commenced, the days were shortening, and heavy, cool shadows had already fallen in the Gap. On the summits, a little sunlight still illuminated the lace-like tips of the hemlocks.

All along the level road, the runaway kept quickening his pace. The driver braced his feet against the front board of the light carryall, sawing the beast's mouth to no avail. On several occasions, as they veered around curves, there had been narrow escapes from upsetting, side-swiping rocks or bumping squarely into trees. The noise of the wagon rattling over the hard road was soft-pedaled by the density of the foliage, and what residuum that carried was drowned by the "chug, chug, click" of the road machine. It seemed only a question of when the inevitable accident would occur; the old man's arms were weakening; it was harder to steer to the middle of the road. There was a bad turn at a gorge known as Painter

Hollow; with these indications, it augured ill to negotiate this letter U which the road made at this point. But old man Frankenberger vowed he would die game. He would fight the runaway to the last moment, and if any dying was done, they would die together. There was a piece of straight road for an eighth of a mile before reaching the "hollow." Here, the runaway gained additional momentum. The carryall never had more than one wheel on the ground at a time; the driver's skill deferred the smash-up. But they were nearing the turn, below which was a precipice of one hundred feet; Indian Run trickled along at the bottom of the gorge. The animal was bowling along at a terrific clip, sending back a mass of foam and dust, with the white-faced driver, his grey beard blowing out behind him, holding the reins as rigid as two rods of iron. They would strike the turn in half a minute more and probably all be reduced to an indiscriminate mass of bones, teeth, kindling wood, and scrap iron. The old man held his breath; he had often wondered how it would feel to die; his query to his soul would find its answer horribly.

Suddenly there was a sound like a heavy bag of meal dropping from a pulley. Something dark landed in the middle of the road. It had come from the limb of a white oak that overhung the drive. It was quiet for a moment, then swelled out and bristled like an angry cat. Old man Frankenberger couldn't help seeing it; the frenzied horse couldn't help seeing it; to the runaway, it magnified twofold. Possessed by a fresh terror, the maddened animal threw back its head, suddenly sinking on its haunches and sliding a full hundred yards before falling over in a limp mass, a victim of exhaustion and fear. The driver had the presence of mind enough; it was his fiftieth runaway, by actual count, to drop the reins and roll over into the wagon box. This saved him from shooting over the dashboard or being hurled into the roadway. The animal in falling ran a broken shaft through its abdomen and was slowly bleeding to death.

Lot Frankenberger had little compassion for a brute that had sought to imperil his life, and besides, he must identify the object or animal which had stopped the runaway at the opportune moment. He climbed out of the wagon and peered up the road. The furry, catlike creature was still squatting, with big glowing eyes turned towards him. From a stationary position, he had no trouble recognizing his deliverer. It was none other than a monster Canada lynx, commonly called a catamount. The animal, alarmed by the noise of the oncoming cavalcade or in the pursuit of some sickly bird, had leaped from its hiding place in the tree into the center of the roadway. But best of all, it had dropped there just when it could save a human life.

"Of all things, to be saved by a mountain cat," ejaculated the horseman after he had recovered himself. "Of all things, this does beat all."

The lynx seemed to realize that it had done something creditable, for it remained where it was in perfect security.

"You are a good pussy; won't you let me stroke you ?" said the old man. The cat smoothed down its spotted, greyish fur, and something like a purr was emitted from its whiskered lips. The old man advanced a few steps as if to stroke it, saying all the while, "I'll reward you for this someday. You've got more sense than most people."

The big cat looked at him in a friendly way but did not seem to require stroking as it got on its feet, which looked like fluffy balls of grey down, and hopped, with ear-tips bobbing, into the hazel thicket at the lower side of the road. Frankenberger returned to his turnout, finding that the horse had expired.

"He's as dead as a mackerel, and I'm glad of it," he exclaimed with a grim smile. Just then, he heard the rumble of wheels; a wagon was approaching. "Now is my first chance to do that mountain cat a good turn. If I say it saved my life, a hundred gunners will be out in the woods by morning to kill it. I'll say the horse stumbled."

A prop timber truck soon hove in sight around the deadly curve. The Leitzell boys were on it and were amazed to see the dead horse, with Lot Frankenberger standing by it.

"We'll be glad to give you a lift back to Indianville; we can't leave you here in the dark," said the good-natured lads. They rolled the dead horse into the ditch, first ripping off his harness. They tied the carryall behind their truck and turned their horses' heads back to Indianville. "An hour later home won't make any matter. We've got a better excuse to tell the old man when we get back."

They were at the Frankenberger farm on the far end of the long, log-cabined street of Indianville within an hour as they kept the team moving at a trot most of the distance. Once over, the old horseman had nothing further to say of the runaway; he laughed about it to his family. That night when he went to bed, he couldn't sleep. It wasn't from the shock of the recent experience. His nerves were of iron. He recollected that they had rolled the disemboweled horse into the ditch. The lynx would undoubtedly make a meal off the remains during the night. When the first lumber trucks passed by at daybreak, the teamsters would notice this. It would start the story that there was a wildcat or a catamount in the Gap; a general hunt would be organized, traps would be set, and the faithful lynx would pay the death penalty for his kindly effort.

Lot Frankenberger was sure that the animal leaped into the roadway purposely to aid him. He had never been a hunter, consequently felt a higher estimation for wild creatures than those whose only interest is to malign them as an excuse for killing. He had heard his old grandmother, who had been born in Germany, tell that the souls of murderers went into wolves, foxes, wildcats, and lynxes; they were given a chance to benefit some human being in this form; if they did so, their sins were forgiven; otherwise, they were doomed to inhabit the bodies of lower animals, such as weasels, polecats, and water rats. The surest way to avoid sleeping too late was to keep awake all night. This the horseman did, with the result that before dawn, he was on the road behind his family horse, an ancient Morgan, which had been temporarily discarded during his infatuation for the calico broncho, bound for the scene of the last night's adventure.

He tied the horse to a tree a goodly distance from the carcass of the runaway so as not to frighten it and advanced on foot. He found things just as he had expected. The hungry lynx had devoured a good part of the dead animal's entrails; blood and fat were everywhere. He dug a good-sized trench in the soft muck below the road and pushed the carcass into it. Then he covered it with heavy stones so nobody would be tempted to pry it out and examine it. He rounded the grave neatly with earth, placing moss, leaves, and twigs over it, so it looked very natural. He cleaned away all the debris left by the lynx; he was discharging his debt of gratitude.

Frankenberger was a man sixty years of age, but life was sweet to him. He had a wife, four daughters, and a beautiful little granddaughter. All this he would have had to leave but for the sagacity of the lynx. He would never forget the animal, come what may. He left the spot feeling happy. He passed through the Gap a number of times afterward but saw nothing of the lynx. The beast was evidently taking a series of delicious cat naps after its feast on the dead horse.

When the cold weather set in, the horseman concluded that it was about time that the mountain cat would be hungry. He noticed that one of the old blue hens was droopy, so he knocked off her head, took her into the horse stable, and picked her. He wanted no feathers found in the woods after the repast he had promised for his animal benefactor. In the evening, he drove through the Gap, ostensibly going on business to Abundance. He stopped under the outspreading white oak where the lynx had been resting the day of the runaway. Taking the dead chicken from under the seat, he trailed it into the woods on the lower side of the road. There, in a secluded nook with some young beeches, with the dun-colored leaves still clinging, he tied the fowl by its feet, a few inches off the ground. When he returned to the spot two days later, it was gone; the lynx had come for its reward.

Pleased by the experiment, he visited the retired spot whenever he found a sick chicken or secured a discarded piece of beef or pork at a neighbor's butchering. Everything disappeared promptly. The lynx, which formerly lived off berries, herbs, roots, and when lucky enough, sick grouse or rabbits, was now being fed "on the fat of the land." It was shrewd enough not to show itself, and its presence in the Gap was not suspected.

In the month of February, stimulated by the action of the county commissioners in awarding a liberal bounty for the scalps of certain miscalled "predatory" animals, a party of idle, intemperate youths from Jacobsburg set up a hunting camp in the Gap. Every night they came to Indianville, carousing at the hotel and insulting women on the streets. They loudly boasted that they were making "easy money," that they would never work while the taxpayers supported them so handsomely. They seemed to know the tricks of trapping, as they captured eight gray foxes the first two weeks they were in the Gap.

Lot Frankenberger was a trifle apprehensive for the safety of his lynx but reassured himself with the thought that it was an uncommonly sagacious beast; perhaps it contained the derelict spirit of Silas Werninger, the outlaw, who had been killed near Robertsburg three years before. The bounty trappers soon caught two big wildcats, which added to the old horseman's fears. After this, the lads had a drunken orgy, wrecking the hotel barroom in their crazy frenzy. They were then forbidden to come to town, which augured ill for the lynx. If half intoxicated all the time, they could secure so many helpless animals; their prowess would increase if alcohol were difficult to obtain. They were in the habit of sending the most reliable of their number to the county seat every time they had a half dozen scalps, and he returned with whiskey and provisions. Despite this, they had made nightly visits to the hotel at Indianville until ordered from the village. They declared that they were the greatest trappers in the Seven Mountains, that they would not leave an animal alive in the entire region. In addition to trapping the proscribed animals, they shot birds indiscriminately, wiping out most of the cheery-voiced Jays which wintered in the Gap. They butchered dozens of useful owls; and many grouse. They caught raccoons, 'possums, muskrats, weasels, and also countless rabbits. They were the sworn foes of every living thing—except themselves. They were typical of the professional hunters which misguided Pennsylvania lawmakers are trying so hard to encourage.

One of the lads, the biggest drinker of the lot, was a taxidermist of some ability, but he never finished anything, wasting scores of rare skins. One sunshiny morning after a heavy snowstorm, old Frankenberger went out on his front porch to catch a breath of air and admire the ice pendants on the trees. Up the street, he noticed a great commotion at the railway station; a crowd had collected. There was still wanting fifteen minutes for the arrival of the train bound for the county seat; it was time to walk to the station and perhaps meet some distinguished traveler, perhaps a United States senator. Putting on his bearskin cap and wrapping his worsted muffler about his neck, he sallied forth into the snow. As he neared the platform, he observed that the throng was centered about a tall young man holding the carcass of some large animal by the ears. He was measuring its length with himself; the animal seemed equally long. The old horseman's heart stood still; could it be that the tall youth was fetching the carcass of the faithful lynx to Jacobsburg to collect the bounty on its scalp and sell the pelt? It could not be that the shrewd creature had been trapped and killed. He was hoping against hope, as he drew near, that it would prove to be a huge wildcat. He recognized the tall young man as the soberest of the roystering crew of trappers camping in the Gap. By the time he reached the steps leading to the platform, he could see that the dead animal was none other than the lynx of Indian-ville Gap. The old man was heartbroken; would the rapacious hunters leave *anything* alive? He mounted the steps and approached the trapper, whom he knew slightly.

"Where did you get the lynx?" he queried.

"We caught him in our biggest trap yesterday noon," was the reply. "He put up a terrible fight before we could kill him."

"Where are you taking him to?" continued the old man. "I am bringing him to the county seat to collect the bounty and sell the hide," said the youth. "I'll get four dollars bounty, and the hide will fetch at least ten dollars, a pretty good day's work, eh?"

"I'll give you twenty dollars as he stands," said Frankenberger with emphasis. The crowd was taken aback; the old farmer and horse dealer were usually close and cared nothing about wild animals.

"It's a go," replied the trapper quickly. The old man fished out a crisp twenty-dollar bill, handing it over. The trapper dropped the fifty-pound carcass to the station platform, where it fell with a dull thud. Just then, the train pulled in, and to the surprise of everyone, Lot Frankenberger climbed into the smoker with the lynx.

"The old man's gone stark crazy," said more than one person as they watched him start on his unusual journey. When the train reached Jacobsburg, it was noticed that he remained on board. He traveled clear to Williamsport that day, returning by way of Montandon. At Williamsport, he left the carcass with a noted taxidermist, with instructions to spare no expense in the mounting. He explained that it should be set in a crouching attitude like he had first seen it in life. As he left the laboratory, he said to the genial naturalist, "that lynx saved my life. I was sorry when the bounty trappers caught him, but it's a long story."

The next day old Frankenberger engaged old Nathan Garis, the only cabinet maker in town, to do some work at his home. He had him erect a large walnut case on the front porch with plate glass front and sides. It stood against the wall; its base rested on a trestle, boarded over, about three feet from the floor. Garis asked no questions, Frankenberger gave no information as to the use in which he intended to put the case. "Seems to me as if he intended keeping store," said the old cabinet maker at the post office that night. The case remained empty until the latter part of April; it was a day when the bluebirds were caroling in the maple trees, and the robins were hopping playfully about on the lawns. There were tulips in bloom. The station agent seeing Lot Frankenberger coming out of the general store, called out that there was a big box for him at the express office. The old horseman looked at it and then went after his horse and carryall.

By noon the box had been opened, and the stuffed effigy of the lynx of Indianville Gap installed in the handsome case. All afternoon a steady stream of callers inspected the crouching, glaring manikin. "It's as natural as life," was the general sentiment expressed. Old Frankenberger had a sad, faraway look in his eyes as he watched the attention the trophy received.

"I owe a lot to the critter," he said to himself. "I'm glad I've got him stuffed since I couldn't keep him alive."

Over fifteen years have passed, and the lynx, faded by the sun and losing hair in some few places, still stares with his glass eyes glowing from the walnut case on Lot Frankenberger's porch. The old man, stooped and very bent, still exhibits pride when strangers stop and ask to look at it. He is less reticent than in the years gone by, but even now, all he will vouchsafe is "the critter saved my life; I owe a lot to him." Sometimes a bond of kindliness draws mankind a trifle nearer to the persecuted kingdom of the animals.

THE OLD ACADEMY

XVI

TURNED TO STONE

(A Story of Naginey Cave)

THOUSANDS of visitors to the wonderful cave of Naginey, near Milroy, have marveled at this superb work of nature with its chambers, its cloisters, its gothic arches, its domes, its walls bush-hammered by the Infinite Architect. They have been amazed at the Indian spring, in the innermost recess of the cavern, with its pool of limpid, transparent water in which rests a small, rounded, yellowed form like a petrified baby. This is the crowning surprise of the cave and well repays the strenuous effort now required to enter it. It seems a pity that the mouth of the cavern has again been allowed to become choked with leaves, that the quarrymen are carrying on their operations so dangerously near as to imperil what a great poet who once visited it styled "the eighth wonder of the world." Twenty years ago, the Naginey cave enjoyed the height of its popularity; those were the days when the Altoona band waked the echoes in its gloomy labyrinths, when picnic parties made use of it every Sunday, all summer long. Now few visit the cave, its fame is fast receding, and the image of the petrified baby rests most of the time undisturbed by mortal eyes.

A legend connected with this cave carries us back nearly a thousand years in the history of the once mighty Lenni-Lenape Indians. It was during the golden age of the noble redmen, centuries before Columbus started his westward voyage. It was long before the humiliating defeat of the Lenni-Lenape by the Susquehannocks at the Battle of the Indian Steps. According to the belief of the Indians living south of the Tussey Mountains, the cavern was erected by the creator of the Lenni-Lenape, Gitche Manitou. It was to be a hidden shrine where the wise men could enter for contemplation, to seek counsel before some great war or migration. It was for the few, the learned and the good only. It must be kept that way as, on rare occasions, the lesser spirits of the realms beyond the grave and even Gitche Manitou himself appeared there. When they came to earth, the gods were possessed of earthly appetites. A spring of purest water welled up in the cave, reserved only for divine users.

According to the belief of the Indians in the Kishoquoquillas country, prayers to spiritual gods could only refer to spiritual wants—soul cravings. When the gods took on physical form, they could be appealed to for physical needs—the restoration of health, the prolongation of life, freedom from disease, and such. To satisfy all the requirements of the faithful, the gods existed part of the time in the flesh. They frequented caves and underground streams when on earth and drank from springs reserved for their use, like the one in the Naginey cavern. The priests and wise men were well aware of these facts, and it was a part of their duties to instruct mortals not to drink from the celestial founts. Ordinary mortals were never allowed to enter the caves where the gods visited, but priests, wise men, and kings could go there during religious festivals. The high priests usually built imposing lodge houses at the mouths of the sacred caverns and claimed to be on speaking terms with the divine spirits. The gods projected themselves into the caves in spiritual form and submerged themselves in the sacred springs, which sustained them in physical form. When they desired to resume their spiritual natures, they refrained from drinking water, and after a certain number of hours, they sank back to a vaporous condition, visible only to the eyes of the soothsayers.

As the faith of the Indians faded through intercourse with the whites, the gods lost their power to take on human form. The greatest wants of the Indians being physical when they had no one to turn to, their people diminished. Such was the theory of the last wise men of the Kishoquoquillas region for the gradual decadence of their culture. The proximity of the early Indians with their gods had a stimulating effect. There could be no agnosticism where the gods were visible at times. The wise men recruited from all the varied castes had the greatest powers of *seeing*. They were most in the presence of the divine rulers. The kings came next in intercourse with the gods. The other castes sometimes saw disembodied spirits, but they were mostly wandering ghosts of plain people like themselves. One thing was certain; the entire Indian culture was in closer tune with the infinite than any white race.

Man may have progressed financially, mechanically, perhaps physically, but he has deteriorated spiritually. The second sight of modern Indians in the west has been ridiculed by government agents and missionaries. But this has been done for selfish reasons; it exists nonetheless. The only real mystery is why such a spiritual culture should have been deserted by their gods when the white men came. As stated before, it must have been caused by a subsiding wave of faith. Some Indians laid it to successive acts of sacrilege by their kings.

One of the early kings of the Kishoquoquillas country named Mallikuwagan was noted for his devotion and piety. His respect for the ancient shrines and customs gave him the name of the Pilsohalgusswagan or "holy one" among the tribesmen. He was married early in life to Ikalissa, a beautiful princess from the Juniata country, and a long and happy life was predicted for the regal couple. The greatest reward that the saintly king desired was a son and heir. He said that if he could have a son, he would be repaid for all his piety and goodness. The priests told him that this wish would be granted, that the gods must look with favor on such a virtuous being. But time went by, and no son was born, and the king, used to having his way in everything, became impatient. Prayers, public and private, proved unavailing; the wisest men from distant parts of the country, from as far south as the Conedogwinet region, were summoned to the royal lodge house to seek the aid of the gods in granting the good king's demand.

Mallikuwagan became very angry with his beautiful young wife, telling her that unless she bore him a son within an allotted time, she must pay for the remissness with her death. The charming young queen, who loved her pious husband devotedly, was taken aback at his unreasonable attitude. He had always seemed so gentle, so anxious to talk about kindliness, unselfishness, his duty to others. She was frightened by his dreadful threat; it preyed on her mind, making her a wreck mentally and physically. The stipulated time passed, and no heir was forthcoming. The king ordered the queen brought before him, telling her that she had been unmindful of her duty to the gods by not blessing their favored monarch, meaning himself, with a son. As a sacrifice to the divine wrath, she must die by slow torture. He was sorry to have to order her to such a punishment, but the gods were angry; he could do nothing else. In all this, he spoke without authority, as the gods were really unconcerned as to whether a son was born to him or not.

The sentence was carried with great barbarity in the presence of the priests and as many of the populace as could be induced to be present. The young queen had been very popular with all classes; her cruel end aroused much private resentment, but the people dared not express their sentiments publicly. *Lese majeste* was an offense invariably punished by death. After the execution, it was whispered about that if the king had been patient a while longer, he might have had an heir. This came to the monarch's ears, and he was secretly smitten with remorse.

He took a second wife within a month to forget such unwholesome feelings. Her name was Sukene. She was of his own rank and came from the distant valley of the Tondoway. She was said to be more beautiful than the first wife. He warned her before the elaborate ceremony that she must speedily bring him a son and heir. She promised to do all in her power if the gods willed it to be. The manner in which he had made this demand on her cooled her ardor for her royal bridegroom. She kept thinking of the wretched fate meted out to her predecessor and secretly feared a similar end for herself. Her entire nervous system became upset, she lost weight and grew sleepless and irritable. The king exhibited no real affection towards her; he only talked of one subject, and that was the heir she must bear him.

In due season a son was born, which seemed to be an unusually handsome, robust infant. The event was the cause of great rejoicing; bonfires were kindled on all of the peaks of the Seven Mountains. The king was overjoyed, spending most of his time fondling and admiring the child. He did not say a single kindly word to the queen, neglecting her for his newfound joy. The infant thrived until it was a month old. Then it was seized with a wasting fever, its chubby little form wearing away to a rack of bones. The king was alarmed and prayed night and day to his gods. The wisemen doctored, and the priests prayed over the infant; human and animal sacrifices were made daily. The child grew worse all the time; the king was in a frenzy. He conceived the horrible plan of sacrificing his young queen, thinking thereby to appease the gods. The poor young woman begged for her life, saying the child would do better with a mother than without one. She said she loved the baby; she could not bear to leave it. She would gladly lay down her life for it when it was a little older. Mallikuwagan sneered at her, remarking that as a choice had to be made, the infant's life was more valuable than the older one. She told him that she could perhaps bear him another heir in case this one died. This infuriated him more than anything else. He said he wanted this child, no other.

When the queen was taken into the forest to be roasted alive by a slow fire, one of her devoted handmaidens, Kimixin, forced herself on the pyre and was burned in her stead. Disguised in her attendant's clothing, she escaped to the north, eventually marrying a chieftain of the Susquehannocks. It is said that she was an ancestor of the great war chief and implacable foe of the Lenni-Lenape, Pipsisseway. The king was kept in ignorance of his queen's escape and expressed great gratification When informed that the execution had been carried out. "Surely the child will recover now," was his comment. But the child failed noticeably after his mother was gone. The gods still frowned. Mallikuwagan fumed and stormed; he would save the child's life, no matter what the means. If the gods would not do it, he would do it himself with the gods' materials. When the wise men broke the news to him that the infant was beyond human aid, he merely clapped his hands with glee.

"I have been waiting to show you pettifoggers that I know far more than all of you combined. I will save the child's life and restore him to perfect health."

The assemblage of high priests, wise men, and soothsayers stood about gasping for breath. How could this king perform the impossible?

"I will bathe my son in the sacred spring," he Went on. "It is the refreshment of the gods; they maintain their human form by drinking it; my son shall be made well by it." The wise men dropped to their knees, imploring their king not to be guilty of such a sacrilege.

"For thousands of years, that spring has been kept for its holy purpose, to preserve our intercourse with the infinite; none but the gods have bathed in it or drank from it. We fear for the safety of a dynasty that would commit such a foul deed." The king, in his anger, struck off the heads of several of the venerable soothsayers and then ranted some more. "My son's life is worth as much as the pleasure of the gods; I shall bathe him in the sacred spring in the cave."

He ordered the puny child to be brought to him and carried it in his arms to the spring. At the risk of their heads, the priests refused to be a party to the sacrilege. Torchbearers and nurses led the way into the labyrinth. Far in its chilly depths lay the crystalline, limpid pool, the fountain of the gods. As they neared the spring, the child began to cry feebly; its unformed intellect was conscious of a great wrong being done.

"In another minute, you will cry no more," said the king with prophetic emphasis. At the brink of the basin, he stooped down, completely immersing the child in the clear depths. He left it there for scarcely half a minute, then started lifting it out. As his hands touched it, they felt as if they clutched cold stone. He tried to raise the body; it was petrified solidly to the bottom of the basin. He called his torchbearers and servants around him, bidding them one by one to try and release the child. They all failed; the baby had been turned to stone and was a part of the base of the spring. The king tried himself again, but when his hands touched the cold mass of stone that had so recently been his hope and joy, his grief knew no bounds. Shrieking with terror and remorse, he fled from the cavern. He never stopped running until he was in his lodge house. He raved all the rest of the day and all night. No one came to comfort him, as all were aware that he was being punished for his horrible sacrilege. Some of the oldest wise men spoke out loudly now.

"We fear the gods will never come to us in human form again; they will never refresh themselves in a spring polluted by mortals. Hereafter we must worship unseen gods; they will answer our spiritual wants, but physically everything will go against us."

In the morning, the king was found to be a raving maniac, and there was a vociferous demand that he be put to death like any of his subjects who might be possessed of devils. His bodyguard, filled with the royal prerogative, rallied around him. The mob overcame them, butchering them all, and somewhere in the melee, the king was felled and cut into pieces. A state of anarchy ruled in the tribes for several months until a clean-cut young warrior named Genamoagan, the son of a wise man, proclaimed himself king, becoming the founder of the new dynasty. But the twilight of the gods became the darkness of the Kishoquoquillas people; henceforth, they fought their battles unaided by divine hands. The gods seemed very far away; no matter how loud they might cry out in their distress, there came no answering voice. Their spiritual prayers were heard, but their earthly demands, more pressing and necessary, were unheeded.

In the gloomy cavern, the little petrified baby rests, the innocent cause of the break between the gods and their chosen people. Those who see its little shrunken, yellow form, anchored fast to the bottom of the shallow pool, wonder at its history, even mistake its identity, its meaning. The Indians of the Seven Mountains handed the story down from father to son. It was the skeleton at every feast. Whenever a battle went against them, or the buffaloes and elks eluded them, or their children died, or their crops failed, they always pointed in the direction of the cliffs of Naginey, saying reverently, "it is the fault of Mallikuwagan, the gods will serve us no longer; they cannot drink of a polluted spring."

XVII

THE DEVIL'S TURNIP PATCH

(An Ancient Legend of the Mingoes)

ACCORDING to the ancient tradition of the Mingoes, the Machtando or Devil, repenting of his evil life, and tiring of the rulership of the dark realms beneath the earth, emerged through a bottomless pit, now known as Winegardner's Cove, near the present village of Naginey, where the lost spirits are said to gaze at the outside world, wailing and moaning on moonlight nights, in the form of a very handsome black man. Seeing all the virtuous beings engaged in agriculture or in the chase, he determined to settle down as a peaceable farmer. He inquired of the first person he met where he could find some vacant land. The Indian received the tall stranger with politeness but said that every spot of ground within the range of his sight was preempted by agriculturalists or hunters. They might be induced to sell; did the black man have any wampum?

As one of the chief attributes of life in the realms below was a complete absence of money and a great plentitude of purchasable articles, the ex-devil in chief had not realized its utility in his new sphere. He replied that he was penniless and did not know how to get any money. The Indian said that he might earn some by labor or by the chase.

The black man became interested, but he demurred when he learned that he would have to work every day for several years to obtain enough to purchase the smallest freehold. He asked for further particulars concerning the chase; it seemed interesting. In his own country, wild animals were always chasing the condemned souls; he would like to reverse the order of things for a while. The Indian explained to him that it would be necessary to purchase or fashion spears, arrow points, and axes in order to kill and skin the beasts. After that, the hides could be sold or exchanged to good advantage. As the demon lacked the money and had not the patience to carve out the weapons, he abandoned the scheme of becoming a hunter.

The Indian told him of the pleasures of fishing; how much cheap food could be drawn from the rivers and ponds. This idea appealed to him until he realized he must buy lines and nets. There was nothing left but to find some spot where there was no population and take up a plot of ground as a farmer. He asked the obliging Indian if he knew where he could find some unoccupied land. The savage pointed to the east.

"Follow this path in the direction of the great river; there are some places where you will not find a single landowner in an hour's walking." In those ancient days, the Indian population was much denser than when the white men first entered the Seven Mountains. Wars, carnage, famine, and pestilence had blazed the way for the newcomers, leaving vacant many fertile fields and hunting grounds. The black man thanked his informant and started for the east. But he was not altogether satisfied. He vowed he would inquire at every lodge house along the way; if his .informant was correct, no harm could be done; if wrong, he might not have to travel so far. As he walked along admiring the beautiful country and basking in the warm sunshine, which was forever absent in the world below, he made sure to stop at every encampment, as well as at each solitary lodge house or hunter's tent, to ask if there was any vacant plot to be had.

The Indians received him courteously; they seemed happy and prosperous, but all told the same story. The country had as much population as it could support; all the land was in the hands of private owners. Perhaps in the east, near the great river, he could find some that was free; it was poor ground, yet an able-bodied man might derive a living from it. A man must live where he can. In the less frequented portions of the way, he often encountered wild animals. They stood across his path, sunning themselves. Unarmed and unaccustomed to their ways, he was powerless to resent their boldness. He had to get out of their way on every occasion. He was impressed by the myriad forms of life which inhabited the forests. There were buffaloes, moose, elk, large and small varieties of deer, brown bears, black bears, black bears with white faces, mountain lions, mountain cats, wildcats, black wolves, brown wolves, grey foxes, white foxes, wolverines, fishers, and countless smaller creatures. Sometimes flocks of birds impeded his way, eagles, buzzards, hawks, owls, pigeons, heath-hens, grouse, herons, pelicans, ravens, and parrots.

The wild creatures, never having seen a black man before, exhibited no fear. They displayed the same unconcern a thousand years later when they saw the white men for the first time. But the whites were armed; they began a merciless slaughter, never ceasing until whole species were annihilated. There seemed to be no end to the occupied country. The wilderness inhabited by the beasts and birds belonged to kings or powerful warriors, who kept it reserved for the chase. The open fields were densely populated; nearly every person was ready to sell; even in those days, the agriculturalists were a dissatisfied class. In the course of his travels, the black man reached a high knob where he could see the great river, the Susquehanna, coiling like an argent serpent at the foot of the mountains. He must be nearing "no man's land," where he would be given a chance to live by his honest toil.

Being in human form, he became beset with hunger. He drank all he could from the copious springs, but he still felt unsatisfied. The fruit was ripening on the trees. At first, he feared it was the private property of the landowners, but hunger at length overcame his scruples, and he tasted the wild apples, persimmons, plums, and grapes.

After inhaling sulfur, soot, and brimstone for centuries, the ex-bad man was happy with these luscious articles of food. He was deeply thankful for this reformation; he was reaping an early reward. When he reached the eastern limit of the mountain top, he realized that his new home must be near. He surveyed the black forest of pine and hemlock, which covered the mountain from the height where he stood clear to the rippling river edge. He met another obliging Indian to whom he explained his situation. He was a stranger from a distant, hot land; he wanted to take up a modest plot of ground and become a farmer.

The Indian told him that he was in the right locality, that a very dense population occupied all the tillable soil not used by the kings and chieftains for their hunting grounds. He pointed to a bench on the slope halfway down the mountain, saying that if he made application to the representative of the king, he could doubtless obtain the right to settle on it. The king's agent lived on the opposite river bank; the accommodating Indian agreed to accompany him there. The path to the foot of the mountain led by the plot which the stranger might occupy; the public road runs by it today, and he had a good chance to look it over. It was shaded by a dense growth of red hemlocks and contained several springs. The ground was covered with huge uneven boulders, which had been cast up when the mountain was formed by a dragon emerging from the bowels of the earth. The devil knew this story well, though he was silent at the time. He had expelled this dragon from the infernal region as an undesirable citizen, and an army of human beings had slain it as its hideous, angry head appeared from the depths.

The Indian guide went on to say that if once the layer of rocks was removed, the plot would make an ideal turnip patch. He explained that turnips were easily raised; the seeds could be found in the open spaces in the forests, and a living could be made off them until he became skilled in raising other plants. At the base of the mountain, a dugout was moored to one of the giant hemlocks; in it, the stranger and his acquaintance crossed the river. The black man was delighted with the smooth, limpid, transparent water, so different from the rivers of fire and steam in his own realm. They found the king's land agent at home. He lived in a cool, commodious lodge house built of white birch logs. He seemed delighted to greet the stranger and accede to his wishes. He could have the land for himself and his heirs forever provided he paid an annual tax amounting to one-tenth of the crops raised. The black man was overjoyed; in his imagination, he fancied himself a respectable subject of the king, with fertile lands and a comfortable income. His past would be forever left behind. He acceded to the agent's terms, stating that he was ready to go to work immediately, clearing the land. The agent asked him if he wished to engage any help. He replied that he was in modest circumstances and would prefer to save his little board by doing the work himself. The agent and the Indian guide re-crossed the river with him and showed him the boundaries of his new domain. The rocks, which covered every inch of it, looked bigger than ever, but the stranger gritted his teeth; he would stand by his bargain. At nightfall, the agent bade him goodbye, congratulating him on his willingness to clear the ground unaided.

"Underneath that layer of stones is good soil; you can begin by raising a bumper crop of turnips." This confirmed what the guide had said and re-awakened his energies. The Indian companion, hating to leave such a respectable-looking person alone in the wilderness, invited him to spend the night at his modest home. The stranger lost no time in accepting—company might drive away thoughts of failure which would crowd into his mind in the weary watches of the night. The Indian's home and tiny farm were situated on the summit of the mountain, about two miles from the devil's turnip patch. It was past dark when they reached it, but the native's watchful squaw had a bonfire of rich pine burning to show the way. The Indian, whose name was Cheerful Dew, had numerous family, including a beautiful young daughter of sixteen summers called Light of the Morning. Like the rest of the young folks, she seemed frightened at the imposing height and dark visage of the unexpected guest. The stranger's manners were easy and affable; he was so confiding that the slim young girl was quite won over before bedtime. She pulled her blanket around herself to dream of him as her dusky lover.

Bright and early next morning, his ex-satanic majesty repaired to his "farm" to commence the clearing operations. Strong as he was, he could not push the aged hemlocks out of root. They gripped the stones with grim stubbornness and had done so for centuries; by nightfall, he had not budged a single tree. As he had been invited to remain with Cheerful Dew and his family as long as he liked, he repaired thither, smiling broadly to hide his chagrin. Of course, they asked him how he had gotten along with his work. He was compelled to tell them that he had made scant headway against the forces of nature. He asked for the loan of some of their implements to fell the trees. His host informed him that the Indians did not possess axes stout enough to chop down such mighty trees; they had knives that girdled the bark. This killed the trees, and they fell out of root in due season. When they died, they lost their needles, letting in the sun on the plantations. "Where I come from, it is very warm, yet we have no sun," said the stranger sardonically. The Indian further explained to him that while he was waiting for the trees to die, he could be digging out the stones. There was undoubtedly plenty to do, but the stranger was undismayed. The next morning, armed with a borrowed scalping knife, he returned to his possessions. After a long day's work, he seemed to have scarcely made any impression on the forest. The circumferences of the ancient hemlocks were so great that it took several hours to cut a ring around a single tree. The genial company of Light of the Morning served to keep up his spirits upon his return; he sought his borrowed blanket cheerfully. For a month, he plied his task faithfully. At the end of that time, he could scarcely notice that he had done anything.

The cold weather was setting in, yet, despite all his exertions, he shivered miserably. He had formed the idea that he would have the land cleared by spring in time to start his first turnip crop; now, if he had all the hemlocks girdled by that time, he would be fortunate. The trees must be dead before he could plant his seeds; turnips would not grow in the shade. But after the trees were dead, he must remove the rocks, as no soil was apparent. He was utterly discouraged; it was galling to his imperious pride to live off the bounty of a poor Indian family with no prospects of ever repaying them. He had about made up his mind to abandon the task and start away on another search for land when a devilish idea entered his head. He was in love with and was evidently loved by the beautiful daughter of his Indian friend. Why not marry her and assist her father on his farm, leaving the turnip patch to lie fallow until a more propitious time? It would be an easy way to escape all his difficulties; he did not mind work, but he was not yet up to the point of accomplishing the impossible.

He took a final look at the interminable proposition; the endless sea of giant hemlocks, which rose from the rocks "as thick as hair on a dog's back," the network of heavy stones, millions of them there seemed on the few acres. The happiness that his new life promised would be slaved away; better to have remained master in his inferno than a drudge in such a desert. He sat and meditated for the rest of the day; life seemed sweet to him again as he was not used to toil.

At dusk, he wended his way to his patron's home. The rest had done him good; his lustrous dark eyes sparkled, as in the days in the world below, his black hair was sleek and straight, a satanically captivating smile played about the corners of his thin lips. He made no advances until after supper. Then he asked the beautiful Light of the Morning to accompany him for a stroll. He wanted her to explain to him the names of the stars; there were none in the deep valley where he had lived. The girl consented with alacrity. He was so elated that he did not stop to note the expressions on the faces of her parents. Very little was said about the names of the stars.

The stranger was not long in opening out with his love story; he had loved her since the first moment he had laid eyes on her when he had come to the house that eventful evening with her generous father. The girl coyly confessed that his odd appearance had frightened her at first, but before that evening was over, she had loved him. Yes, she had loved him truly ever since. Moreover, he was her first love; she had never seen a man before who had attracted her. She had grieved over his non-success on the turnip patch; as his wife, she would help him with his toil and sympathize with him in his disappointments. He allowed the sweet creature to say no more. Catching her in his arms, he thanked her for her self-expressed willingness to be his wife. Then hand in hand, they had not gone very far; they returned to Cheerful Dew's lodge house to obtain the parental blessing. The suave Indian listened attentively to the black man's request for his daughter's hand in marriage. Then his face darkened like a thundercloud; his wife looked equally unfriendly.

"I cannot allow my daughter to marry a person about whom we know nothing," he replied decisively. "Tell me first about yourself, your former home, and parentage; as matters stand now, you can never obtain my consent." This speech, unlooked for, literally knocked the props from under the devil's feet. He was too taken aback to make up a false story of his life.

"I am a respectable stranger," he faltered. "I can only say that I will make your daughter a good husband."

"Tell me your antecedents, and I will consider the matter," rejoined Cheerful Dew, scowling fiercely, "otherwise, *never*."

"My life here speaks volumes," pleaded the black man. "Have I not been industrious and steady ?"

Here the Indian signaled that he had heard enough and, drawing his buffalo blanket over his head, lay down on the floor of the lodge house.

The vigorous squaw next took the case in hand. First, she ordered the stranger from the house, then told the girl to get her blanket, lie down, and go to sleep. The stranger sheepishly wandered out into the night, his head full of confusion. Were it not that he had reformed, he might have murdered the old Indians and stolen the girl. In his belt hung the sharp scalping knife he had used to girdle the ancient hemlocks. But he had reformed. His first impulse was to quit the hateful region; it had been unlucky to him from the first day. He soon quelled this longing, as he could not bear the thought of never seeing Light of the Morning again. He would compromise by lurking in the woods until he could have a last look, a last kiss. He would like to run away with her, but to where? He had no money nor ability to provide for her, even if he eloped with her. If they stole her father's dugout and started down the stream, hunger would compel them to seek shore; it was now almost winter, nuts were scarce, and there was no more fruit on the trees. He had not thought that perhaps Light of the Morning was a huntress and could provide for them on their way. If she was skilled in the chase, it would be a great help; anyway, he would watch for her, and matters would adjust themselves if they could meet face to face.

Evidently, the young girl's parents suspected he would attempt a clandestine meeting, as it was nearly two weeks before he could see her. In the meantime, he almost froze to death, sleeping on the rocks; he missed Cheerful Dew's cozy quarters. His only food was chestnuts and a few frozen wild apples and plums. He was attacked by wolves and mountain lions. He was gaunt, yet traces of his old charm remained as he arose from behind a boulder to greet her. The girl out gathering nuts seemed overjoyed to see him and sprang into his arms with all the agility of a fawn. She said that her parents had held her captive for ten days but at length had concluded that the cold weather had driven the stranger to seek warmer climes.

The black man explained to her that he was penniless and no hunter, that if she went away with him in her father's dugout, he would support her in some habitable region in the east. But en route, if she possessed any aptitude as a huntress, she could assist greatly by providing food for them both. The young girl burst into tears. Between sobs, she said

RHODODENDRON AND TAMARACK   (Photo by S. W. Smith)

that she had never even killed a chipmunk or a hummingbird; she knew nothing of the methods of the chase.

"Why don't you take me to *your* country," she wailed. "You lived there comfortably before you came here; no matter where it is, take me to it."

The stranger was silenced by her plea.

He hung his dark head and, then, speaking very softly, replied: "I did not dare tell your parents who I was because I am the former ruler of the realms under the earth. I could not take you to the inferno."

Light of the Morning clasped him tighter than before, crying, "take me there; I would be happy anywhere with *you*."

"Do you understand fully what I meant?" said the devil, abashed by the extent of her love. "Do you realize my home is the abode of lost souls writhing in everlasting torment? You would have to witness terrible scenes; you would never smile again! You could never return."

"I don't care what is there. I love you; I would never smile if you went away without me," said Light of the Morning.

If you are determined, then we shall go there at once. All this repentance with starvation and humiliation as the reward counts for nothing; I will improve in goodness in inferno with you at my side, quicker than as a lowly toiler in some field of rocks."

Taking her by the hand, they started in a westerly direction along the summit of the lofty mountain. They had strolled along for several hours, often stopping to kiss and embrace, when the preternaturally keen ears of the black man detected the sound of footsteps on the brittle leaves on the path some distance behind. He whispered the news to his exquisite companion, who suggested that they leave the trail and go down the side of the mountain to elude the pursuer—who was undoubtedly Cheerful Dew. For a time, they went their way towards the valley, apparently unmolested. But again, the black man heard pursuing footsteps. They quickened their pace, but the sound of feet pattering on dry leaves grew plainer and plainer. By the time they reached the valley, their pursuers seemed to be only several hundred yards in the rear. Coming to an open space where the timber had been burned away by successive fires, they noticed Cheerful Dew and several other warriors armed with spears, emerging from the woods. Flight was no longer possible; a conflict was imminent. It could but result in favor of Cheerful Dew and his henchmen as the black man was armed only with a scalping knife.

In the forest into which the eloping couple now fled was a wide black chasm; it was the air hole of some subterranean labyrinth or a sink from a cave-in. It loomed before them as a haven of refuge. Fate had sent them there, it seemed. Before the eyes of their enemies, they plunged into the black hole; they were in the underworld, free, forever. Just as Cheerful Dew and his supporters reached the opening, rocks fell into it, making it impossible to descend. The deserted father fell in a swoon and was carried back to his lodge house. He never recovered from the shock and was weak and nervous to the end of his days. The black man and his beautiful love were never seen again. From that day on, the valley where they disappeared became known as Black Hole Valley; doubtless, the backsliding Machtando and Light of the Morning are happy in the profound abyss. Perhaps, for this reason, the tortures of the inferno have lessened in their severity. The arch-fiend has learned from personal contact the failings and temptations of mankind. But humanity, less fearful of tortures to come, regarding sin with less loathing, has sunk into depths of villainy that the ancient Indians would have abhorred. Persons passing through the beautiful Black Hole Valley little guess as to its sinister history, of it being the scene of the evil one's ungraceful exit from the living world which he sought to grace.

XVIII

STORY OF THE CANNON HOLE

(A Legend of the Invasion of 1756)

WHEN the vanguard of the invading force of French and Indians started down the West Branch of the Susquehanna in the early summer of 1756, determined to destroy Fort Augusta and the adjoining English settlements, the first raft was commanded by the young Viscount Emile Malartie. He was the ranking officer of the flotilla, which numbered twenty rafts and bateaux. Most of the five hundred French trappers and soldiers rode in the boats, while the thousand Indians who accompanied them marched along on the shores as an armed bodyguard. The raft on which the commandant made his headquarters contained a heavy brass cannon that had seen service in the Thirty Years' War. It was to be used to demolish the British forts and bring the helpless settlers to a point where they would be ready to sue for peace. After leaving the present site of Williamsport, the leading raft seemed to catch the current better than the rest, for it swirled along at a rate where it distanced the others and, above all, the Indian guards. The invading force had met with no opposition thus far. The few pioneers who had erected cabins on the Sinnemahoning and the West Branch fled at the sight of this formidable armada. Some French trappers who had been harassed by the English scouts who sought to drive them from the region offered their arms to Malartie and accompanied him on his raft as expert guides.

In the fertile Muncy Valley, a number of settlers, Germans, Scotch-Irish, and Quakers, had established themselves and built comfortable houses and barns. They feared that they would be dispossessed by the French invaders, who, if luck favored them, might reduce Fort Augusta, which was the key of the entire situation. These frontiersmen formed a private company of defense and elected a North of Ireland man named Fitz Hugh Jemison as their captain. They would frighten the invaders by a show of force, perhaps turn them back without firing a shot at Colonel Hunter garrison. They rigged themselves out in red coats in imitation of aggressively attired British soldiers. These coats were made by sewing on the outside of their homespun jackets, the materials from their red undershirts. They covered their caps with the same goods and, when half hidden by the forest, could not be taken for anything else but real soldiers of King George.

When the raft containing Viscount Malartie and his brother officers reached a point in the river where the water was very deep—sixty feet in high water, it is said—the "redcoats appeared among the tangle of vines and bushes by the north bank and began an active fusillade. The Frenchmen were so taken aback that they lost their presence of mind, but only for a second. They rushed to the side of the raft nearest the shore and began firing at the supposed British force. There was a circular current at this spot and the steering oar, abandoned for an instant, caused the raft to veer about. The cannon happened to incline towards the side to which the Frenchmen had gone; the combined weight was too much, the raft upset in midstream. As the Frenchmen floundered about in the water, the sharpshooters on the bank picked them off, one by one, until all were apparently dead men. The cannon, which was nailed to the flooring of the raft, carried the entire barge to the bottom. In its capsized state, it rested there, with the cannon on the bottom side, rapidly sinking into the muck. In very low water, modern raftsmen say that their rowers have struck the platform of the raft, under which the cannon from the Thirty Years' War lies submerged in this distant land. Ever since that time, the point where the disaster occurred has been called "the cannon hole."

The rafts further up the river and the Indians along the shore were thrown into a state of panic by the sudden annihilation of the commanding barge. All the commissioned officers were aboard it. To their frightened senses, they imagined a force of several thousand British troops were massed along the river, ready to destroy each craft as it passed. The noncommissioned officers commanding the other rafts veered them into shore, compelling the Indians to drag them on the beach and construct them into an improvised stockade. They would meet the British in a state of preparedness this time. Several days passed, and no signs of attack materialized. Indian scouts were sent out, but they could locate no British force. At the time, none of them suspected the ruse which had been played so skillfully by the farmers. It was decided that it would be a dangerous plan to re-embark on the rafts, yet if they returned without making a show of strength against Fort Augusta, there might be a general court-martial. With no commissioned officers, no one cared to take responsibility. Swift runners were dispatched to Lake Erie to find out what should be done. The delay caused general dissatisfaction among the Indians. They had started on the expedition reluctantly; they wanted to do some fighting to justify the long trip.

Disobeying orders, five hundred of them started overland in the direction of Fort Augusta. Their route was across the Bald Eagle Mountains, planning to attack the fort from the Blue Hill on the opposite side of the river. History records that they fired a few shots and, after seeing the impenetrability of the fortified position, slunk back into the forests. Meanwhile, the runners returned to the camp with instructions to the force to return at once to Lake Erie. In the excitement of the sortie from the shore, one man from the officers' raft apparently escaped alive.

He happened to be Viscount Malartie, the first in command. He had fallen into the river when the raft capsized, been hit on the head by a corner of it, and knocked senseless. He had floated downstream submerged and been overlooked by the sharpshooters' bullets. The cool water had brought him to his senses a few minutes after he had drifted into an eddy on the Bald Eagle Mountain side of the river. There was a terrible gash on the side of his head; he was bruised from head to foot; his mind was dazed. When he was able to get to his feet, the instinct of self-preservation goaded him to wander along the face of the mountain, gradually ascending it. The echoes of the awful fusillade which had slain his companions were still ringing in his ears. He imagined that the rafts, one after another as they appeared, had been wrecked and destroyed by the British soldiery. As he carried valuable maps and orders in his pockets, he fancied that his only safety lay in flight. His compass had been lost; the day was foggy; he was ignorant to a great extent as to where he was traveling. If he could go West or south, he would fall in with friendly Indians or French officers or trappers. He was humiliated at the sudden defeat of his flotilla; he had dreamed much of its chances of success. He had pictured in his thoughts Colonel Hunter capitulating, the victorious fleet sweeping eastward, the French firmly established in the entire middle and western part of Pennsylvania. Now probably every man of his command, except himself, was dead; it would be horrible news to the ambitious leaders on Lake Erie. He was too heartbroken, too upset physically to feel hunger or thirst; all he cared to do was to go on, on, on. Night set in, and he dropped into a dizzy stupor among some leaves. He awakened while it was still dark, hearing wolves howling dangerously near to him; he realized that he had lost his pistol in the water; he only carried a slim sword. He got up and plunged forward into the darkness. Often he could have dropped in his tracks, but he felt himself too high on the social scale to become a feast for wolves. As a child, he had been surrounded by a pack of wolves on his father's estate in Clermont-Ferrand; he would have been devoured had it not been for the timely appearance of a gamekeeper. It seemed that wolves were his Nemesis.

Daylight appeared through the tops of the tall pines; the sun did not remain long, and lowery clouds like the day before prevailed, adding considerably to his melancholy. He sat down frequently to rest, each time getting up a trifle refreshed. His physical hurts were abating, though he was weak from loss of blood. He felt thirst and later hunger, signs of returning vigor. He drank copiously from the springs and ate some wild leeks, strong as they were, to allay his demand for food. He had noted the direction where the sun had risen; he decided to move in a directly opposite route. With the inherent courage of a well-bred man, he covered an incredible distance that day. He passed over the headwaters of Buffalo Creek into the region of Laurel Run, which is a tributary of Penn's Creek. He tried to sleep in a hollow in the rocks, which was filled almost to the surface with leaves; it was as soft as a feather bed. The wolves had followed him, for they circled about his refuge, barking like fiends. Malartie drew his rapier; he would pierce any beast which came too near. They made no move to attack him yet remained in his proximity until daybreak, when they trotted away, looking back and wagging their tails like friendly dogs.

Hunger and nervous exhaustion were beginning to tell on the young officer; he found that he could not travel as well as on the day before. At times his legs acted unsteadily; he saw black before his eyes. The sun shone at times this day, which was an aid spiritually.

At about noon, he saw, to his surprise, a solitary cabin built of black birch logs, roofed with pine boughs. It stood in the center of a small clearing planted with hills of Indian corn. The young man, ragged, swarthy, and bearded, presented an ill-favored appearance, but he approached the door of the hut. Inside, seated on a bench, weaving, was a young Indian girl of probably twenty years. She was tawny colored, black-haired, and her eyes were long and narrow, like those of an Oriental. The Frenchman knew several Indian dialects, but he chose to speak to her in French lest she mistake him for an English spy and have him murdered. The girl indicated that she did not understand French yet appreciated the fact that he was not a foe. He then spoke to her in the language of the Mingoes, to which she replied cordially. He told her of the great disaster which had overtaken the French and Indian allies at the Susquehanna three days before, of his escape, his hunger, his fatigue. He noticed that the young woman's eyes and lips quivered as he related the story; tears stood out in her long eyes when he had finished. She said that she could sympathize with him in his trouble, that she had been left a widow a month previously, her husband being murdered in cold blood by scouts in the employ of the English after he had refused them information concerning the movements of the French. She had buried him with her own hands among the yellow pines back of the clearing. After his death, an infant was born. She showed him the papoose strapped to a board, hanging from a peg on the wall. She had hoped that the young warrior's cruel death would be avenged when the allies attacked Fort Augusta, but now a wholesale calamity had been added to the weight of her sorrows. She said her name was Asteria; her husband's name had been Wuh-hala.

The common misfortune created a bond of sympathy between Malartie and the lovely Indian widow. She invited him to remain at her cabin until his wound was healed and he became strong enough to endure the tramp to the West. She would gladly put him on a trail known as the Buffalo Path, which would lead him across the mountains in the direction of the Sinnemahoning.

The officer was extremely grateful for her kindly treatment, especially so as on the next day, he found himself so stiffened from his hardships that he could proceed no further. The young woman rubbed his limbs with bear's grease, but it was two days before he felt able to resume the journey. The morning on which he had planned to start, he was aroused by Asteria's little half-wild dog barking furiously. Without looking outside, the girl whispered to him the words "English scouts." He lay flat in the far corner of the cabin while his good angel piled buffalo robes and bear hides over him. Then she walked boldly to the door. She was correct in her surmise as three powerfully built Germans came across the cornfield and saluted her. They told her that the French and Indians had been defeated with great loss, that bands of scattered Indians were everywhere in the forests. They demanded to know if she had seen or harbored any of them.

"You must not forget your husband's fate," said the spokesman of the party, whom she recognized as one of her husband's slayers. Malartie, hidden under the huge pile of hides, could hear parts of the conversation, but he trusted Asteria's shrewdness to save the situation. The girl informed them that she had seen no Indians since the time indicated, that if she did, she would send them on their way; she had learned a sufficient lesson to remain neutral. The Germans said that they were hungry, that they smelled cooking. Asteria served them a pot of corn soup which they ate ravenously. Their stomachs satisfied, they became more sociable, especially after the girl had filled their pipes with some of her late husband's choicest tobacco. They smoked and chatted until late in the afternoon, when, with profuse thanks for the courtesies displayed, they took themselves off into the forest. After they had gone a sufficient length of time, Asteria unrolled the young officer from under the pile of blankets. He was as white as a sheet and violently ill as a result of his suffocating position.

The girl told him that the men were Busse, Faust, and Knauer, three scouts in the service of Colonel Conrad Weiser, the chief Indian agent of the colony. They seemed like jovial fellows but were quick-tempered when crossed. Busse had ordered her husband's death; someday, she would revenge herself on him; an Indian never forgot a wrong. Yet it was policy to be pleasant to him when he had her in his power. She strongly advised the young man not to attempt to leave for the west inside of a week. The German scouts had a habit of lurking about certain neighborhoods when their suspicions were aroused. They trusted first impressions; they hated to change their minds. Undoubtedly, Indians retreating westward from the silly "attack" at Shamokin would pass through the Laurel Run country; the scouts knew their favored routes to the west.

Malartie was perfectly contented to remain under Asteria's comfortable roof. She was good to look upon, had all the refinement of the ancient Indians, was kinder to him than any woman had been before. A soldier since he was fourteen, wandering and fighting, he had seen little of the finer aspects of women's natures. The idea of marrying and settling down had never before appealed to him. Now it took full possession of his nature; it was the awakening of love. He knew he would probably spend the remainder of his life in the French service in America; a beautiful Indian wife would make his days in the wilderness tolerable. He waited until the day appointed for his departure to impart the story of his love. Asteria must care for him; she had been so anxious to keep him with her; it would be worth trying anyway. He felt very ill at ease during the intervening period; the words of love were ever at the tip of his tongue; he could hardly force himself to discuss formal topics. All the while, he was watching the girl; to find confirmation of his belief that she cared for him. He selected as the best time the walk that they were to take together when she was to put him on the trail which led to the Sinnemahoning country. It was a rainy morning; the water poured off the roof in cascades. Asteria looked out, shaking her head.

"My friend," she said softly, "you had better remain another day under my roof. I will gladly accompany you to the northern trail, but what is the use of hurrying away in such dreadful weather?"

This seemed to strengthen Malartie's theory that she would like him to remain with her. The Frenchman laid aside the buffalo cloak he had intended to wear and sat on a stool made of stags' horns just inside the door.

"I will stay another day," he said, taking in his the hand of the Indian girl who stood beside him. "But when I go, I want you to accompany me and become my wife. I love you with all my heart; I cannot leave you and your baby here alone."

"I am very, very sorry," said Asteria. "I think that I love you, but I could never leave the grave of my poor husband. When I buried him with my own hands, I swore before my Gitche Manitou that I would remain nearby as long as there was life in my body. It is our faith never to abandon our dead."

"But can you see me go away never to meet again while you remain in this unfriendly country, liable to the treachery of German scouts, the attacks of wild beasts, and wretched loneliness?"

"I realized all that when I made my vow; of course, I never dreamed of meeting *you*, but the words have been said; I am here for my lifetime." She was silent for a minute, hanging her pretty head. Then she spoke again. "If you love me, why can't *you* remain here?"

The young officer was amazed at this, but he had to reply. "Dearest Asteria," he said, "much as I love you, I cannot rest here, a deserter in a hostile region. My duty to my king is to report as quickly as possible to my commanding officer. It will be hard enough to explain how I came to be the sole survivor of my barge, how I led my force into such a trap."

"I should not have asked you to remain," replied Asteria, "knowing you are an officer. I fear our fates must follow separate channels, yet neither of us can be happy again."

"What you say is in perfect truth," said Malartie, "my career is ended; I cannot be happy without you." Then he was lost in thought for several moments. "I have a splendid idea," he said at length, his dark eyes lighting with enthusiasm. "I will report to my superior officer, and then after my defeat has been explained to his satisfaction, I will resign my commission and return to you."

"Your plan is wonderful," said Asteria, leaning over and kissing his bearded cheek. The young man arose from the bench.

"I think I will be off, rain or no rain; I must accomplish our destiny quickly."

Asteria threw a tawny panther hide about her shoulders and went with him into the rain, which now showed signs of lessening. They parted with many kisses and protestations of love at the crossways. The happy soldier hurried to the north, reaching his destination in five days. To his relief, he found matters not so bad as he had feared. The other rafts had not been wrecked; most Indians who had disobeyed orders and attempted to attack Fort Augusta were coming back in small parties. The only loss was the one raft with its group of officers, scouts, and the brass cannon from the Thirty Years' War.

Within three months, his resignation had been accepted provisionally: he was granted three months' leave of absence until his honorable discharge could be received from Versailles. When the leave of absence was allowed, he at once started for the lonely cabin on the headwaters of Laurel Run. It was a perilous trip through a hostile country, but love gave him added caution and speed.

Within a week, he reached the little clearing. To his horror, naught but ashes and ruins of the cabin remained. The cornfield was trampled down as if a force had occupied it. All was desolation and loneliness. In his absence, the hut had b«en burned to the ground; the occupants were gone. He searched among the debris for signs that Asteria and her child had perished with it; there were none; they had probably fled before the flames or had been carried away by the cruel English conquerors. Even the grave of the murdered husband, Wuh-hala, had been pillaged.

Stern veteran that he was, the Viscount Malartie fell on his knees and wept. When he recovered himself, he resolved to search the Seven Mountains for his missing love. He had to move about by stealth, as the territory was under English rule. He met many friendly Indians, but all of them disclaimed knowledge of the fate of Asteria. He spent his entire leave of absence in the search, having many narrow escapes from the German scouts and hostile natives. Even the wolves troubled him every night, but he feared to shoot because of the noise. Reluctantly he returned to Lake Erie in time to receive his accepted resignation. He bade farewell to his companions and started for his home in Clermont-Ferrand. The voyage set him to thinking, and when he returned to his parental chateau, he was bright and cheerful. He said he had fought enough; henceforward, he was to be a man of peace. He married within two years to a young lady of his own caste and became the father of several children. It is said that his eldest son, the Viscount Francois-Marie Malartie traveled extensively in the United States shortly after the Revolutionary War. One of the localities he visited, looking at with interest, was where his father's barge had been wrecked in the depths of the Cannon Hole on the West Branch.

XIX

THE GHOSTLY LIGHTS

(A Story of an Ancient Public House)

THE old-fashioned town of Indianville consists of a single long street, lined on both sides by primitive log cabins. It is a street nearly a mile in length, but the yards about the cozy little dwellings are so spacious that the number of houses is not as numerous as might be supposed. In the southern end of the town, which is nearest the L&T railway station, half a dozen of the log cabins have been weather-boarded porches added, the trees on their lawns trimmed and otherwise modernized. They do not add to the charm of the village and are best forgotten by anyone wishing to create a mental picture of it. At the northern end, near where Indian Run surges out from the narrow gap, a number of the cabins are deserted. The mountain-ash trees in the yards are dead, most of the gates are unhinged, whole panels of yard fences are down. It is a woe-begone, desolate scene, especially on a dark, bleak day.

A furlong beyond the last cottage, at the mouth of the gap, stands the ruined public house, once known as the Last Chief Tavern. It was abandoned by the last tenant as long ago as 1892, although the tavern sign, the wrought iron figure of an Indian in full regalia, with the date 1801 below, swung to the breeze in a much-rusted condition until six years later. A relic hunter from Pittsburgh saw it, hunted up the owner, and bought it for fifteen dollars. The existence of two more up-to-date hotels nearer the railway station was the ostensible reason for the crowding out of the old-time hostelry. The public always fancied public houses close to the busy centers—they always preferred the new instead of the old, even though the rooms in the newer hotels were smaller. But there were other reasons which conspired to close the ancient stand.

The story was rumored about that it was haunted. Before the new hotels went up, visitors were willing to put up with ghosts; afterward, they were glad to shun their habitations. The ghosts which flitted about the Last Chief were almost as old as the building itself. They dated back to the first quarter of the nineteenth century, as far back as the oldest inhabitants of Indianville could remember. A few years ago, there were three aged men living in the village who were old enough to recollect the events which caused the haunting of the old hotel. They were Uncle Dan McChesney, Pappy Himmelreich, and Daddy Sweitzer. All three were veterans of the Mexican War, which stamped them as persons of reliability. There were few permanent residents of Indianville who had not seen the ghosts, or rather the ghostly lights. Belief in the supernatural is almost a part of the everyday conversation of dwellers in the Seven Mountains; voices are lowered slightly when it is discussed, but it is regarded as accepted fact. Perhaps it will be by everyone everywhere a hundred years hence.

Science is confirming belief in ghosts; their position as part of our national life grows stronger every year. Belated travelers from Abundance at the north side of the gap invariably saw the lights; loving couples straying too far up the road after church would see them; boys and girls out on Halloween larks prided themselves on their bravery to take a "look;" the old folks to confirm their early faith wandered up that way after nightfall at regular intervals. The ghostly manifestations consisted of two lights, like the uncertain yellow and blue centered flame of tallow candles, which came out of the side doors, one from each end of the house at a little before midnight, and ascended as if by invisible ladders to the roof. They remained motionless for several minutes, one at each end of the roof as if resting against the giant chimneys. Then they would advance towards one another, flickering and swaying, as if in combat; this would continue for a minute until one would go out; the other remained burning a minute, then extinguished. A traveler timed the proceedings as six minutes from the first appearance of the lights until the last one was extinguished. When the tavern was occupied, there were stories of divers rappings and moanings, of cold draughts of air, of closed doors opening unexpectedly, and the like.

Over the mirror back of the bar was the mounted head of a black wolf, said to be that of the last of its kind ever killed in the Seven Mountains. Its glass eyes grew alive towards the hour of midnight. Sleepless visitors sometimes encountered the beast on the stairs. A fat man, hunting for the upper porch to get a breath of air one hot August night, met it in the hallway, becoming so frightened that he fell downstairs, breaking both his legs and dying shortly afterward. From that time on, his bare feet could be heard every night on the oilcloth floors chasing the wolf. But these were only minor spooks; presumably, they faded away when the hotel was closed.

The ghostly lights remained; they even grew brighter with the passing years. A strange part of it all was that nobody feared the lights; they were as much a part of the town's life as the arrival of the mail train from Montandon or the rising of the moon from behind Mount Petersburg. Many residents tell the story of Indianville; although the old men who were alive at the time the "ghostly lights" began are all resting beneath tiny American flags on the hill; it came direct from their lips and is singularly free of variations. It is a ghost story first-hand. Most such tales begin by "I knew a person who heard someone say;" in this case, the haunted tavern is the best answer to doubters.

It appears that seventy-five years ago, Jake Stackhouse and his circus were well known in the Seven Mountains and far into western Pennsylvania as well. It was a "one-horse" affair, judged by modern standards, but was the marvel of its day. Stackhouse was a middle-aged German, hard-fisted, selfish, mean, but he possessed the faculty of amusing—or fooling, the easily satisfied public. The outfit consisted of three wagons, gaudily painted, the first one hauled by two Conestoga stallions, a white pony, and an elk, harnessed abreast. The elk, a native of the Seven Mountains, had been captured as a calf; its mother had been killed. Like the wolf which years later graced the barroom of the Last Chief, it was the last of its species. The elks lingered longer in the Black Forest and at the headwaters of Bennett's Branch of the Sinnemahoning than in the Seven Mountains—but their name lives on in the numerous Elk Creeks which percolate through the southerly valleys.

Jake Stackhouse's captive elk, to be exact, was caught in the mountains south of Tylersville. It had been driven to bay on elk rocks with its parents after a long chase by a pack of hounds. The elk rocks, which were plentiful in the forests, were strongholds for these animals, where they retreated to fight off wolves and other enemies. The poor, browbeaten animal, with its rangy horns and protruding ribs, had a habit of looking people in the eyes; the glances from those dark brown, liquid orbs lingered in the memories of the most callous; yet no one attempted to buy the wretched creature its freedom.

The other wagons, also garishly painted, were drawn by calico horses, miscalled by the showmen Arabians, which were then novelties in the east. The trained dogs, which were tied to the frames of the vehicles, trotted contentedly underneath. The elk was trained to dance on the bottom of a bucket; the pony stood on his hind feet, the spotted horses and dogs performed tricks; every person connected with the show was a performer. Stackhouse had a wife, a good-looking, black-haired woman much younger than himself. Many stories were told about her, that she had Indian blood, that she had been the wife of another man. Divorces were looked upon with holy horror in the Seven Mountains; it was hinted that this was a divorced woman.

When the tent was pitched, Jake, who had been connected with a circus in the old country, acted as ringmaster. He wore a mustache, the only man in the region who had one at that time; it caused many to say that this was sure proof of his being a black leg. His wife sold the tickets, and yokels often complained of being short-changed. The circus was not a popular institution in the mountains, but it was patronized because it offered something different from the humdrum life of the wilderness. It was the desire of folks to do something which the preachers told them was wrong.

One beautiful afternoon in late August, in the height of the golden hour, when every leaf and twig was clearly outlined, Jake and his circus emerged from the shadowy, cool depths of Indianville Gap. There was a flat or common directly across the public road from the Last Chief Tavern, where gypsies and circuses usually located; it stretched clear to the bank of Indian Run. It was pastured by half the cows in the village until it was so smooth that the weazened hemlock stumps stood up like miniature church spires; the tall mulleins and milkweeds resembled little trees. It was an ideal spot for an encampment; it had been big enough to hold the maneuvers of the local military company at their semi-yearly drills. As soon as the wagons were driven on the green, Jake had the horses unharnessed and picketed, and they were soon munching away contentedly. The elk was tethered to a slight wisp of a white pine by the fence and amused himself by rolling his brown eyes at the small boys who flocked to admire him. Jake's wife and a couple of other women became busily engaged cooking supper; a red fire sent up a blue tail of smoke in true gypsy fashion. The showman ordered that the tent must go up before anyone would get any supper so that clowns, tumblers, glass-eaters, and mountebanks generally fell to the task with a will.

The crisp, ozone-laden air of the gap had made everybody ravenously hungry. There was to be no performance that night, but the showman had his own ideas about getting things in readiness. It was pitchy dark before supper was served, but the circus was ready for the next afternoon's exhibition. On account of scanty lights and difficulty of travel for the patrons after dark, shows were always given by daylight. After supper, Jake and his motley crew adjourned across the road to the public house. They felt entitled to a few drinks of Ferguson's Valley whiskey.

The barroom was a plain affair compared to the mirrors and carvings of its later days. Instead of the looking-glass back of the bar, there was a row of walnut shelves, on which stood curious old-fashioned "Black Betties," jugs, flasks, and some shells. Above them was nailed a wide-spreading set of elk horns. Landlord McCay greeted the showman effusively; he would make business lively during the next twenty-four hours. They always commented on the elk horns above the bar.

"They are the horns of your elk's daddy," the landlord would repeat proudly. "Mike Barner killed him and his mate and roped the one you have—he was a little calf at the time. He gave me the horns himself; a fine young man is Mike Barner. I heard tell that he killed three panthers in the east end of Sugar Valley last winter; few hunters can beat him."

Talk like this stimulated business in the barroom and added a halo of romance about the circus. Mountaineers came in to see the proprietor of the show, and by ten o'clock, the low-roofed room was crowded to suffocation. Jake Stackhouse had taken too many drinks to be good for him,

(Photo by S. W. Smith)

PENN'S CAVE HOTEL

and he leaned against the crude wooden bar unsteadily, his tongue running like a "clapper." Usually, when he drank, he got in an ugly humor, but he always had to be provoked over something. When in his cups, he beat his horses and dogs and sometimes struck his wife. He had been in many barroom brawls, and once, an Indiana county trapper stabbed him through the left arm. He had the proverbial chip on his shoulder this evening; only no one cared to knock it off.

Shortly after ten-thirty, the narrow door opened, and a big lean man with a big unshaven face entered. He had been drinking and, like the showman, looked ready for a fight. Jake looked around as he came in, recognizing him instantly. Of all persons to meet this night, this was Lewis Miller, his wife's former husband.

Since the woman had eloped with the showman fifteen years before, her first husband had been going "downhill." He had been a respectable carpenter in Frankstown but had taken to drink in hopes of forgetting his great sorrow. He could not keep a position and became a wanderer in the mountains. As he had some proficiency as a wood carver, he used it to make elaborately decorated canes, which he sold or exchanged for board and lodging. It was the year of a presidential campaign, and he carried a recently finished hickory stick adorned with the head of Andrew Jackson. The two men glared at one another like angry wolves. The crowd soon understood the situation, passing the story from man to man and watching in breathless excitement.

Miller of the two was the least prosperous, the most desperate, the most long-suffering. His chance had come to even matters. Suddenly raising the heavy walking stick, he brought it down with a thud on the showman's head. Although he wore a felt hat, the victim reeled and would have fallen to the floor had not some of the bystanders caught him by the arms. When he recovered his senses, he was full of fight and sought to spring at his enemy. Landlord McCay pinioned his arms behind him, whispering in his ears that he had always run a respectable place; if he wished to fight, he could go outside. Brawling was offensive to his Scotch-Irish probity. Before the showman left the barroom, one of Miller's supporters came over telling him that the woodcarver wished to challenge him to a duel, to be fought to a finish at midnight. Stackhouse was satisfied to fight; as challenged party, he would have the right to choose the weapons. Miller had gone outside; the showman quickly followed into the darkness. On the front steps, he informed the henchman that he accepted Miller's challenge; he would fight him with case knives on the roof of the hotel at twelve o'clock.

The landlord little suspected what was "in the air;" it was past eleven o'clock, the official closing time, and he hurried the other customers into the yard, barring the doors. Miller's seconds wondered how they could get to the roof without arousing the landlord; it almost caused a hitch in the proceedings. But the showman had noticed a tall ladder leaning against an old pear tree in the corner of the yard. He pointed it out to his adversary's seconds, who quietly placed it against the wall. Miller ascended it with a lighted candle in his mouth and took his place astride the ridge pole, leaning against one of the ponderous chimneys. Stackhouse's seconds carried the ladder to the other end of the house, and he ascended it with flickering candle in his mouth, taking his place astride the ridge and leaning against the other chimney. As there was no one among the motley half-intoxicated crowd who would be suitable to both combatants as referee or to give the signal to begin the duel, a novel scheme was devised. When the two men had taken their places on the roof, their seconds were to knock loudly on the front door of the hotel. When the landlord would come to the door to find out what was wrong, they were to tell him that the showman and Miller were about to begin a fight on the roof. Naturally, the landlord would run out in the yard and shout to them to come down; this was to be the signal to begin hostilities.

The seconds hammered on the door, and in a minute, the proprietor in his nightshirt and cap appeared, demanding to know the cause of the disturbance. The men told him what was about to happen on the roof. McCay, thinking that the seconds were genuinely anxious to prevent a duel, bounded out into the yard in his bare feet. He yelled to the duellists to get off his roof at once. The signal having been given, the men moved towards one another. Miller was far the quicker of the two; his intoxication had been earlier in the evening; it was pretty well worn away. Before the showman could poise his knife, the deserted husband plunged his blade up to the hilt in his heart. It was over so quickly that the corpse of the victim, with the candle still sticking between his teeth, was lying in the grass in front of the landlord before he fully grasped what had happened. When the victim's circus employees came to their senses, they looked to see what had become of Miller. He had slid down the rear slope of the roof, gotten on the porch roof, and from there dropped to the ground, escaping into the trackless forests. The excitement aroused the dead showman's wife. She came across the road and knelt by her husband's body. Those who saw her thought she took his demise rather cooly.

Stackhouse wore a red plush vest at the time of his death; the widow had it made into a bodice that she wore for many years. During the eventful moments, the elk escaped, but it was eventually restored to the widow, who sold it to another wandering circus. Lewis Miller was never captured by the authorities, though it is doubtful if they made a systematic effort to find him. Public sympathy ran with the murderer; he had been wronged; the victim was a foreigner. As he was already practically demented from his sorrows, no jury would have convicted him. But he never returned to civilization, living for fifteen years in a cave not far from Detwiler's Hollow. As he grew older, he was called "the wild man." He certainly looked it with his unkempt beard, bloodshot eyes, and tattered raiment. In the hot weather, he went about scantily clad, frightening travelers, berry-pickers, and children. He was the bugaboo of every child in the Seven Mountains for generations. A few faithful friends knew his whereabouts and brought him provisions. On one occasion, some berry-pickers saw him devouring a live rabbit. He also subsisted to a considerable extent on berries, nuts, and roots. Tales of his fantastic appearance and conduct are numerous in all the country adjacent to the Seven Mountains. He lived to be nearly sixty years of age; his friends eventually found him dead, probably from exposure, within his cave in the rocks. He was brought to Indianville and buried in the juniper-shaded graveyard on the hill. Many followed his body to the tomb. The night of his funeral, the ghostly lights on the hotel roof were noticed for the first time by some young men at the creek gigging for eels. They communicated it to their elders, and soon the story was known to everyone in Indianville.

The landlord at the time of the duel, McCay, was long since dead and had been succeeded by a man named Fleck. The new landlord noticed the lights but accepted them as one of the events of life. Guests offered no objections until after the new hotels were built when they suddenly began to show a dislike for ghostly surroundings. The older generation remained loyal to the Last Chief, but as they died off, patronage dwindled to almost nothing. Landlord Fleck passed away in the spring of 1892, and no one appeared willing to renew the license. The house was abandoned to the ghosts, who have doubtless held high revels there ever since. Now it is rumored that the ancient snuff factory, once the pride of Indianville, is to be rebuilt on the foundations of the ancient hostelry, and if this comes to pass, the ghostly lights will shine for the last time. With gleaming knives, the two enemies will be wafted to some distant sphere to right the wrong that wrecked the lives of both. Meanwhile, the creek bubbles on, the dark pines loom as of yore, the lonely street is just as deserted. As the midnight hour draws near, the wavering candles of the ghostly duellists mount to the ridge pole to wait a moment before they advance towards one another, like the collision of two meteors.

XX

THE OLD FORT

(The Story of an Early French Enterprise)

WHEN William Penn ascended the West Branch of the Susquehanna as far as the Cherry Tree in 1700, he was particularly interested in the sight of a French fort and furnace at the mouth of Wolf Run, not far from the present town of Muncy. He had his flotilla of canoes stopped at the settlement, making the acquaintance of the garrison. The party was ostensibly commanded by a young French nobleman named Baron Boaz de Grison, a nephew of a Parisian banker who was often of service to the king. The real moving spirit, however, was an older man, a French-Swiss named Alois Duhain, a veteran of many years in the French civil service, who at the fort held the titular rank of lieutenant. Silver ore had been discovered in the Bald Eagle Mountains across the river, and the great trading company had made a large investment to open the industry. Old Duhain confided to Penn that young Baron de Grison was very wild, which was a cause of considerable worry to his wealthy uncle, who was childless, and whose heir he was to be. To sober the young fellow, he had been sent to America and put in nominal charge of the silver mining enterprise. It had turned out to be a flat failure.

The Indians who sold the first ores to the Frenchmen now refused to bring any more or to reveal the whereabouts of the mines. Threats to torture them proved futile, as they said they would transfer their allegiance to the English, who were steadily moving their boundaries westward if ill-treated. As the trading company's strict orders were to conciliate the red- men, nothing further could be done in this direction. There was no more ore to be refined; efforts had failed to procure a fresh supply, even at advanced rates; the young baron was restless and discontented. As Duhain was growing old, he feared for the safety of his position if he allowed the young man to abandon the fort and start for Philadelphia. He had tried every scheme imaginable to please his charge; hunting was good, but he could not induce him to touch a firearm, fishing was excellent, but he would not handle a net; there were many Indian girls in the neighborhood who were good to look at, but he paid no attention to them.

Penn listened attentively to this tale of woe, encouraging the old man to go into all details. The great Quaker was secretly pleased with all he heard. It would be only a question of a few weeks when his authority over the river would be firmly established; if the Wolf Run enterprise could break up of its own volition, it would save the negotiations and expense of their removal through diplomatic agencies. He also believed that his friendliness with the Indians would induce them to reveal the secret of the silver mines, especially as they had threatened to ally themselves with the Quakers if harshly treated by the French. It was all very good news, which probably accounted for his excessive geniality while the guest of the Frenchmen. After resting a night at the fort and tasting, for politeness' sake, some real French wine, which the young baron had in a specially constructed cellar, the great peacemaker resumed his journey to the Cherry Tree. His negotiations for added territory with Connoondaghtoh, King of the Susquehannahs, were very successful, partly due to the presence of a very intelligent Indian princess named Rose-Marie, who had been educated by the French in Canada, and who superseded the itinerant interpreters who accompanied the party.

On the eastward voyage, Penn was anxious to travel faster, and he only stopped at Wolf Run long enough to shake hands with the officers. He could see that the bottle of French wine opened on the night of his previous visit had been the beginning of a protracted spree; young Baron de Grison looked much the worse for wear. As Penn climbed into his canoe, the youth said to him, "May I call to pay my respects to you in Philadelphia next month?"

The Quaker replied that he would be delighted, but he noticed the old civil employe's face whiten during the brief conversation. All the way down the river, Penn thought of the unfortunate young man, wondering if he would have courage enough to leave his prison and start for a land of social gaieties. Perhaps the old Swiss encouraged him to drink to weaken his willpower and handle him more easily. Several months passed, and the young baron did not put in an appearance. He was gradually forgotten, and Penn was too busy to think further about the silver mines. The first permanent settlers at Monsey Town discovered the abandoned furnace; it was the cause of much comment. It is mentioned by the historians of the West Branch, Meginness, and Gernerd. Very little light has been shed on the subject, despite its apparent importance. After Penn's visit, the history of the spot as a silver mine ceases. Henceforth it becomes solely the story of the unhappy young Frenchman, Baron de Grison.

The revelry, which had begun so harmlessly by the opening of a bottle of wine in honor of the Quaker visitor, had been prolonged into a spree that lasted until the last bottle was emptied. Perhaps Penn was right in supposing that the old Swiss was encouraging the insobriety; one thing was certain, as long as the baron drank, he uttered no threats about leaving for Philadelphia. If the rich uncle could have seen his nephew's wretched condition in the wilderness, he would have much preferred his ruining his physical life in the gilded vices of the court. When the last bottle was thrown into the river, the young man's senses became very alert. Where would he get more; he would either go after it himself to Philadelphia or have it brought to him from somewhere. He must have it quickly. He became ill-natured and, at times, violent as his unsatisfied thirst burned within him. He said that he was dying of ennui; he must go somewhere for a change of scene and sound. He was tired of looking at mountains, tired of listening to the mournful crying of the loons on the river at night. He might remain longer if wine was brought him, but it must come soon.

Old Duhain was at his wit's end. There was no place nearer than Philadelphia to send for a fresh supply; he knew that the Indians made several kinds of alcoholic decoctions, but they were vile-tasting and would not please the youthful nobleman's cultivated taste. The Indians shunned the fort ever since they had been threatened with torture; it would be difficult to get them to part with any of their spirits. Several days of bickering went by, but the situation was becoming critical. At length, the baron ordered his servants to prepare his belongings for a long journey. This was a sure sign that he intended starting for civilization. The old Swiss realized it would be useless to plead with him further; he was resigned to losing his charge, his billet, everything. If the old man could have found something to drink, he would have imbibed to drown his sorrows. He found a vial of laudanum, but the dose was not enough to ease the misery which oppressed him.

On a bright, crisp morning, when the maples were gold and scarlet, the baron had his canoe brought to the wharf. He was having his effects packed in it when a strange pirogue, occupied by three Indians, was seen coming down the stream. Old Duhain hailed them, as was his custom, and they replied to the signal by heading their boat towards the shore. The old man was delighted; the arrival of these strangers might divert the baron to such an extent that he would postpone his departure for another day. The Indians, who were stalwart braves, said that they had come all the way from the headwaters of the Genessee. They had made a portage at the summit across to the waters of Little Kettle Creek and from thence into the Susquehanna. They were Senecas and had no knowledge of Duhain's recent unpleasantness with the local Indians. They recognized the fort as a French institution that stood for friendliness. They explained that they were on their way to a famous Indian distillery, situated in the Bare Meadows, near the sources of Spring Creek and Sinking Creek, where, according to a formula given him by an Irish Quaker, an old chief named Tengettik was making a life-giving liquor from potatoes. On account of being at war with the tribes occupying the territory along Bald Eagle Creek, the Indians intended to reach the Seven Mountains country by way of the Karoondinah or Penn's Creek, of which Sinking Creek was a tributary, and would take them directly to the distillery. This was an even easier route than through the Bald Eagle Valley.

The young baron had come down to the landing to see the savages and was amazed at what they had to say. Here he had been suffering untold tortures from his thirst, with a distillery only about fifty miles away. Before he could open his mouth, old Duhain spoke out. Addressing the most intelligent-looking Indian, he said, "if we give you wampum, and in addition, pay you for your time and trouble, will you bring us back a supply of whiskey?" The thirsty baron did not give the Indian time to answer.

"My friends," he said, addressing the Indians, if you will allow me, I will accompany you to the distillery. To compensate you for your company, I will buy you all the whiskey you require; the trip will not cost you a single stick of wampum."

The savages seemed pleased at this prospect and said that they would gladly take him with them. At this point, old Duhain was heard again. He said that, of course, the young man, being a personage of high rank, must have his two servants accompany him. The Indians did not seem to object to this, but the baron replied firmly that he would not take the servants along.

"My Indian friends are sufficient bodyguards," was how he settled the matter. He ordered the servants to remove much of the baggage from his canoe and asked one of the Indians to paddle it for him. The sight of the unloading of the baggage allayed old Duhain's most serious fears. He had rightly suspected that if the baron went to Philadelphia, he would never return; the loading of all his belongings gave color to this. Now he was starting away with only a small supply of clothing; it meant he was coming back. He could understand now that if his charge had plenty of stimulants on hand, he would remain in the wilderness as long as his uncle wished. The old man saw visions of his easy berth on Wolf Run extending several years into the future.

The two canoes started downstream. The first was occupied by two Indians, the second by the baron, and the other Indian as rower. Old Duhain was a very happy man; it looked as if things were coming his way. The young Frenchman enjoyed the voyage very much. There had been some heavy rains, so their canoes traveled from the Karoondinah into Sinking Creek without any trouble. The scenery was wild and picturesque. There was much game along the way, and the expectant travelers had meals of wild turkeys, heath-hens, and fawns which could be only described as banquets. The flesh of the heath-hen appealed especially to the young Frenchman. It reminded him greatly of the *grande outarde*, which his father used to kill on the arid plains of Champagne.

This heath-hen is now extinct, but it was once so plentiful that it was fed to the slaves.

When they came in sight of the distillery, they found that it occupied the center of a formidable encampment. It stood on a high hill, with the waters of the two creeks, Sinking and Spring, running from copious fountains on either side. All the timber had been burned off the entire mountain, which had been planted thickly with potatoes and Indian corn. The distillery, which was as big as any chief's council house, was built of logs; on the roof was a tall pole made of white pine, from which floated an Indian banner of many colors. This was hoisted on lodge houses occupied by chiefs of distinction. The thirsty pilgrims had left their canoes at the furthest navigable point, and their climb up the steep hillside further aroused their desire for liquid refreshments. It was a wonderful sight, this promised land, and to their parched imaginations, stillhouse, banner, and encampment seemed of gigantic proportions.

The leading pilgrim handed a beautifully inlaid calumet or peace pipe, as a mark of goodwill, to the doorkeeper of the distillery and asked to be presented to the celebrated proprietor. Tengettik, a weasened mite of humanity, advanced to meet the visitors. His face wore a broad smile, especially when he noticed that a white man was in the party. He thanked the strangers for their gifts and invited them to feel at home.

"I have many visitors at present," he said proudly. "The famous chief Connoondaghtah is here with his beautiful daughter Rose-Marie. These Indians recently had the honor of entertaining the great white father William Penn at their encampment at the Cherry Tree."

This was interesting information for the baron, as he had entertained the same white father himself, and he had been the innocent cause of his- prolonged spree. "I recently entertained Father Penn," said the young baron, "he is a very liberal-minded gentleman." Old Tengettik smiled more broadly, saying, "come into my council room and become acquainted with Connoondaghtah and his daughter."

The party of four followed the old distiller through a long gallery filled with red earthen pots in which the liquor was being distilled to a spacious apartment, the walls of which were hung with the skins of wild animals. Seated on the floor, wrapped in the same grass-green blanket that had so captivated the sedate Penn, was the beautiful Indian girl, Rose-Marie. By her side sat her father, a huge lean warrior with a big head, small eyes, and an enormous predacious nose.

Seeing that one of the newcomers was a European, Rose-Marie spoke to him in French before the distiller had time to make the introductions. The Frenchman replied in his native language, bowing profoundly. The girl had liked his appearance from the first, but when Tengettik explained that he was a nobleman, the commander of the fort at Wolf Run, her manner became more engaging. Nothing succeeds like prestige. Yet foe was an attractive young fellow, even if stripped of rank and power. He was of medium height, erect and slender, with the golden brown hair, keen blue eyes, and clear-cut features so characteristic of natives of the northeasterly parts of France.

Rose-Marie was slightly below the average in size but wonderfully formed. Her black hair was soft and inclined to curl, her eyes were wide apart, her nose short but with a haughty arch to the bridge. She put much vermillion on her lips, according to an Indian custom later very popular on the European continent. Her complexion was not dark, and her French pronunciation so good that it was small wonder there was a persistent rumor of her having European blood in her veins. She invited the young baron to sit beside her, and they were soon engaged in an intimate conversation. Meanwhile the old distiller had a servant bring in a deerskin filled with the oldest whiskey, which was poured into gourds, and handed around among the guests. It is an unpleasant thing to say, but all, including Rose-Marie, partook too freely of the spirits. They were like one family by nightfall. The beautiful girl was lying in the Frenchman's arms, and he was pouring stories of his great love for her, of his desire to have her marry him, into her shell-like ears. The girl was anxious to marry him, and they made and unmade many plans in their maudlin state as to the place and date for the ceremony. The next day, after they had slept off their over-indulgence, more potato whiskey was consumed. All were again put to sleep by it. This kind of thing continued for several days until the Seneca Indians said that they must be returning homeward.

Rose-Marie broke the news of her engagement to her father. He was pleased, but he whispered to her, "what will Gischigu say?" This was the name of a fierce and vengeful warrior who had loved Rose-Marie for several years. She had encouraged his attention at first and then rejected him. He had threatened to kill her if she ever married anyone else. He was horribly jealous and often followed her in the forest.

"I don't care what he will say," said the girl defiantly. But later in the day, she thought the matter over, concluding that it would be wisest not to return to the Cherry Tree with her intended husband; it was too near Gischigu's bailiwick. She would go with the baron to Wolf Run and marry there. After that, she did not care. She confided this to her father, who commended her on another exhibition of her usual good judgment. He said he would go with her to the fort and give her away in marriage. He selected a bodyguard of a dozen picked braves to accompany them. Rose-Marie informed her lover that she would prefer to be married at Wolf Run. This pleased him as he dreaded the tedious overland journey to the Cherry Tree. He had gotten his fill of spirits; he was to have a beautiful wife, he wanted the marriage accomplished as soon as possible. Accordingly, they bade goodbye to the distiller, who gave them all as many deerskins filled with whiskey as they could carry, refusing any payment.

The departing band consisted of the baron and his bride-to-be, the three Senecas, Chief Connoondaghtah, and his twelve bodyguards. They found Little Kingfisher, the celebrated canoe builder who lived near the Rising Springs and purchased enough boats from him to convey them all to Wolf Run. The trip promised to be a memorable one as everybody was happy. Wide as was Penn's Creek, hemlock boughs completely arched it. They swept along with the current, singing songs as if none of them had a care in the world. All went well until they reached a point a short distance below the confluence of Pine and Penn's Creeks, at the base of what is now called Volkenburg Mountain. Without a warning of any kind, a bowman concealed somewhere on the side of the mountain sent an arrow on its silent way, which struck the gay young baron, piercing his jugular vein. With a cry of despair and pain, he fell forward against his sweetheart, death ensuing a minute after the canoe was beached. He would have died even if not hit in a vital spot as the arrow point was poisoned. As the vengeful Gischigu was noted for his skillful archery,

Connoondaghtah and Rose-Marie instantly suspected him. He had evidently followed the girl from the Cherry Tree. In some way, he had learned of her impending marriage and had gone on ahead, concealing himself in a place where he knew the canoes would pass.

The happy travelers were now plunged into the deepest gloom and fear. They knew that if they proceeded up the Susquehanna minus Baron de Grison, they would be accused of his murder by the garrison at Wolf Run. They would doubtless get into trouble anyhow, conceal the misfortune as they may. The Senecas held a council with Connoondaghtah and his daughter, the result of which was that they decided to abandon their canoes and cargo of whiskey and proceed overland to the Cherry Tree. The Senecas were disguised as bodyguards of the King of the Susquehannahs so they could pass unmolested through the hostile region in the Bald Eagle Valley. The canoes and whiskey were sunk in the creek; the body of the young Frenchman was wrapped in his sweetheart's grass-green blanket and interred on a little knoll near where he breathed his last. At the head of the mound, Rose-Marie placed a tiny cross of aspen twigs bound together by a heavy lock of her dark hair. At the fort at the mouth of Wolf Run, old Alois Duhain waited and waited. When no tidings of the missing young man were heard in six months, he concluded that he had changed his mind and struck out for Philadelphia. The old man abandoned the furnace and fortifications and started for Lake Erie. At the French headquarters, nothing was known of the baron; thus ingloriously ended the mining operations at Wolf Run.

XXI

AN EPISODE OF '65 FLOOD

(A Little Romance of Success)

A NEW and spacious mansion of cement, painted white, with colonial pillars, was being erected on the hill overlooking Indianville. It was the most up-to-date and striking-looking structure, not only in the valley but in the entire region of the Seven Mountains. When completed, it was to be occupied by Darius Cammerdiner, the Pittsburgh coke millionaire. This wealthy man, who had been born in Indianville, was early left an orphan and worked for several years as a farmhand in the valley and across the mountains by the Susquehanna. He had drifted to the Smoky City, amassed a fortune, married, and then decided to spend his summers amid the scenes of his childhood in preference to Sewickley or Cape May.

The natives, proud to welcome him back to their midst, were surprised to see how well he remembered everyone. He had not changed much since he went away a sandy-haired Dutch boy; he was only bigger and stouter, but he was as good-natured as ever. The county papers published cuts of the mansion as it would look when finished; it seemed to auger a renaissance for the little town which contained but one industry, a small sawmill since the snuff factory had burned down fifty years before. To be exact, it had been destroyed the year before Darius Cammerdiner's birth. Now on top of his return, it was reported that the snuff factory was to be rebuilt, and a creamery as well. Truly golden days for Indianville. But what interested the villagers mostly was the romance connected with the life of the rich man. He had married when well past thirty, after his fortune was well established, to the daughter of the wealthy landowner for whom he had worked as a stableboy in the beginning of his teens. The wife, who took an active interest in the construction and beautifying of the new estate, seemed to be devoted to her successful husband; it was evidently a love match. The couple had two small children, so small that the residents of Indianville, who invariably married early, said that the ceremony had been performed ten years too late.

On winter evenings, the life story of the great millionaire was told and re-told around the huge whitewashed stove in the general store. It was of far more absorbing interest than the rebuilding of the snuff factory of the projected creamery. According to the general statement, Darius Cammerdiner was the son of very poor parents; they had lived at the log cabin furthest up the road, next door to the Last Chief Tavern. The father, Jehiel Cammerdiner, once worked in the snuff factory—old Jonas Cleon had worked beside him, but he had not done much after it burned down. He had become a hunter but got one of his feet caught in a bear trap, becoming a cripple. He drank a lot, dying when Darius was five years old. The mother had struggled on a few years longer, sewing and eventually taking in washing. She died of throat trouble when less than thirty years of age. Darius, the eight-year-old orphan, was adopted by an elderly spinster. This estimable lady died when he was thirteen, turning him adrift again. The prominent McClintock family who lived at *Swatragh*, a brick manse by the Susquehanna, sent for the boy, and he tended 'Squire McClintock's pet Hambletonian stallion for a time. He remained at *Swatragh* until after the big flood on St. Patrick's Day, 1865.

After that, his whereabouts were undiscoverable until his former schoolmaster at Indianville, during a visit to Pittsburg, recognized his name and called to see him in his magnificent suite of offices in the Frick building. The wealthy man, surrounded by secretaries and stenographers, had received his aged teacher cordially, and the talk drifted back to old Indianville. Cammerdiner had expressed a desire to see the place, which he had not revisited since he left it, a boy of thirteen in Squire McClintock's buggy. He told the teacher that he had married the Squire's daughter, which further proved his upward course in the world. He promised to visit Indianville the following summer to see if his early impressions would be verified. True to his word, he wrote to the old schoolmaster that he was coming, and one hot July evening, he stepped off the train from the west.

He expressed regret that the Last Chief Tavern was closed; it was so near his birthplace and put up at one of the newer hotels. Accompanied by the teacher, he drove around the valley all the next day in a livery turnout. He expressed great delight at everything he saw. When he departed the next morning, he said he would return in a month, bringing his wife. Again he was true to his word and returned to Indianville with his life's companion. They spent a day driving about, passing several hours on the round hill at the base of the Petersburg, which is backed by such a grand grove of volunteer sap-pines. It commanded a splendid view of the majestic Seven Mountains; it would be an ideal spot for a summer home. Several sweet springs ran out of the sandy soil below the young pines, which grew as thick as a "black forest." Not long after this, the Pittsburgh millionaire returned a third time to Indianville. This time he took title to five hundred acres of land, including the round hill and the stand of white pines. After that, he came back every week, usually accompanied by architects or builders. By the first of October, ground was broken for the new home, the greatest event that had ever happened in the remote little hamlet.

One winter evening, while Cammerdiner was sitting in the corner of the hotel lobby, puffing at his W. H. Mayer cigar, conversing with his old friend, the schoolmaster, he told the story of his life from the time he first left Indianville; it sounded like a romance of success. Squire McClintock, the master of *Swatragh*, had put him at heavy work for a boy of his years, but he had taken to every task cheerfully. There were several boys, Pennsylvania German lads, from the valleys like himself, engaged in similar capacities, but he could always accomplish twice what they did. Several times the dignified landowner singled him out and praised him. This did not turn his head; it only made him work harder. The Squire had a daughter named Ernestine, a girl a couple of years younger than the German chore boy; she was very pretty and winsome, was a general favorite. She often accompanied her father during his drives about the estate, invariably speaking pleasantly to the hired help. She always had a smile for Darius, who sometimes handed her small bouquets of wildflowers. During the two and a half years he worked on the place, he got to know her as well as their different stations in life would allow. She was not at all snobbish or reserved but had the same dignified charm which characterized her father and mother. Although he was a very young boy, Darius secretly loved his highborn friend. He was wise enough to bide a time when he could express himself; he was too young and too ignoble to make any advances now. Once or twice children's parties were given at the big house, and the hired boys were admitted. He was thus enabled to dance a few times with his unacknowledged sweetheart. The other boys were much too shy to attempt this, but Darius, with an assurance of future success, seemed to be perfectly at ease in her society. She was always very nice to him, but he had no way of divining how much or how little she cared for him. Matters drifted along like this until St. Patrick's Day, 1865. This was always a gala day at *Swatragh*.

Although the MeClintocks were of North of Ireland Presbyterian stock, they cherished an affection for the Emerald Isle. The interior of the manse was decorated with green ribbons, and an Irish flag hung above the framed lithograph of Governor Curtin in the library. That day also happened to be the birthday of little Phoebe McAmbley, Ernestine's most intimate friend. She lived half a mile inland from *Swatragh*, which manse had been built on the riverbank; it had been erected in 1808 before the reckless cutting of timber had increased the dangers from floods. After breakfast, the little girl, dressed in her widest spreading skirt and strawberry-box hat, strolled out the lane to spend the day with her friend. She carried a tiny umbrella and walked along with all the dignity of a grown-up lady. Darius happened to be grooming the Hambletonian stallion as she passed the barn, and he gazed after her until she was hidden among the bare locust trees which lined the narrow path. It was a warm day for the time of year, and the sun was often obscured by dark clouds. The rains of the previous week had made the river "bank high," but no further rise was anticipated. It seemed that Ernestine had barely reached her friend's home when another heavy rain began. The water literally fell in "buckets-full," the river began rising again. After dinner, there was a let-up, so the 'Squire sent for Darius and told him to hurry out the lane and tell Ernestine to come home at once. He gave him a big umbrella and a great coat to put over her.

Before the boy reached the McAmbley mansion, the storm began with redoubled fury; there were several terrific peals of thunder and flashes of lightning, the latter shattering several of the original white pines which still remained along the river bank. It had evidently been raining more heavily "up country" as the river swept over its banks and spread out through the fields. When the little girl saw the hired boy, she said she was sure the storm would stop if she waited, but she was anxious to obey her family. The McAmbley household urged her to remain, but go she would. When the couple had gone about a quarter of a mile, they saw the brown flood waters sweeping toward them. The chocolate-colored tide was frothing white at the edges; it looked forbidding and dirty, to say the least.

There was a big black walnut tree along the lane; it had wide-spreading branches; to the little girl, it offered a temporary refuge. The stake-and-rider fence ran beside it; it would be easy to climb into; there was a temporary refuge in the fork. Darius suggested that he help Ernestine into this refuge and then wade through the water to the barn and come after her with one of the horses. She demurred at first—it was a little way she had—but she let him assist her to the point of comfort and safety. Then the boy struck out boldly into the seething torrent, which was now licking about the butt of the tree. The flood had occurred so suddenly that neither of the young people could realize that it would prove lasting or serious. But the water was rising with incredible rapidity. Before the boy had gone a hundred yards, it was up to his armpits, and the driving rain beating in his face blinded him. A few saw-logs were floating dangerously near, bumping into the fences and trees. Ernestine saw the danger and called to Darius to come back at once to the sheltering walnut. He realized it would be useless to go further, especially as he could not swim. It was lucky that he turned back when he did, as the water was up to his neck by the time he seized the top rail of the stake-and-rider fence and drew himself to safety. He climbed into the fork of the big tree, where he sat with the little girl, watching the water raising on all sides. The manse was obscured from view by many old trees, but doubtless, the Squire had already gone out to search for his beloved child. Even if he had found a skiff and was poling about in search of her, the rain was so terrific that it was impossible to see through it. Coupled with this, the skies were as dark as night; it looked like the end of the world.

The water was now on a level with the top of the fence and was dangerously full of huge logs and drift. There was nothing to do but to make the best of conditions, to accept a drenching and wait for the morrow. Ernestine worried considerably lest her father would go to the McAmbley home and, not finding her there, be frightfully worried. She urged Darius to call out loudly, which he did, as he had a stout pair of lungs. His voice was drowned in the roar of the storm.

Some of the saw-logs moved with considerable swiftness; they broke off most of the slender locust trees which lined the lane at the rear of the manse. They could hear the logs bumping together, or breaking off trees, or pushing over fences; it was a horrid splitting, banging, booming sound; the young people in their snug sanctuary shuddered and drew closer together. The atmosphere seemed to be growing darker all the time; they looked in vain for a light to shine out between the trees from one of the upper windows of the manse. It was too dark; there was too much rain to enable candlelight to penetrate the gloom. The roar of the flood, and the breaking of trees, amounted to a tempest.

Occasionally portions of sheds and, in several instances, chicken coops bumped against the tree. Perched on the roof of one of these structures, they could make out a much bedraggled Greeley rooster. Darius leaned down to try and grab the poor bird, but his reach was not long enough. A wild pigeon lit on the tree not far from the young couple. Ernestine said it reminded her of the dove that came to Noah's Ark, which she had read about in her little blue Bible book. They almost smiled at the droll conceit. The boy and girl were drenched to the skin, yet they remained calm and cheerful through it all. Once Darius took Ernestine's little hand to see if it felt cold, she made no effort to take it away; he held it tighter. Then he managed to put his other arm around her waist; she snuggled a little closer to him and soon laid her curly head on his shoulder. With such encouragement, he knew he could speak what had been in his heart for so long. Though he was only fifteen, hardships and self-reliance had given him the poise of a man twice his years.

He told her that he loved her, to which she replied that she loved him and proved the truth of her statement by kissing his wet cheek twice. He said that he realized it would be some years before they could marry, but it was lucky they were both so young. If she waited for him, he would go west, make a fortune, and come back and marry her. This would equalize their different positions in the world. She pressed her head more tightly against his shoulder by way of answer. He cemented his promise by a closer embrace and several heartfelt kisses. They were one in heart and spirit, out there in the flood center. They no longer heard the roar of the storm, the bumping together of saw logs, the crash of falling trees and buildings. The darkness was a cloak of intimacy to their romance. They were silent at times, thinking over their great joy. At other times the boy broke the silence to explain how it would be difficult for him to remain on the farm as her lover; he would leave the following week if they got out of their trying predicament in safety.

They were in the tree all night; morning dawned a little brighter; the storm had spent most of its fury. The river still rose, but with a cessation of the rain, rescuers could get about a little. As they had feared, the Squire and his good wife were terribly concerned over the safety of Ernestine and the hired boy also, as they were humane, Christian people. He had tried to seek them on foot and horseback, but the oncoming flood turned him back. He poled about all night in a skiff, not daring to go far from the manse on account of the drift piles and the darkness. At dawn, when the rain abated, he had poled to the McAmbley home, where they told him that the hired boy had left with little Ernestine after dinner the day before. The fond parent was in a quandary of fears and hopes; either the young people were lost in the storm or had found some sanctuary. The McAmbley family urged him to believe that they were marooned somewhere, possibly in the fork of a tree, that all was well. He went away in his boat, gazing anxiously at every tree he passed. About nine o'clock, he saw the missing pair, looking like drowned rats, huddled among the branches of the huge walnut. He gave a cry of delight, which was answered by the boy and girl who saw him at the same moment. He brought his boat over to them, and they dropped into it, drenched but happy.

There was much to be told of the recent adventure, which was related good-naturedly. It was a joyous sight when the little girl was restored to her mother's arms. The water, which was now beginning to recede slowly, was up to the level of the second-story windows of the manse; it was three feet higher than the mark made by the flood of 1847. The Squire was so delighted over the safety of his child that he passed over the loss of the Hambletonian stallion and all his other livestock, which had been engulfed in the barn while he was out looking for his daughter.

Darius was highly commended for his admirable protection of Ernestine but bore his honors modestly. He remained on the estate for a month after the flood, helping to bury the drowned livestock, clear away drift piles, build fences and get the place ready to resume farming. Then he said he was going west to make his way in the world. The Squire admired his courage, bade him go, but said he parted with such a likely lad with regrets. Ernestine was in the carriage which drove him to the railway station and waved her checked handkerchief as he boarded the train which connected for the west. The morning of his departure, he had met her under the grape arbor for a goodbye kiss, and she renewed her promise to wait for him.

His career in the west was a checkered one. His first work was as a farmhand in Illinois; he became a section hand on the railroad, then a freight brakeman. He learned telegraphy and drifted to Ohio. There he secured a situation in the freight office of another railway. He resigned to become a head bookkeeper for a wholesale firm of coal dealers. He saved a little money and invested in coal lands in western Pennsylvania. He moved to Pittsburgh and opened an office. He fell in with many ambitious young men; they made deals together, which turned out well. He prospered; everything came easy; he was nearly a millionaire when less than thirty-five years of age. Several times he had been on the point of writing but hesitated until his fortune was assured.

Meanwhile Ernestine, confiding in no one, not even in Phoebe McAmbley, was waiting patiently at the manse. She moved in the best society in the county; she had the prestige of beauty and wealth; she had many admirers and, of course, marriage proposals. She turned a deaf ear to all, saying she would die an old maid. Her parents urged her to marry, but she had the same retort for them. She was cheerful and contented; she did not miss masculine society; she had perfect faith in one man.

Often she wondered why Darius was so silent; he might have dropped her a line once in a while; perhaps his struggle was harder than

ROAD TO THE NARROWS

he expected; it might be many years before he could call himself a success. But her mind had been made up that eventful night when they escaped from death on the fork of the old walnut tree; it was too momentous an occasion to discard for a milder destiny. She would marry a man who *tried* rather than one who *had* or *was*.

One evening her father returned from the post office with a bundle of letters. He was growing old, and little things aroused his curiosity more than formerly. He held up an envelope addressed to Ernestine; on the upper left-hand corner was printed "Darius Cammerdiner Coke Co., Pittsburgh, Pa." saying, "that's the same name as that hired boy we had; he was with you the night of the flood in the walnut tree, but this one must be a big businessman." The girl grasped the letter with strange eagerness; she tore it open, holding it before the lamp to read. The old people looked at her in wonderment.

"He's coming here next week," she gasped. "I'm going to marry him; he's made a great success in life."

"What do you mean, a man coming to see you," gasped Mother McClintock.

"That's what I said," whispered the girl. "I promised Darius Cammerdiner I'd marry him when he made a success in life, and he surely has."

XXII

AT THE GATE OF THE DEAD

(A Story of Winegardner's Cove)

WITHIN almost a stone's throw of the Xaginey Cave, with all its mystic associations, on the crest of the same hill yawns the mouth-like s ink called Winegardner's Cove. It has been a popular resort for the curious for years, as it retains its ice formations during the summer months. Beneath the shelving masses of rock where the ice is conserved, the fissures stretch underground to incredible depths. In former years the surroundings of the "cove" were much more entrancing than at present. Walled in by a forest of hemlock and pine, its steep sides were overgrown with rare and strange-looking mosses. Once, a buffalo herd, driven from its pastures along Honey Creek by rival bands of Indian hunters, stampeded and ran until they fell pell-mell into the sink. Many of their bones are still to be found, wedged in among the crevices. Most of the timber has now been removed from the vicinity, and were it not for a few thrifty young white pines and hardwoods, which fringe its edges, one could hardly tell its location from the surrounding hilltop field. A string of barbed wire was placed around the circular opening to prevent cattle from falling into it.

Once a blind mare fell in, and efforts were made to lift her out with rope and tackle. She struggled so unwisely that it was decided to shoot her, and her bones are mingled with those of the ancient buffaloes. Several landslides have marred the symmetry of the sink; it is fast filling with logs and debris so that fewer visitors are apt to go there as the years progress. In this manner, time, circular in its movements, will restore it to the condition it was in during Indian days, shunned by everyone. There was no more mysterious and weirdsome spot in the entire region of the Seven Mountains than this gateway into the realms below. Many legends clustered about it, all terrible enough to cause the superstitious Indians to keep far away from its baleful precincts. When the Machtando or Devil repented for a brief time and visited the outer world, he emerged through this opening. When he returned to the depths, it was by a different route, but he carried with him a very beautiful Indian maiden named Light of the Morning, whose parents never ceased regretting her horrible fate. It was said that their ghosts came nearer to the edge of this abyss than almost any living person; they had the courage of despair. In Indian days the cove was known as the Gate of the Dead.

Swept into the world below through divers caverns, sinks, lost creeks, and airholes, the sentences of lost souls were for eternity. But they possessed the ability to come to the mouth of Winegardner's sink on clear nights and gaze up at the world where they had missed their opportunities, the beautiful world that they had failed to appreciate when in the flesh. They would look on the grand old trees which hung over the chasm, with the stars and sometimes the moon, glancing down on them with cold unconcern from the silver-grey dome above. They could hear the songs of night birds, the loon on the creek, the whippoorwill in the persimmon tree, the screech owl in the hemlock, the great horned owl in the white pine. The wolf's call would echo from the top of Sample Knob, the panther's love song from Jack's Mountain. The little crickets and the katydids would sing melodiously, a minor variant to the murmur of the forest wind. They would catch faint breaths of the pure air, so different from their fetid atmosphere. All these familiar sounds and odors would make them wish they were back on earth, which seemed so near, yet was unattainable. They were doomed to starve spiritually in sight of plentitude. Every moment while they peered aloft, they felt themselves stone dead, crushed beneath the .inexorable. Their bold, dead breaths formed the ice which choked the crannies of the sink; an odor like from a morgue rose from the unhappy place; it would be deadly to any human being breathing it.

The whole hill was shunned by the canny Indians; they knew they could not help the dead who looked out from the abyss; they dreaded lest they stumbled and fell into the clutches of this horrid Golgotha. The priests kept urging them to stay away, painting vivid word pictures of the horrors of the region. They exhorted the natives to lead good lives, to pass after death into a land of milk and honey, of perpetual sunshine, where game of all kinds abounded, where there was happy warfare all the time. The priests had an added reason for keeping their people off the hill; the sacred cave was near at hand, where the gods refreshed themselves in the crystal springs during their visits to the world. The giant forces of good and evil, the propelling powers of life and death, were very near together. It might have been properly called the hill of alpha and omega. As it was, it went by the name of the Hill of the Thousand Wishes, meaning all that passed through the mind of man. There never was a place in the history of mankind that was forbidden but which was eventually violated by some foolish soul. A vainglorious Indian king penetrated the sacred cave and was promptly punished; an unstable warrior crept to the brink of the Gate of the Dead—his history will follow. Around the marshy source of Muddy Creek was an encampment of considerable importance.

A small but warlike tribe called the Bald Faced Stags lived there; they had maintained their independence for untold centuries. They took their name owing to their pale complexions, which were slightly darker than those of Europeans. Added to this, their eyes were a pale blue, their hair brownish. The warriors always dressed in deerskins, with the antlered heads of the stags as caps, presented an odd and never-to-be-forgotten appearance. The chief wore the horns of the royal stag; that is, antlers with more than five points. They evidently sprang from the same stock as the Lenni-Lenape and other leading races of Indians, as their religion was identical. The women were particularly beautiful, some having light brown, others dun-colored hair, always with pale blue eyes. They were attired in the skins of female deer or fawns.

Foremost among the young warriors of this strange aggregation was a brave called Stag-of-the-Cliff; he was handsome and engaging, a noted hunter among a people of great hunters. He was a youth of strong passions; that is, he threw his whole soul into every undertaking, being successful with most. As the chief of the tribe was feeble and childless, Stag-of-the-Cliff's name was often mentioned as his most fitting successor. He was proud of his physical beauty and, somewhere, obtained considerable gold leaf, with which he gilded the stag horns of his helmet.

It was only natural that such a beautiful youth should love the fairest maiden in the tribe. Her name was Colia, and she was distantly related to the aged chief. This would have made her a suitable wife for the bold young warrior; in case of his being elected as chieftain, Colia was even more blonde than most of her kind. Hers was a dull, dun color, hair, lips, complexion, not at all the vivid blondness of the Anglo-Saxon, but entrancing from its very uniqueness. Her eyes, which were inclined to be small, were more of a pale hazel than a bine, but at times they shone with a bluish tint, like the sun on limestone water. She was very tall and slender, wonderfully graceful and alert in her movements, a perfect Diana in type. From her earliest girlhood, she had been attracted by the stalwart Stag-of-the-Cliff; it seemed a foregone conclusion that they would be married. It seemed so inevitable that neither appeared to be in a hurry.

It was customary every spring for the Bald-Faced Stags to camp on the main fork of Standing Stone Creek and engage in a salmon fishing operation. Thousands of these delicious fish were seined and carefully dried and salted by the squaws. These made a pleasant variation to the diet of venison, elk meat, wild turkeys, and heath hens, usually consumed by the warriors during the winter months. Muddy Run empties into Standing Stone not far from the present town of McAlevy's Fort, and it was several miles below this confluence where the fishing camp was located. Every evening Stag-of-the-Cliff returned to the main encampment in the mountains to bring news of the day's doings to the old chief, who was unable to his lodge house. He went most of the way by canoe; was almost as easy a trip against the current as with it. It was nearly midnight when he returned, letting his pirogue slip along with the tide while he sat in the stern, bathed in the rays of the silvery moon. He had perfect faith in his sweetheart, and his thoughts when away from her were full of love and hopes for the future.

One night he started on his return voyage to the fish camp an hour earlier than usual. The aged chief was sleepy and did not care to listen to the story of the day's catch. The fishing expeditions were regulated by the moon, consequently, barring storms, it was always moonlight during his canoe trips. He had passed out of Muddy into Standing Stone and was floating along past open fields, which had been cleared and tilled by Indians for many years. Masses of cat-tails and cane and a few willow trees lined the shores, allowing the moon to show in all her grandeur on the tranquil scene. As he swept along, night herons rose up squawking, frogs croaked, and crickets chirped; there was just enough sound to swell the harmony of the ripples on his graceful craft.

As he neared a giant forked willow tree, he thought he could make out two forms standing behind it. They seemed to be very close together, very unmindful of his presence. Fearing that they were spies from some hostile tribe, conferring over some plan of attack, he boldly steered his canoe into the reeds, which extended out fifty feet into the brook. When the pirogue struck bottom, he leaped out of it and, drawing his tomahawk, advanced on the couple. As he drew near to them, his surprise and grief knew no bounds. Instead of spies, they proved to be his false sweetheart held in the tight embrace of a strange brave of another Kishoquoquillas tribe.

The moonlight showed this Indian to be Stag- of-the-Cliff's inferior in every way. He was short, flat-faced, heavy-jawed, thoroughly ill-favored.

As the unwritten law of the Bald-Faced Stags was that they should never marry outside their tribe, and infidelity was looked upon with loathing, he raised his tomahawk and cleft the skulls of his false love and her ugly charmer. It was all over so quickly that neither of them was aware of what had happened; perhaps they were too dazed to realize the identity of their slayer. He had some difficulty in breaking the tight grasp of the dead man, so he cut off his arms at the shoulders. Then he collected some heavy stones and fastened them to the corpses. He placed them in his canoe and paddled them upstream to where Muddy and Standing Stone come together. There is a point where the water is quite deep with revolving currents, where it is constantly forming bubbles; it was here that he threw them overboard to sleep their last sleep in the muddy depths.

It was with feelings of satisfaction that he floated down to the fishing camp that night. He had righted three wrongs, one against his tribe, another against honor, still another against his personal pride. He slept the sleep of the just. The parents and friends of Colia soon missed her fair presence and set up lamentations. No one had seen her leave the camp; she had dropped completely out of sight. A search was made, with no avail; it was concluded that she had been devoured by some skulking panther or run away. The last version was the most popular. It was broadly hinted about the camp that she had another lover; soon, sympathy ran high for Stag-of-the-Cliff. He seemed to be much dejected. As time wore on, a genuine sorrow replaced his sense of injured pride. He missed the fair, frail spirit; he almost condoned her wrong. He knew that for her sins against the tribal honor, her spirit had been wafted to the underworld. He wondered how she liked it there, if she felt lonely for him and would like to see his face again. Perhaps he had acted hastily in slaying her.

The stranger who had broken in on his happiness might have put a spell on the beautiful girl; her presence in his arms might not have been voluntary. He would forgive her; he would give anything only to see her again. Across the mountains was the baleful hill where the Gate of the Dead opened out on the happy world. Would he dare to go there, to brave the foul marasmus, to break the will of the priests, and gaze into the beloved and lost face to ask her why she had treated him with such lack of faith? But he had his position to uphold; he was loyal to his religion and its traditions. Six months came and went. Not a single hour passed, but Stag-of-the-Cliff failed to think of his departed sweetheart, of his murderous deed.

At the end of this period, the old chief passed away; the bold young warrior, as generally expected, was elected as his successor. On the night of his election, there was great rejoicing among the tribe; it augured well to have such a brave young spirit as their leader. Bonfires were lit on the highest ridges; their flames seemed to mount to the very heavens! Stag-of-the-Cliff wondered if the dead Colia, peering from the deep sink, could see these signs of his triumph. He wished she were with him and could share the honors and probably the next day become his wife. It cast a gloomy pall over his happiness.

As the night, which was beautifully clear, advanced, he was overcome by an unconquerable desire to creep across the mountains and risk everything for just one glimpse of his doomed sweetheart's face. Was it vanity or love, or both, he could not tell, but he must see her on the great night of his life. He stole away from the merrymakers and, finding a well-known path, traveled breathlessly across the high ridges. As he was starting downward on the last one, an eighteen-pronged stag, the biggest he had ever seen, barred his way. This animal, the harbinger of the good fortune of his tribe, sought to stop him from going to the sink. Instead of feeling a sense of gratitude and retracing his steps, he cleft the handsome creature's skull and, in the moonlight, stripped off his hide and head and placed it on his sinewy, manly form, the emblem of his new authority. He now looked every inch a chief; the hot blood surged in his veins as he thought of his eyes meeting the wistful gaze of Colia, away down in her dismal prison. It was not long before he reached the Hill of the Thousand Wishes. The tall pines and hemlocks grew so thick that they almost shut out the moon's effulgence.

As he neared the summit, he was nearly prostrated by the foul, reeking effluvia that arose from the abyss. He heard doleful cries and groans like souls in torment. He reached the brink, got down on his knees, and peered in. The full moon was directly above the opening; its clear rays shone into every nook and recess of the sink. Over against the rim of the tree tops, he could see the reflection of the ruddy bonfires, the signals of his honor. His heart beat fast as he gazed at the many upturned faces in the depths below, all looking upwards with sad, wistful eyes, many of them weeping and wailing as if their hearts would break. Face after face, he scanned; all so white, so dead, so cold, with grey lips articulating their sorrows.

At last, he saw the beloved countenance in the full moonlight; it was ghastly yellow, pitifully emaciated, its eyes were focused upon the flaming reflections on the sky. They turned suddenly; their dead gaze met his; he looked more closely. Beside her, resting against the pit-hole in the abyss, was the hated stranger, his arm around her, in a close embrace. The two were united in the world of shades, but were they happy?

If thoughts of the living can penetrate dead brains, they surely did on this occasion. Colia turned her dead eyes from her murderer, from the reflection of his glory, and leaning close to the stranger, kissed him passionately. High up on the brink of the abyss came a cry more hideous and pain-racked than any in the underworld. As it was uttered, the dead lips of Colia kissed her homely adorer again and again.

Staggering to his feet, Stag-of-the-Cliff attempted to leave the horrible spot. He reeled, striving to save himself from falling into the pit by clutching at one of the giant hemlocks; he fell heavily, cracking his skull on a jagged root and rolling away into the forest.

Death came to him slowly, partly from his wound, partly from the foul gases of the abyss. He breathed his last just as the sun rose and the last reflections of the bonfires died down behind the timberline. Now the Indians say that his unquiet spirit has met an awful torment; it must watch, during all eternity, the faithless Colia demonstrating her love for the ill-favored stranger. He cannot turn his eyes from her; he cannot get near to her; he seems to be always leaning over the edge of the sink, she with her lover in the depths below. When Machtando or Devil emerged, the unhappy shade caught him by his reeking garment, imploring him to lighten the sentence, but the spirit, of evil, turned his face away. After the evil one had returned with his beautiful prize, Light of the Morning, who languished happily in his arms, Stag-of-the-Cliff uttered a cry that is still echoing down eternity: it was the cry of baffled hopes, of envy, malice, despair.

Finis

Made in United States
Troutdale, OR
12/15/2023

15925380R00137